Our Beautiful Game

D1332187

Lou Kuenzler

faber

First published in 2021
by Faber & Faber Limited
Bloomsbury House,
74–77 Great Russell Street
London, WC1B 3DA
faberchildrens.co.uk

Typeset by M Rules
Printed and bound by CPI Group (UK) Ltd, Croydon, CR0 4YY

A CIP record for this book
is available from the British Library

ISBN 978-0-571-36500-5

2 4 6 8 10 9 7 5 3 1

To my Lily.
Love, Mum

*The game of football is quite unsuitable for females
and ought not to be encouraged.*

THE FOOTBALL ASSOCIATION,
5TH DECEMBER 1921

It is our duty to inspire young girls to play a sport.

STEPH HOUGHTON MBE,
ENGLAND'S TOP SCORER AT THE
2012 OLYMPICS
AND CAPTAIN OF ENGLAND WOMEN'S
NATIONAL FOOTBALL TEAM SINCE 2014

Author's Note

I have changed names and invented places, but all the key events in this novel are based on the actual experiences of munitions workers and/or female football players during and just after the Great War. All the quotations I use from official sources, such as the Football Association, are verbatim, to stand as a true record of exactly what was said at the time. Through my central character Polly I have echoed the life of the famous footballer Lily Parr. One of eight children from a working-class Lancashire family, Lily began her professional playing career aged fourteen and went on to score over nine hundred goals for her team and country.

PART I

CHAPTER ONE

Lowcross, Lancashire
July 1917

Polly charged across the back yard, flicked the football on to the toe of her left boot and eyed up the goal. All that stood between her and victory were three fat piglets, the washing tub and a gaggle of chicks.

She darted forward, weaved between two of the chicks, and thundered down the right-hand side of the yard. Polly was about to take a shot at goal, which was a narrow slit between two clean sheets hanging on the washing line, when out of nowhere the fattest of the piglets blocked her path. She almost lost control of the ball in a puddle of slops and slippery potato peel.

'Oh no you don't!' She slithered sideways, flicking the ball upwards in the nick of time, before skidding to the ground. Her nostrils filled with the familiar stench of pig muck and rotting veg, but it was worth it. The ball sailed through the air. 'Goal!' She smiled as it disappeared between the sheets, then waited, expecting to hear the satisfying thud of leather on wood as it hit the back gate

But the thud never came.

Instead, Joe, the eldest of her five brothers, appeared.

'Hello, Pol. You lost something?' He smiled down at her, holding the muddy ball.

'Give it here!' said Polly, sitting up and trying not to gawp.

Joe was in his new army uniform. She'd never seen him look so smart. She couldn't remember a time when anyone in their family had ever had new clothes.

'What do you reckon?' Joe beamed as he took one hand off the ball to salute her.

'Not too shabby, I suppose.' Polly heaved herself up off the filthy ground.

Her fingers were covered in muck but she wanted to reach out and touch his jacket. It was brown, like the colour of strong tea, and so stiff it looked more as though it was made of cardboard than cloth.

Polly was twelve years old and tall for her age, especially for a girl, as people never tired of telling her. She was nearly the same height as Joe, even though he had just turned eighteen and had shoulders as broad as a bear. Yet, all trussed up in his fancy clothes, he seemed young somehow, like a little boy. His big ears were sticking out from under his cap and his bristly chin was shaved clean. Apart from the thick soldier's belt around his middle, he looked as if he was off to church, not away to fight a war.

Polly made a swipe for the ball, waving her grimy paws at him. 'Hand it over then, unless you want to get muddy,' she said.

'Get away, Pol.' Joe marched past her, dunked the leather football in the pigs' water trough and shook it dry. 'This old beauty's coming with me.'

'What?' Polly's mouth fell open in disbelief. 'You can't take my ball to the war.'

Joe raised an eyebrow.

'All right, *your* ball,' said Polly, weakly. Joe had won it in a game of poker off a lad at the works, and she knew it. But that wasn't going to stop her. 'You're supposed to be out there fighting Jerry, not playing football,' she said.

'Ah! That's where you're wrong.' Joe leaned up against the wall and took out a smoke, with the ball wedged safely under his boot. 'Haven't you ever heard of no man's land?'

'Course I have,' said Polly. 'It's the scrap of ground that runs between the trenches. The German ones and the ones our boys are stuck in.' She'd heard enough stories about the war to know that.

'Exactly.' Joe pointed to the pigs' water trough. 'Say that over there is our lads' trench, then this here . . .' He kicked the long narrow slop feeder with his boot. 'This here is Jerry's!'

Polly laughed as the gaggle of chicks waddled merrily between the trough and the feeder. 'In that case, someone ought to tell those little beggars they're right in the middle of no man's land!'

'They wouldn't last long,' said Joe gravely. 'It's where you get yourself blown up, Pol.' She saw him swallow hard. 'That rotten little strip of land's what we're all fighting over.'

'Like a football pitch,' said Polly with a shudder.

'Reckon you might be right,' Joe agreed. 'The trenches are like goals and each team is trying to fire their shots into the other's.'

Except it's bombs and shells they're shooting, not footballs, thought Polly. But neither of them needed to hear that said out loud. Not when Joe was shipping off to the battlefield in just a few hours' time.

He had stubbed out his cigarette but was still

chewing his lip.

'I don't see what any of that's got to do with you taking *my* ball,' said Polly with a cheeky grin. Inside, she felt all shivery at the thought of Joe going away, but she was desperate to lift the mood. She and Joe had never had a serious conversation in their whole lives. It certainly didn't seem like a good moment to start.

'*My* ball!' said Joe firmly, but he was grinning now too. Although Joe was the eldest of her five brothers, Polly felt closer to him than any of the others. You could tell at a glance they were related. They had the same wild black hair, deep-set grey eyes and big, wide mouths. 'The point is this, Pol.' Joe kicked the ball lightly from one foot to the other. 'If you've heard of no man's land, then you must have heard of the Christmas football matches.'

Polly had. But she let him tell her anyway. 'It was 1914, the first year of the war,' Joe said. He always told a good story and his eyes sparkled as he spoke. 'The two sides decided to call a truce. Just for a few hours, they all stopped fighting because it was Christmas time and they probably missed home like billy-o.' Joe's voice was sing-song, as if he was telling some magical fairy tale. 'There was frost in the air and the lads on both sides sung carols between the trenches. Then someone lobbed a ball into no man's land and they all had a bit of a kick-about . . .'

'That's as may be. You still can't have my ball,' said Polly, folding her arms, when Joe was finished. 'From what I hear, lads aren't larking around out there playing football these days. They're too busy killing each other.'

The moment the words were out, Polly wished she could stuff them back in again. She saw Joe's face turn white as the sheets on the line. She'd only meant to tease him, hoping he'd let her keep the ball. But now she'd said that awful thing about killing. And it was true – Joe wasn't going to be playing football for a very long time. He'd be too busy fighting in the endless, horrible, stupid war.

Me and my big gob, she thought. Why did she never think before she spoke? 'Keep the rotten ball, Joe.'

'Why?' He glared at her, his grey eyes dark. 'Out of pity? Cos you figure I might go out there and die?'

'No!' said Polly quickly. Her tummy flipped over and a hot blush burned her face. She couldn't let Joe see that was exactly what she had been thinking.

'There's only one way to settle this,' she said, standing tall and pushing back her shoulders. 'I'm a striker and you reckon yourself a great goalie. Let's shoot it out! Winner keeps the ball.'

'You're on.' There was a glint in Joe's eye again. He unbuttoned his smart new jacket, took off his cap and hung them on the back doorknob. 'Let's be clear, though,' he said. 'To be a goal, the ball needs to go under the washing line and if it touches the sheets on either side then it doesn't count.'

'I know!' Polly felt a flash of irritation. Why did her brothers always treat her as if she didn't understand the rules? She'd played more football in this back yard than any of them.

Joe pushed the sheets apart like curtains and stood between them, his arms outstretched.

'Wait!' cried Polly, running hither and thither, scooping up chicks and putting them in an empty bucket, as they cheeped and tumbled over each other like a swarm of angry bees. 'I don't want to squish any of this little lot with my great, clod-hopping feet!' She glanced down at the enormous pair of tatty, hand-me-down boots she had inherited from her second eldest brother, Walter. He was fifteen but Polly had nearly outgrown them already.

'Fair do,' said Joe. He wasn't really listening. His eyebrows were knitted together and he had the serious, tight-faced look he always had when he was in goal.

Good, thought Polly. If he was concentrating on winning the ball, at least he was no longer dwelling on the war and the dreadful thing she'd said.

Although she'd finished moving the chicks out of the way, there was nothing she could do about the piglets. They would just have to take their chances – or more likely she would have to take hers. She'd been tripped up by piglets more than once while playing football out here, and had the scars on her knees to prove it.

Polly hitched up her skirt and tucked it into her knickers. 'Stupid thing,' she mumbled. Boys didn't know how lucky they were. No one could take a serious shot at goal if they were wearing a skirt. Then she flattened herself against the wall of the house. It was nothing like as far as the twelve yards from goal allowed for a penalty kick in a real football match, but it was all they could manage in the small back yard.

'Best of three. Winner keeps the ball,' she said.

'Deal!' Joe agreed.

Polly glanced quickly at her feet, more to check there weren't any piglets in the way than anything else. Then she kept her eyes on the goal.

Thwack!

The ball sailed through the air, arching to the left. Joe was stretching upwards but not high enough or fast enough to save it. The top of the ball grazed the washing line but flew underneath and smashed through the gap in the sheets, hitting the wooden gate.

'Goal!' Polly cheered.

'One-nil to the lady.' Joe gave a little a nod of respect.

'Ha!' Polly spluttered with laughter, tucking her skirt back into her knickers. 'I don't see any lady here!'

'Me neither, now you mention it!' Joe laughed too, but not unkindly. He was never one for picking on his sister or being mean just because she was big or awkward or a girl.

Polly curtsied like a queen. She was trying to put him off his mark. She could feel the blood thumping inside her ears, as she always did when there was a challenge on. She needed to win this. If Joe took the ball away to war she'd have nothing to play with. A new ball was sixpence at least. She didn't have that kind of money. She didn't have any money – and, even if she did, Mam would only nick it to pay the rent man. She was going to have to win this battered old football the hard way.

Polly pushed her hair out of her eyes, leaped over a piglet and fetched the ball back to the shooting spot. 'Where've you been this morning, anyway?' she asked. 'Mam was fit to burst when she couldn't find you.

Walter reckoned you must have slipped out last night and gone drinking with your pals.'

'I was just saying goodbye to the old haunts,' said Joe, but the tips of his ears had turned pink. He was lying about something.

'The smelly old canal and Duke's pub?' Polly sniffed. 'That can't have taken more than five minutes!'

'Are we playing football or nattering?' Joe asked. It was clear he wanted to change the subject. But then he added quietly, 'It might be the last time I see those rotten old places, Pol.'

Polly decided with a shiver that he probably had been telling the truth. She wondered what she'd do if she ever got to leave Lowcross for good. *Spit in the canal and run as fast as the wind!* she thought. But nobody was asking her to go off and fight the Germans.

The ball was barely in front of her feet before she was aiming for the goal. If she was quick, she could catch Joe off guard. Just one more shot like that first one and the ball was hers.

Thwack!

Too low, too weak, too central. Polly clutched her head. She'd rushed it.

'Ha!' cried Joe, closing his arms around the ball as he hugged it to his stomach. 'One to the gents,

I believe!'

He bounced the ball off his knee, kicked it with the edge of his heel and headed it back her way.

'One-all!' said Polly, pushing up her sleeves. There was just one shot left to decide it.

She stretched her arms up into the air, bent down and touched her toes, jogged on the spot and shook her head from side to side.

Joe sighed impatiently.

'What's the hurry? Got a war to get to?' Polly laughed. She wasn't going to rush it this time. Joe could wait. She stretched again, lifting her arms towards the tiny patch of grey sky above the yard and gulping a great big breath of smelly, soot-filled air from the factories over the way.

Then she kicked, right-footed for once. That was cunning. She'd only recently been practising that. Joe wouldn't expect it. The ball flew through the air. Joe leaned right. The ball arched left. It was good ... surely, it was good ...

Joe dived sideways and stretched out his great, long arms.

'No!' For a moment Polly thought he was going to reach it. But the ball grazed the top of his fingers and sailed into the goal.

'Yes!' Polly threw her arms in the air. She'd done it! She'd won! She'd beaten Joe, even though he was eighteen and a cracking goalie. The ball was hers to keep. Joe lay sprawled flat out on the floor of the yard.

'What you lying in the muck for?' Polly laughed. 'Looking for worms?'

'Blast!' said Joe, sitting up. Polly gasped. His spanking-new army shirt and trousers were all covered in mud. He looked like he'd just played two full halves for Lowcross United.

'Crikey! Now we've gone and done it.' Polly glanced towards the house.

'I just hope it was worth it,' said Joe. He stood up with a wet, squelchy sound and sighed. Polly could see it wasn't just the mud – his pride was hurt too, but she couldn't help grinning like a cat who'd got the cream.

'Oh, it was definitely worth it!' She tucked the mucky football under her arm.

'I didn't think you stood a chance or I'd never have let you challenge me,' Joe snapped. He was a decent fellow but he still didn't like being beaten by his little sister.

'Why? Because I'm younger than you?' said Polly. 'Or because I'm a girl?'

Joe said nothing. He didn't need to.

'Well, you'd better get used to it.' Polly turned her back and gently lifted the chicks from the bucket, placing them back on the ground. 'I'm growing up fast,' she told him. 'I plan to go on beating you boys from now on, no matter how big and strong and tough you think you are. Just you wait and see.'

CHAPTER TWO

'What were you thinking of, Polly?' Her brother Walter loomed over her as she knelt, furiously trying to scrub the mud off Joe's clothes with a wet, soapy brush. 'Trust you to make trouble on a day like this!'

'Me?' Polly might have known she'd get all the blame. She looked imploringly at Joe, standing by the fire with a blanket wrapped around him like an emperor's cape. 'It wasn't just me. Our Joe—'

'Our Joe is going off to war, in case you'd forgotten. Now his smart new clothes are filthy and it's all your fault.' Walter was enjoying himself. He was nothing but a bully, desperate to prove to everyone what a big man he could be. 'You're more trouble than you're worth, Polly Nabb.'

Polly stuck her tongue out, but snapped it in again as she heard a rasping cough and saw a shadow fall across the open doorway.

'What've you gone and done this time, Polly?' grunted Mam, dropping a sack of coal on the step. 'Come on, speak up!'

'It's nothing,' said Polly, edging backwards. 'Honestly.'

Mam looked worn out. She was pregnant again but had been up since dawn delivering coal because Dad had one of his glum moods today and couldn't shift. 'I know trouble when I see it!' she said, resting one hand on her swollen belly and the other in the small of her back. Tired as she was, she was still fierce as a pit bull terrier. Her eyes were darting backwards and forwards between Polly, the scrubbing brush and Joe's grubby uniform. She missed nothing.

'Polly was playing football in the yard,' blurted Ernie. Polly glared at him. He was the next youngest after her and always quick to tell a tale. 'She made our Joe fall in pig poo!'

'Pig poo! Pig poo! Pig poo!' shouted their little brother Tommy, toddling forward delightedly. Polly couldn't help giggling as he flung his arms around her leg.

Mam grabbed her by the ear and marched her across the room towards the fireplace.

'Ouch! Let go … Please, Mam!' Even though she

was a good head taller than her mother, Polly knew better than to wriggle. She'd been grabbed by the ear too many times to try that. If she wriggled, Mam would only pull harder.

'Do you see this, do you?' Mam pointed a coal-blackened finger at the clock, which stood in pride of place on the mantelpiece.

'Yes!' screeched Polly. 'I see it.' When she was little, Polly had thought the clock was made of real silver. She knew now it was only pewter, which was just some sort of swanky tin, but it was still the finest and most valuable thing the Nabbs owned.

'You can tell the time, I suppose? You did learn something at that school of yours?' asked Mam, with another sharp tug on Polly's earlobe.

'Course I can,' Polly squawked. 'It's half past three!'

'Exactly!' Mam swung Polly round to face Joe. 'That daft beggar's supposed to be at the train station by a quarter past four.'

'You'll be lucky if you can get his clothes clean and dry in time,' chimed in Walter – as if he knew anything about washing!

'Don't fuss,' said Joe. 'Just give them here and I'll be on my way.'

'What? So folk can say the Nabbs don't send their

boys off looking right?' Mam's cheeks were blazing. 'I'll not have this family disrespected.' She was on her high horse now. Everyone knew to keep quiet. Even Polly. 'We may be poor but we look after our men and we do what's proper,' she thundered.

Normally Mam would have gone on like that for half an hour, but this pregnancy had not been an easy one. She slumped down in a chair, kicked off her clogs and sighed.

'Now look what you've done,' hissed Walter, narrowing his eyes at Polly. 'Mam's run off her feet and Dad's having one of his turns.'

Polly glanced at their father. With all the clamour and noise in the cramped back room, she had barely noticed him sitting in the dark corner by the stairs. He was hunched in his armchair, nursing a tiny chick with a broken wing. Bob, the baby of the family, was crawling round his feet in the sawdust, which they put down to try and keep the floor clean.

'Gently does it.' Dad sighed. Polly wasn't sure if he was speaking to the wounded bird or his baby son.

'I don't see how I'm to blame for Dad's moods,' she whispered, scowling at Walter. Dad had injured his back carrying bricks on building sites for twenty years. Now his whole body ached and he grew sad and lifeless sometimes. Soot moods, Polly called them to herself – as if a thick, dark dust had settled on him, like the ashes left in the grate after the fire had burned out. Dad was never violent or mean – he didn't beat his wife or children, or take to drink like some of the fathers round here. He just sat in his chair like that. He couldn't get up and go to work. When it was really bad, he couldn't even speak.

'Fancy squabbling with our Joe on the day he's off to fight,' said Walter, raising his voice again so Mam would hear.

'Squabbling?' Polly wasn't having that. 'We were playing football!'

'You and that blasted game.' Mam sighed, rubbing the side of her head as if a full-blown football match was going on inside there right now. 'You'd think a big lass like you could find better things to do. Like bringing the washing in from the yard.'

Washing? Polly wanted to scream. There was always washing to be done – and always her who had to do it. She didn't see Walter or Ernie out there with the sheets, their hands bright red from the freezing water and their knuckles rubbed raw from the scrubbing brush.

'We were deciding who'd get to keep the ball. I won,' she said, wishing she could make her family see why that old football was so precious to her, though she knew they'd never understand. Her brothers could have a kick-about anytime they wanted, just by strolling up Link Street or hanging around on the gravel patch outside Duke's pub.

But Polly needed that ball to start a game. Boys were happy to play with her then. Without it, she had to beg and wheedle just to be allowed to join in. Half the lads wouldn't let her because she was a girl and they thought she wouldn't play properly. The other half wouldn't let her because she was a girl and they knew she'd beat them.

'I bet our Joe played soft,' said Ernie. 'I bet he let you win. Football's a boy's game, everyone knows that.' He folded his arms as if the matter was closed.

'Then how come he ended up face first in the muck?' snapped Polly. 'Tell him, Joe. Tell him how I beat you fair and square.'

Joe mumbled something under his breath.

'Aren't you going to give the ball back?' Ernie sounded genuinely shocked.

'No!' said Polly, stubbornness rising inside her. 'I told you. I won it fair and square.'

Mam raised herself up out of her seat and glared at Polly. 'You should never have taken it from him in the first place,' she said, stomping over to the bowl of soapy water and beginning to scrub Joe's shirt. 'Not when our Joe's off to fight and might …' Her voice seemed to catch in her throat.

Polly dug her nails into her palm. She had never heard Mam struggle for words before.

'Sometimes I wonder if you've got a woman's heart in that chest of yours, Polly.' Mam thumped the front of her own coal-stained pinafore as if to stress the point.

'That's not fair,' said Polly, her cheeks burning.

'Course it is! There's nothing in your chest except a dried-up leather football!' said Walter, smirking at everyone as he realised how clever he'd been.

Polly ignored him but took a step closer to Mam. 'Please …' Prickles of heat burned the back of her neck. She knew lots of girls would cry if their mam had said something like that to them. Perhaps that's what everyone wanted. Perhaps all would be forgiven then. But Polly couldn't cry. She never cried. Instead, she just felt hot and furious and guilty all at once. 'I'm sorry Joe's swanky clothes got filthy,' she said. 'But I'm not sorry I beat him. It was a fair game and the mud'll wash off—'

'It's not Polly's fault. It was me who suggested we have a contest,' said Joe, the lie making him blush.

'That's as may be.' Mam sighed. 'But Polly's a lass.

She should have had more sense than to take you up on it!'

'She's getting above herself,' agreed Walter. 'Challenging the men in the family like that.'

Polly wished she could run outside and throw herself in the pigs' water trough to cool off. A girl getting above herself was never a good thing. She was supposed to cook and clean and take second place to men, not fight things out in a silly football game. But they were wrong! Football wasn't silly – not to her, and not to Joe either. They'd both felt free and happy while they played and they'd almost forgotten about war and trenches and guns. If she'd given in and let Joe keep the ball, it wouldn't have been right. Not that any of the others would understand that.

By the time Polly looked up again, the flush had gone from her cheeks and Joe was pulling his jacket over the damp shirt.

'Reckon I best be off then,' he said glancing at the clock. 'Don't come and see me to the station. I don't want a fuss.'

As he stepped past Polly, he stopped and ruffled her hair. 'Just mind you look after that ball for me.'

With that he was gone. Striding away through the back yard, ducking under the washing line. Off to war.

'Bye, lad.'

'Show Jerry what for.'

'See you home by Christmas, I hope.'

The others all called their goodbyes.

'Joe …' Polly wished she hadn't spent this last precious time arguing with everyone. She tried to shout something funny. Or rude. Or clever. She found she couldn't think of anything. For once, she was lost for words. But as the gate slammed shut behind him, she knew she'd done a terrible thing. She picked up the ball and ran as fast as her legs would carry her.

'Joe!' she yelled. 'Come back'

CHAPTER THREE

Polly hurtled across the yard. Mam and Walter were right. She should have let Joe take the ball! She felt a tight, panicky feeling in her chest. How could she have been so selfish? She'd been so busy thinking how much *she* needed the ball she hadn't been thinking straight.

Now he was really leaving, she couldn't bear the thought of Joe having nothing to kick around. What if there was a Christmas Day match in no man's land after all? He'd need a ball to play with then. He needed a ball whatever happened. Joe loved football almost as much as she did – and there'd be precious few pleasures where he was going.

'Where are you off to?' Mam bellowed from the doorway, but Polly flew out of the back gate before anyone could stop her, clasping the precious football under one arm.

'Joe?' she yelled. But he was already gone.

She ran on down the narrow passage behind the yard. As she reached the top of Link Street, she glanced towards the patch of gravel outside Duke's pub. Frank Cogley, who lived two houses down from them, was kicking an old tin can about with one of his little brothers.

'Hey, Polly! Give us your ball,' cried Frank. 'We'll let you play with us if you do!'

'No chance!' Polly didn't even glance back.

She pelted on down North Road. She dodged past a mother with a big pram, as if avoiding a defender in midfield, and leaped over a milk churn that had fallen on its side.

'Joe!' she cried, catching sight of him ahead of her at last. 'Joe, wait up!'

But one of the new motor omnibuses was clattering past and there was too much noise for him to hear her.

As she reached the junction at Railway Street, Joe started running too. She glanced at the big station clock. It was gone ten past four already – less than five minutes until his train.

'Blast!' she cried, almost dropping the ball as she stumbled over the gutter at the edge of the road. In the time she'd taken to glance up at the clock, she'd lost sight of the back of Joe's head amongst the gathering crowds around the station. Once she was inside the big, high-roofed building it was even worse. There was a mass of people all milling about at the end of the platform, all dressed in their Sunday best, all come to see their lads off to fight.

Polly saw a few of the women scowling at her, shooting sideways glances at her torn, muddy dress as she pushed past them.

'Fancy coming to wave our boys off dressed like that,' said a smart lady in a big purple hat. Polly wished she'd stopped to grab a shawl to cover her dress, or brushed her tangled hair at least. But there was no time to worry about that now. She had to get the ball to Joe.

'Excuse me!' Polly put her head down and pushed through the waving crowds, some of them clinging to each other and crying. 'Please! I need to get through!'

The roaring train was already shuddering and billowing steam like a dragon as it waited on the platform.

'Joe!' Polly screamed. Young men hung out of every window, waving and blowing kisses to their loved ones through the smoke. Every one of them was wearing a brown army jacket and cap, identical to Joe's. She couldn't make out his face anywhere.

'Joe!' she cried again, running along beside the waiting train.

Then suddenly she saw him. He was leaning out of the window in the next-to-last carriage. She'd recognise that messy black hair anywhere. He was waving his cap at her.

'Here!' she cried. Then she realised with a jolt that it wasn't her Joe was waving at. She stopped running and hung back.

A slim figure in factory overalls was pelting along the platform ahead of her. For a moment – because of the trousers – Polly thought it was a lad ... but it a was a lass, with short brown hair.

Joe stretched his arms out of the window. 'Hello, you!' He beamed with the biggest, brightest smile Polly had ever seen from him. 'You made it. I knew you would,' he cried.

Joe grabbed the girl round the shoulders, gathered her up and drew her close. Then he kissed her on the lips.

Polly froze. No wonder Joe had wanted to come to the station on his own. He'd wanted to have this girl all to himself. His secret sweetheart! A knot of jealousy twisted in her gut.

Polly backed away.

But it was too late. Joe had spotted her.

'Pol? What are you doing here?' he said, his eyes wide with shock.

Polly wished the platform would swallow her up.

''Ello!' said the girl. Her accent sounded strange. She wasn't from Lowcross, that was for sure. Polly forced herself to look up and smile.

'Blimey!' she gasped. The girl was pretty – like a fairy or an elf – with big green sparkling eyes ... but that wasn't why Polly was staring at her with her mouth wide open. It was the girl's skin. It was bright yellow.

'Pleased to meet you!' The girl winked, holding out a little yellow hand. Her grip was surprisingly strong as she pumped Polly's arm up and down. 'I'm Daph!'

'Daff?' Polly blurted out. 'Is that short for Daffodil?'

'No, it is not! You're only saying that cos I'm yellow as a flower.' The girl laughed – a big, loud chuckle, which Polly found hard to believe had come from her tiny frame. 'It's short for Daphne, as it happens. Daphne Jenkins.'

'Daph works at the munitions factory,' said Joe, finding his voice again at last.

'It's the chemicals they put in the shells to make them explode,' Daph explained. 'It turns all the girls in my section yellow.'

'Canaries!' cried Polly excitedly. She'd heard somewhere that's what the girls who worked in the bomb factories were called, because their skin turned yellow as a canary's feather.

'Charming! First I'm a flower, now I'm a bloomin' bird!' said Daph.

'Sorry …' Polly's own face burned red as a robin's breast. It wouldn't have been so bad if Daph had just looked hurt or angry – instead she was laughing her head off. Joe was laughing too – both of them so big and grown up, as if Polly was some sort of idiotic kid.

Then suddenly a whistle blew.

Joe's face turned from laughter to panic in a second.

The train belched steam.

'Mind your backs, please, ladies and gents. Mind your backs,' bellowed a porter as he hurried along the platform.

Joe pulled Daph towards him and kissed her again.

Lots of the other lads were kissing girls too.

'Goodbye!' Joe said as the train began to move. He looked up quickly and smiled at Polly. But he wasn't thinking about her. She knew that. He was leaning right out of the window and his hand stayed in Daph's for as long as it possibly could, holding just the very tips of her yellow fingers as the train moved away. Polly felt the tight twist of jealousy in her tummy again.

'Goodbye!' she called.

'Bye, Joey-boy! Stay out of trouble!' Daph leaped up and down, waving both hands in the air when she couldn't hold on any longer.

'Wait!' Polly suddenly remembered why she had come. The football was still wedged under her arm. 'Here!' she bellowed, sprinting along the platform. 'Take the ball. It's yours, Joe. I should have let you have it all along.'

'What?' Joe seemed confused.

He was too far away from her already. Even if she threw the ball, it would never stand a chance of reaching him.

Suddenly, Polly knew what she had to do. Joe might be too far ahead for her to throw the ball to him, but she could kick it. It would be some sort of miracle if it reached him.

The shot would have to be accurate, right on the mark . . . But it was worth a try.

Trusting her instinct, Polly dropped the ball to the platform and kicked, keeping her eyes on the target, aiming for the small square window where Joe's face was still grinning out at her in surprise. 'Save it, Joe!'

she cried, and she saw the flash of recognition on his face and his hands shoot out through the gap in the window.

'Whoa!' cheered the departing carriage of soldiers as the ball flew past their gawping faces.

'Yes!' An even louder cheer split the air as Joe caught the ball, squashing it between one free hand and his cap in the other.

For a moment, Polly thought he might fumble and drop it, but Joe held tight, his chest and shoulders hanging right out of the window.

'Well saved, mate!' cheered a young solider with a ginger moustache.

Polly ran like the wind. As she pelted along the platform beside the chugging train, she heard Joe's voice louder than any of the others, shouting above the din.

'That's my sister! The best striker I know,' he roared.

Polly beamed with pride.

'Look after *my* ball!' she cried cheekily. But Joe was already too far away to hear her.

Chapter Four

Polly was right about what not having a ball would mean. In the weeks after Joe left for the Front, she barely got a kick-about let alone a proper game. As summer continued in a disappointing drizzle, she was reduced to hanging around the rough gravel pitch outside Duke's pub, begging anyone with a ball to let her join in.

One rare sunny afternoon, she'd managed to escape from home after an endless day of doing laundry and was more desperate than ever for a game.

'Hey, there!' she cried, as she spotted Frank Cogley kicking his old tin can around with two or three of his little brothers and a gaggle of cousins too. 'Let me play,' she begged. Polly knew the can made a hopeless football, but would settle for anything she could get. 'I know where there's a rotten hen's egg in the back of our yard. You can throw it at the wall if you like.'

'Fine!' said Frank, wearily. 'Just don't kick too hard, you'll bend the blooming can.'

'Better try and stop me, then,' Polly cried, leaping into the middle of the fray. Most of the ragged Cogley clan only came up to her waist. All the same, it was fun to be part of a makeshift game at last, even if she did get confused about which of the little lads were supposed to be on her team. There were even more Cogleys than there were Nabbs. All of them boys, all skinny, and all with sticky-out ears and freckles on their noses.

'Not to him, you daft lass,' cried one small angry gap-toothed boy as she made a pass with the rattling tin can. 'He's on Frank's team. Pass to me.'

'Right!' said Polly, charging forward and regaining the can in one swift tackle.

'Blimey!' gasped the gap-toothed boy. 'You're all right, you are. For a girl!'

'And you're all right, for a tiny gnome!' said Polly, grinning as she weaved past him. She was doing all this in a skirt too – she'd like to see Frank and his clan try that. She'd folded it over at the waist three times to make it as short as possible, but couldn't tuck it into her knickers like she would at home.

'Oi!' cried the gap-toothed boy furiously. 'Aren't you going to pass to me?'

'Nope!' said Polly, charging away. She smashed the can between the beer-barrel goalposts and scored.

'Watch it!' cried Frank, as the can bounced off the brick wall of the pub behind. 'I told you not to kick too hard! It doesn't roll right if it's dented.'

'Can't you just get another tin can?' asked Polly, as Frank barged past her to inspect the damage.

'How? Do you think condensed milk grows on trees?' Frank snapped.

Polly shrugged. It was a fair point.

'It's my lucky can, isn't it,' said Frank, a pink glow creeping up behind his freckles.

'Lucky can?' Polly was about to explode in fits of laughter. What sort of lad has a lucky tin can? But something in Frank's expression stopped her.

'My dad brought it back for me on his last leave,' he said quietly, his cheeks now bright pink.

Polly was pleased she hadn't laughed. Frank's dad was serving at the Front. Same battalion as Joe. Everyone was superstitious while the men were away. Some people had horrid little fluffy rabbits' feet, which they kept in their pockets and were supposed to bring good luck. Others wore St Christopher charms around their necks – if Frank felt an old tin can was special, who was Polly to laugh at him?

'Liar!' Polly gave Frank a gentle shove. She knew he wouldn't want to seem soppy about the can. 'Do you expect me to believe your dad gave you a whole tin of condensed milk? All to yourself?'

'He blooming did!'

Polly smiled to herself as she saw embarrassment change to indignation and Frank clenched his fists.

'Are we going to play or chinwag?' cried another of the tiny cousins. 'That's the trouble with girls, they always want to chatter!'

'Too right!' echoed Frank, who'd finished inspecting the can and seemed to have decided it was all right. 'The big lads will be down here any minute and they'll kick us off the pitch.'

'What're you waiting for, then?' Polly slipped the can out from under Frank's feet. 'My side are already two-one up.' She charged away across the gravel. But she hadn't got far when she heard a voice at the edge of the pitch.

'Scram!'

Polly glanced over and saw a tall, beefy young man in work overalls. She recognised Don Sharples, the lad Joe had won his precious football from. It must be letting-out time for his shift at the factory up the road.

'Move!' Don barked. He had a new, shiny,

chestnut-coloured leather football wedged under his muscly arm. 'You kiddies are going to have to clear out and let the big boys play.'

'Sorry, Don.' Frank and his cousins scuttled off the pitch like mice fleeing from a cat in a barn. Polly didn't budge. This wasn't fair.

'Can't we finish our game?' she said. As she glanced over the canal, she could see Don's mates still sauntering down the long lane towards the pub in twos and threes. 'Your lot aren't even all here yet. What's it to you if we play a couple more minutes?'

'What's it to me?' Don took a step forward. 'I'll tell you what. First, I don't appreciate getting lip from a kid like you. If I say scram, you scram, right?'

Polly still didn't budge, even though her heart was pounding. She knew bullies. She'd lived with their Walter long enough. The more you showed them you were scared, the more fun they got tormenting you. Don had a stupid grin on his face, like a Halloween turnip, and kept glancing over his shoulder, putting on a show for the few lads who had arrived.

'Second,' he said, thrusting two rude fingers right in Polly's face – this got a big cheer from his mates. 'Second ...' He waited for the laughter to die down, working the crowd. 'You're a girl! Girls don't belong on a football pitch!' There was more laughter and even a wolf whistle this time, but Polly didn't look at the gathering crowd. She kept her eyes on Don. There was something about being on a football pitch – even a scrap of waste ground like Duke's – which made her feel bold, like she belonged. She wasn't going to be pushed around, not even by a big lad like Don, a year or so older than Joe and mean with it.

'I'm surprised you even bother with this place?' she said, spreading her arms to take in the whole ragged rectangle of gravel. A rickety fence ran along one side of the makeshift pitch, which was all that stopped balls flying into the stinky canal – although they frequently did, and someone had to wade in to rescue them. On the other side, there was a low wall along the edge of the road, where lads gathered to sit and watch. The goals were two old beer barrels at the pub end and a whitewashed outline someone had painted on the back of the tumbledown garages at the other. 'If your game's so important, shouldn't you be up at Lowcross United?' Polly asked cheekily. 'They've got a man who mows the grass and real goalposts and everything, you know!'

'Yeah! And no girls!' snorted Don. 'Perhaps I will get myself up there.' She could see Frank and the others, perched on the spectators' wall, beckoning her to hurry up. More older lads had arrived too and were milling around the edge of the pitch. Polly knew there was no point in standing her ground any longer – their game was over. She shrugged and struck her chin in the air as if she didn't care, although she was still burning with fury at being pushed about.

She was so busy keeping her head held high, she didn't notice her bootlace had come undone, until she nearly tripped over it.

'Steady!' said Don.

Polly smiled, a flash of devilment rising inside her. She stopped right there in the middle of the pitch, bent down and started to tie the lace. Very slowly . . .

'Get a move on!' bellowed Don. Polly could tell she was getting under his skin at last.

'Why?' she grinned at him, innocent as a baby. Now it was her turn to work the audience. 'What's the big rush, Don? Does your mammy want you home for tea?'

That did it! Frank and his little band of boys collapsed in wild, horrified giggles. And a roar of laughter went up from the factory lads too.

'Where's your mammy, Don?' taunted one fair-haired chap with oil on his face.

Don said nothing. He stared hard at Polly as she sauntered across the pitch towards him. She knew she'd made a mistake, but she had to keep looking him straight in the eye. Don waited until she was about five yards away, then he dropped the hard leather football and kicked it so close to her head that she could hear the wind whistle as it flew by.

As she passed him, Don grabbed hold of her sleeve. 'Watch yourself, Polly Nabb!' he hissed. 'I've got my eye on you.'

He was so near, Polly could smell the sour mix of onions and tobacco on his breath. She knew she had made a new enemy – as if she didn't have enough trouble in her life already – and this one was dangerous.

CHAPTER FIVE

Polly's heart was still pounding as she stood watching Don Sharples and the other lads sorting themselves into teams. It was a tradition in these games at Duke's that the married men played against the unmarried ones. Before he went off to Europe, Joe had been the unofficial captain and goalie for the unmarried team. If ever there was a spare slot, he'd let Polly take a place on the side, especially as more and more of the young men were called away to fight.

And fewer and fewer come back – at least not in one piece, thought Polly. Fear flared up like a burning match inside her. She tried to snuff it out, stuffing it deep down into the black fog of worry that had been lying in her tummy ever since Joe had gone. Instead, she tried to concentrate on who else, apart from Don, had turned up to play today.

Mr Graves, the local vicar, was captain of the married men, and his job for the church meant he would never have to go off and fight. Polly watched him strutting up and down the pitch now and smiled to herself. He was as tall and bony as a skeleton and always dressed from head to foot in black, even when playing football.

He flapped his arms at Frank and the rest of the Cogley clan, still gathered in a huddle at the other end of the low wall. 'Run along now! Haven't you urchins got somewhere better to go?' he said in his posh, wheezy voice. 'And you, Miss Nabb,' he added, spotting Polly a little distance away. 'I hope you're not going to loiter. Your interest in football is most un-ladylike, you know!'

'Just watching the game for a moment,' said Polly, smiling politely at the old hypocrite. He'd used her once or twice to make up numbers on his married men's team when he was desperate. He hadn't seemed to mind that she was a 'lady' then.

Today, it was clear he wasn't going to need her. His side was well supported, but Don was at least two players down.

Polly watched the shiny chestnut football sail through the air as Harry Gobin, the unmarried's best remaining striker, took a practice shot at the empty goal and missed. He was a nice lad, Harry. But last year, before so many of the boys went off to the Somme, he'd barely ever got a game. He couldn't hit a barn door with a football, let alone a goal. Polly sighed and turned to go. Even with the likes of Harry as his best hope, Don wouldn't ask her to play today. That was for sure. Not if she was the last person standing.

'You off, then?' said a voice behind her.

Polly looked round and her face broke into a smile. 'Alfie!' She was surprised to find Joe's best friend hanging back, standing under a tree at the edge of the road. 'It's so good to see you. I thought you were still in France,' she said excitedly.

'*Non!* It's *au revoir* to all zat, for *moi*,' he said in a daft French accent, which even Polly knew was hopeless. Alfie was laughing as he spoke, but the laugh sounded hollow and strained. He was half turned away, hiding under the shadows of the tree. He wouldn't look her in the eye and kept pulling his cap down over his face. 'I thought you might have heard,' he said, using his own down-to-earth Lowcross voice again.

'No!' Polly shook her head. She felt the sense of uneasiness rising inside her. Alfie wasn't wearing his uniform, just a thin grey suit. It was the sort of thing men were given vouchers for when they left the army for good. Even on a dreary summer's day like this, the material looked shoddy and cheap. *Not thick enough to cover a flea's backside!* thought Polly. The pale cloth was getting spattered darker grey with spots of rain as it started to drizzle again.

'It looks set to pour,' she said, glancing up at the clouds. Alfie stepped out from under the tree and stared upwards too.

'Oh!' Polly gasped, catching sight of the whole of Alfie's face for the first time. She didn't mean to cry out, but it was too late – the little yelp of shock escaped her lips before she could stop it.

'I'm no oil painting, am I?' Alfie gave another hollow laugh. The left-hand side of his face, which had once been chubby and bright, was sunken inwards and covered in a mass of pale scars, like spider webs. A chunk of his ear was missing too. 'I had a bit of a tussle with one of Jerry's shells,' he said.

'Oh, Alf!' Polly tried not to stare, but as she dropped her eyes from his face, she realised with a jolt that there was no arm inside the left sleeve of his jacket either. She hadn't noticed while he was hiding in the shadows, but the thin material was hanging loose, fluttering in the breeze like a flag.

Polly lifted her eyes again quickly, pretending to peer

through the drizzle at the game, but she had already given herself away.

'I'm thinking I might get myself a hook,' said Alfie with a lopsided wink. He lifted the empty sleeve with his good hand and wiggled it at her. 'Do you reckon it would suit me?'

'Of course!' Polly tried to pull herself together. 'You'll be like a blooming pirate!'

That seemed to cheer Alfie up and he laughed properly for a moment, before adding, 'At least I don't need a peg leg too. Not quite, anyway, though I think my days of playing footie are over.' He took a few steps forwards as if to demonstrate. Polly saw that he walked with a limp. He'd once been the best goal scorer on the whole unmarried team. 'Sharples there won't be picking me for his side again.' Alfie sighed.

'Me neither!' said Polly as they watched Don beckon Frank and his tiny gap-toothed cousin on to the pitch.

'Come on! You lads'll have to do!' he barked.

'See!' said Polly, indignant. 'He'd rather have that little gnome than let a girl on his team.'

'Or a cripple,' said Alfie dryly.

Polly flinched at the word – it sounded so cruel. 'Only because Don Sharples is an idiot,' she spat. But she knew it was true. Alfie wouldn't be asked to play football with the lads any more.

They stood in silence after that. Polly couldn't think of anything else to say. Most of the time she was busy blurting her mouth off, saying the wrong thing – now she was tongue-tied. She splashed her feet in a puddle and looked at the ripples they made.

'Don't worry, lass!' said Alfie at last. 'I won't hold you to your promise, if that's what you're thinking.'

'What promise?' asked Polly. Had she sworn she'd have a kick-about with him when he got home? She wouldn't mind that, if Alfie was up for it.

'Don't you remember?' His eyes were twinkling at last. 'You made a vow you'd marry me. Joe was my witness.'

'Oh, that!' Polly spluttered. She remembered the big boys teasing her when she was little and how she'd solemnly sworn to be Alfie's bride, sitting on the lock by the canal. There'd even been a ring made out of grass.

'If I was going to marry anyone, it'd be you, Alfie,' she said. She meant it too. Alfie was kind, with a wicked, rude sense of humour. He'd always looked out for her, just like Joe. 'It doesn't matter to me one bit that you're . . .' Polly waved hopelessly towards his damaged body. Yet again, she felt lost for words. She couldn't bear to call him 'crippled', even though that's how Alfie had described himself. *Broken* was the word which kept pushing itself forward – not because of his injuries, but the way it seemed as if his whole spirit was shattered. All the light had gone out of his cheeky face. '…wounded!' she said at last. She hoped this didn't just sound like a brush-off. It was true. She didn't want to get married to anyone. Ever.

Alfie smiled at her through the drizzle. 'Don't worry, I'm only teasing, Pol. You're still a kid!'

'I know,' said Polly, feeling more stupid than before. Of course Alfie wouldn't want to marry her – a great, strapping, awkward lass who was taller than he was already. Even with one arm and scars down his face, he could do better than her.

'Look at the old vicar run,' chuckled Alfie. They turned back to the game in relief and watched as Mr Graves swooped across the pitch like a black crow. He tackled Frank's tiny cousin savagely and shoved him into a muddy puddle. There was no umpire to call a foul, and the game went on – though Mr Graves missed an easy goal.

'Blast!' gasped Polly, wiping rain from her eyes. It was properly bucketing now and water had run all down the back of her neck. 'I've got to go!'

'What is it?' asked Alfie, but she was already speeding away.

'The laundry,' she cried over her shoulder. 'I left it hanging in the yard. Mam will crucify me!'

She pelted round the corner into Link Street and ran smack-bang into Walter.

'There you are!' he snapped. 'I've been looking everywhere for you.'

'I know,' she said, pushing past him. 'The sheets. I've got to get them in.' Trust Walter to come looking for her rather than take them off the line himself.

'Never mind the laundry,' he said. 'It's Mam. She's having the baby.'

CHAPTER SIX

Polly stared at her brother. He'd come out without a cap and his dark, mud-coloured hair was plastered flat against his head in the rain.

'Hurry!' he said desperately. 'The baby's on its way.'

'Why'd you come looking for me?' asked Polly, as he grabbed her arm and pulled her along Link Street. 'What am I supposed to do?' Just because she was a girl, she didn't know anything about having babies. Then it dawned on her. 'Of course! You want me to look after the little ones. You couldn't even do that.'

'No!' Walter dragged her through the gate and across the yard. 'Ernie's taken them up the park to keep them out the way. They can shelter in the bandstand if the rain gets worse.'

'What do you want me for, then?' said Polly, panic

rising in her chest as they stepped into the house. The back room was deserted.

'You've got to help deliver the baby, that's what,' said Walter. 'Dad's out on the coal round and there's no one else.'

A low groaning sound was coming from upstairs.

'Didn't you go for Mrs Cogley?' hissed Polly. Frank's mam had trained as a nurse before she got married and delivered all the babies round here.

'She was out,' said Walter. 'There's a lady on Mortimer Road having twins.'

The low groan turned into a loud bellow.

'Go on,' he said, giving her a gentle shove. For once he didn't seem to be trying to wind her up. He was properly scared. 'There's nobody else, Pol.'

'Right!' said Polly, swallowing hard. 'Put some coal on the range and boil plenty of hot water – we'll need that.' She had no idea what for, but remembered Mrs Cogley shouting for basins of the stuff when Tommy and Bob were born. 'And towels too.'

'Got it!' Walter grabbed the coal scuttle and charged out to the yard.

'And bring the washing in,' bellowed Polly.

She put one foot on the bottom step and stood in the darkness for a moment, listening to the sound of

Mam's moans. Every instinct made Polly want to run in the opposite direction – away down Link Street, back to Duke's, all the way to France if she had to. She'd rather face one of Jerry's shells than whatever was waiting for her at the top of those stairs. But she had no choice.

'Mam?' she said, quietly pushing open the bedroom door. 'How you doing?'

'You took your time!' Mam barked. She was soaked in sweat and her thick wet nightie was stuck to her round belly so tightly that it looked like the skin on top of a jug of old milk. Mam's knees were pulled up underneath her. Her thick hair had fallen out of its usual bun and was spread over the pillows in long damp strands.

'What should I do?' asked Polly.

But Mam let out another long groan, which seemed to mean she couldn't talk.

Polly saw a pan of water and a rag by the side of the bed. Perhaps Mam had fetched it for herself earlier on. She grabbed the rag and dunked it in. The water was cold.

Instinctively, Polly mopped Mam's brow.

'This'll be nice and cool,' she said. Whatever had Mrs Cogley wanted all that steaming water for? Mam was as hot as a furnace. The last thing she needed was any more heat.

'Thank you!' Mam breathed, as another wave of pain seemed to pass. 'That's lovely, that is, pet.'

Polly beamed with pride. She was doing something right after all. She couldn't remember the last time Mam had spoken to her so softly – or let Polly touch her like this. Mam wasn't usually one for hugs and cuddles.

She grabbed Polly's hand and squeezed tightly as a fresh spasm of pain made her face scrunch into a ball.

'You're doing so well,' said Polly, pushing the hair back from Mam's face.

Mam shoved her roughly away. 'I should think so! I have done this six times before, you know.'

There was a timid knock on the door and Walter poked his frightened face into the room.

'Get out!' bellowed Mam as he left a pot of steaming water and a pile of towels at the end of the bed. Walter didn't wait to be told twice. He shot away like a frightened rabbit.

'A birthing room's no place for a man,' snapped Mam angrily.

'It's not much of a place for a girl either,' said Polly with an anxious laugh. She wished Mrs Cogley would turn up and take over.

'Don't be stupid!' Mam snapped. 'You'll have to do this yourself one day. You might as well learn.'

'Oh no!' said Polly firmly. 'I'm never going to have children.'

'Pah!' Mam raised her head off the pillow and looked Polly straight in the eye. 'You say that now, young lady, but just wait till some handsome young soldier comes courting you in a few years' time. Or some hefty-looking lad with a job at the brewery.' She let out a loud bellow and sank down on to the pillow again.

Polly sighed. She knew there was no use arguing about it, especially now.

Mam was squeezing her hand so hard, tears came to Polly's eyes.

'Do you think the baby's going to be a boy or a girl?' she asked suddenly.

'How the blazes should I know?' Mam growled through gritted teeth.

Polly hadn't really thought about it properly until then. There were so many boys in the Nabb family, she had just assumed this baby would be a boy too. They always were. Mum let out another loud groan and Polly mopped her brow.

'I'd like a sister,' she said. But as soon as she'd spoken, she changed her mind. 'No, actually, another brother would be best.' Boys made more sense around here. A girl would only grow up to wash sheets, peel spuds and have babies of her own one day. *What's the point in that?* thought Polly furiously.

'Well, whatever this baby is, it's on its way,' said Mam. 'Lift my nightie and have a look will you?'

'Me?' Polly leaped to her feet, ready to bolt for the door, but she knew there was nobody else. 'Blimey!' she cried as she peered between Mam's legs. 'I can see the head.'

'Good!' Mam was panting like a dog in the sun. 'Lay a couple of those towels down, Pol. You and me'll get this done.' Then, in a great, slippery mess and a wild scream from Mam, it was all over. A tiny, wet, red baby was lying on the bed.

'It's a girl,' cried Polly, staring down. The baby was so small she looked like a bird, her skin as dark and blotchy as a bruise. She seemed so tiny and frail, Polly couldn't believe that all that pain and noise and pushing had been for this.

'Is she dead?' Polly asked in panic, until she saw that the baby's papery chest was heaving up and down.

Her little sister let out a tiny sound, no louder than the chicks cheeping in the yard.

'Good girl!' cheered Polly, darting forward and

wrapping the baby in a towel. 'You cry, little one. You cry just as loud as you want.'

Then the door burst open and Mrs Cogley came thundering in.

'Well done, lass,' she said, pushing Polly aside. 'You've done a grand job here.'

'I was glad to have her with me,' agreed Mam, weakly.

'Really?' Polly swelled with pride again, but her throat tightened as she stepped back and watched Mrs Cogley and Mam look down at the new baby.

Both women shook their heads. They sighed and tutted as if they were examining a scrawny chicken at the butcher's or a wilted cabbage on the greengrocer's cart. Whatever they were seeing, it wasn't good enough.

'This one'll be lucky to make it,' said Mam.

Mrs Cogley nodded. 'Some of them just aren't meant for this world.'

'Don't say that,' cried Polly. 'She's just a little weak, that's all.' She thought of the injured chicks Dad had nursed back to health. 'I'll look after her. I'll make her grow big and strong, I promise.'

'I don't rate your chances.' Mrs Cogley passed Polly the towel-wrapped bundle as she fussed round the bed, seeing to Mam.

Polly sat on the edge of the windowsill, watching

the rain splatter against the glass and rocking her tiny sister in her arms.

'Listen to me,' she whispered. 'You can be anything you like, if you just live long enough. You can be Queen of England if you want to.'

'Ha!' Mam pulled herself up on the pillows. 'Hark at you, Polly Nabb. Talking nonsense as usual.'

Polly blushed. She hadn't realised she'd been speaking loud enough for anyone except the baby to hear her.

Mam chuckled. 'I suppose we better call her Queenie, then.'

Polly beamed and looked down at the tiny baby. 'Hello, our Queenie,' she said.

CHAPTER SEVEN

Everyone in the house was sound asleep. Everyone except Polly.

How could they just drop off like that? she wondered as she lay awake, anxiously listening to the faint rattling sounds of baby Queenie breathing through the night. The frail newborn had been laid in an empty drawer padded with blankets and put on the floor between Mam and Dad's bed and the mattress Polly shared with Ernie, Tommy and Bob.

As Ernie rolled over and stuck his big foot in her face, Polly thought of Walter sleeping like a lord on the other side of the thin wall. Nothing would disturb his sleep. He used to share the narrow box room with Joe, but he had it all to himself now. Polly had tried to move Ernie in there the day Joe left, but Walter wasn't having it. 'Mam and Dad's room is the place for kids and girls!' he'd said.

That was all very well, but at nine years old, Ernie was like a young calf – all long legs, bony elbows and huge, stinky feet.

'Budge over!' Polly hissed. Three-year-old Tommy – who was up the same end of the bed as her – had wet himself in the night and there was a great damp patch next to her head. Little Bob, meanwhile, was supposed to have his head down next to Ernie, but had crawled up to her end and spread himself out like a starfish.

One day, Polly thought, *I'll have a big bed all of my own.*

'No! Better than that,' she promised under her breath as she heard a loud snore coming through the wall from Walter. 'I'll have my very own room!'

Mam was snoring too, like a great factory siren, and Dad mumbled all night long as if running through an anxious list of things that needed checking but never came to an end.

Polly tried to ignore all other sounds except for Queenie's tiny, fluttering breaths. It would have been all right if they'd been regular, like a ticking clock. Instead, the baby seemed to fill her shaky lungs with air and puff it out in little pants and gasps. Then silence followed, sometimes for what seemed like minutes, until she wheezed again, like a rusty hinge squeaking in the wind.

Two or three times Polly leaped out of bed to kneel beside the drawer, sure her sister was stone-cold dead, until suddenly Queenie breathed again. Polly realised she was holding her own breath each time too, just waiting for the little rattling sounds to start up. She laid her hand on her sister's chest, so thin and hollow it felt like a birdcage.

In the end, Polly gave up on sleep herself. Someone had to watch over baby Queenie. She wrapped a shawl around her shoulders and sat on the floor next to the makeshift cot, keeping vigil.

At last, Polly must have dozed off, lying on the bare floorboards. When she woke, the drawer was empty and Queenie was gone.

'Mam?' she gasped in panic. But Mam was still snoring. Dawn light was creeping though the gap in the two old bedsheets that hung across the window as curtains. Polly saw that Dad was up and gone. Scrambling to her feet, she darted down the stairs.

'Dad,' she hissed, blinking in the murky light of the back room. 'Dad! Is the baby still alive?'

'Don't fret,' said Dad from his usual chair in the darkest corner. 'I've got her.' Polly opened the back door to let some light in from the yard. She saw that Dad had baby Queenie bundled up on his knee and was rocking her gently back and forward.

'Look on the top shelf there, Pol,' he said. 'Above the stove. That's it. Behind the salt. You should find a little tot of brandy.'

'This?' Polly held up a dusty glass bottle with a cork stopper. There was a dribble of pale honey-coloured liquid in the bottom. 'There's not much left.'

Dad dipped his little finger in and let the baby suck. 'That'll put fire in your belly, my Queenie,' he murmured. Dad always seemed to be at his best when helping something small and frail.

Polly knelt down beside him and laid her hand on her sister's soft black hair.

'Why does everything always have to be such a battle?' Dad sighed.

Polly hoped he wasn't giving up already. She wasn't going to quit. Whatever it took, she was going to fight to make Queenie strong.

'We'll win this one, Dad,' she said. 'Just imagine our Joe's face when he comes back from war and realises he's got a new sister to bother him!' The thought of

that really did make Polly smile. 'Double trouble!'
She giggled

'I suppose you'll teach her to play football,' said Dad.

'Just you try and stop me!' Polly grinned.

Polly stayed close to Queenie's side all day.

'Stop gawping at that baby,' said Mam irritably,
almost tripping over Polly crouched on the floor beside
her makeshift crib. 'You needn't worry. I've sent Ernie
for the vicar, just in case.'

'Just in case of what?' asked Polly.

'To christen her, of course,' said Walter. 'Mr Graves
is coming here, to save us going all the way to church in
case ...' Even Walter dropped his voice as he explained,
'in case our Queenie doesn't make it, Pol. Babies stand
a better chance of getting into heaven if they've got a
proper Christian name.'

Polly rolled her eyes. 'What a lot of nonsense!'

A doctor would be more help than a vicar, she thought.
But she knew they couldn't afford the medical fees. No
one on Link Street ever could.

'Queenie's not going to die anyway,' she said
defiantly. The baby had fed well all morning and was
getting stronger by the hour.

'Get upstairs and put a clean shirt on,' said Mam,

bustling Walter away. 'And Polly, you get outside and scrape that muck off the yard. We can't have the vicar thinking we live like pigs.' She thrust a shovel into Polly's hands.

'Why can't Walter clear the yard?' Polly groaned. 'Or Ernie.' She hadn't seen either of them lift a finger to help since the baby was born. Even Dad was back with his chicks again.

'Can you never just do as you're told …?' roared Mam. She had returned to her full fiery force already.

'All right.' Polly ducked before Mam could clip her round the ear. 'I'm going.' She stumbled out of the door, taking the shovel with her

But it was too late.

Mr Graves was already coming through the back gate and stepping straight in an enormous pile of steaming poo.

'Lord alive!' he cried, letting out a howl of anguish.

'Now see what you've done,' hissed Mam as Polly stuffed a fist into her mouth and tried not to laugh.

'Pig poo! Pig poo! Pig poo!' shouted Tommy in delight.

'I do apologise, Vicar,' said Mam in the strange, pinched voice she always used to talk to educated people like churchmen or teachers. 'I had asked my daughter to prepare a pathway, but ... she's that stroppy, she won't be told!' She slipped back into her own voice again as frustration bubbled over.

'Hmm!' The vicar glared at Polly as Mam offered him a pail of water to clean his shoe. 'These are the things which are sent to try us, Mrs Nabb.' It was clear from the way he was wrinkling his nose, he didn't plan to hang around the tumbledown yard any longer than he had to. 'We had better get this infant christened,' he said, holding a white handkerchief to his face. 'Though heaven knows, if she lives, she'll only be another mouth for you to feed.'

Polly couldn't believe her ears. How dare the vicious old crow talk about their Queenie like that? As if the baby was nothing but a burden – to be clothed and fed and paid for – not a human life at all.

She turned, expecting to see fury on Mam's face too. No one insulted the Nabbs like that and got away with it. But she was shocked to see Mam nodding in agreement at the vicar's cruel words.

'I don't know how we'll manage.' She sighed as she led Mr Graves into the house.

Polly was stunned. Were things as bad as that?

'Perhaps it's time to put your older daughter out to work,' Polly heard the vicar say. 'It would bring in a little extra money and teach her some manners too.'

'Our Polly? That's not a bad notion, Vicar ...' said Mam, back to her plummiest voice.

Polly froze. Trust that rotten crow to interfere. She didn't want a job. She wasn't old enough yet.

CHAPTER EIGHT

For the first faltering weeks of the tiny baby's life, Polly barely let Queenie out of her sight. She even stopped slipping out to try and find a game of football at every opportunity.

The rest of the family could shake their heads all they liked, and say how small and weak the baby was, but Polly wouldn't listen. She stubbornly believed her sister would grow strong and well by the time Joe came home from the war.

Little by little, rosy colour did start to creep into Queenie's cheeks and she grew fatter too, gripping Polly's finger with an iron grasp.

'You've done well with her, I'll give you that,' admitted Mam.

Polly kept her head down and tried not to fuss too much over chores either, hoping that if she made herself useful, Mam might forget about finding her a job. The idea hadn't been mentioned again since the day of the christening. But when September came, Mam told Polly she needn't bother going back to school.

'It's a waste of time for a lass like you,' she said firmly. 'You're better off here helping me.'

'You mean, never go back at all?' asked Polly. She was supposed to stay on at school at least part-time until she was fourteen, though the inspectors weren't checking up much with the war on.

'What does a lass like you need with any more learning?' said Mam.

Polly shrugged. She knew her teacher Miss Divilly would agree. She wasn't like Walter who had a scholarship to stay till the end of secondary because he was good at sums and might get a job as a bookkeeper one day.

'That's it, then. No more school for me!' She grinned as Mam heaved a sack of coal on to her back. Dad was having another of his bad days. His face was turned to the wall in the bed upstairs and he hadn't even got up to feed his chicks.

'Give Queenie a bit of wet rag to suck on if she fusses for milk before I'm back,' Mam shouted as she clattered away down the lane. 'And watch the little ones . . .'

For a moment Polly felt wildly happy and free. Never

again would Miss Divilly whack her over the knuckles with her birch cane just for fidgeting or answering back. There'd be no more endless reciting how many pints make a quart and how many quarts make a gallon, or stumbling through dates of great battles of the British Empire.

It wasn't like Polly had friends to play with at school either. The girls her age thought she was rough and rude. They didn't even jump the big skipping rope together like they had when they were younger. Mostly, the others just stood around in tight little groups, playing cat's cradle with knitting wool and chatting at playtime, while Polly was forced to listen to cheers of exhilaration and the thud of a football being kicked in the boys' playground on the other side of the wall.

I shan't miss it one bit! she thought.

Then she stared down at the big, wet mound of laundry Mam had left for her to hang up on the line, and her heart sank.

She sighed, picking up an enormous, dripping-wet pair of Mam's knickers, just as Frank Cogley poked his head round the back gate.

'How do, Polly?' He grinned, obviously bunking off school himself. 'Fancy a kick-about?'

'Do you even need to ask?' Polly flung the soggy bloomers back on the pile of wet laundry.

She'd have to take baby Queenie and the boys with her, but as she turned to grab them, she paused. 'I suppose you've only got that daft condensed-milk tin of yours to use as a ball?' Mam would skin her alive if the laundry got left ... Perhaps it wasn't worth it just to kick around a battered old tin can.

'That's where'd you'd be wrong.' Frank was grinning as if he'd won fifty pounds at the dog races. 'I got this, see. I scooped it out the canal just now!'

He stepped out from behind the gate and kicked a soggy football from one foot to the other.

'A real ball?' cried Polly. No matter that it was sodden-wet and caved in on one side like a half moon. 'Give me one minute!'

She dashed inside, knocking over a chair as she crashed around, grabbing a woollen bonnet for Bob, a cap for Tommy and a shawl to keep Queenie warm.

'Let's go, you lot!' she said, pulling the cap on to Tommy's head and scooping Bob and Queenie into her arms. They wouldn't be long. She could do the laundry later. 'We're going to play football!'

'What's this?' roared Mam.

It was already afternoon by the time Polly came home and found her standing with her hands on her hips, staring down at the soggy pile of laundry still sitting in a tub in the middle of the yard. The piglets had run off with Mam's gigantic knickers and a couple of sheets had been dragged through the mud too.

'Well . . . I . . . er . . .' Polly's brain was whirling like a windmill. She hadn't meant to stay out nearly so long, but she and Frank had had the pitch to themselves for once and had kicked about for hours. Polly pretended she was the famous local striker, Ned Shorrock, Joe's favourite player, who had scored a hat-trick of legendary goals to win the FA Cup.

'Thing is,' she said, inspiration flashing into her mind. 'Frank Cogley called by. One of his dad's racing pigeons had escaped. So we had to run over to the allotments where we thought it might be roosting and . . .'

'Polly Nabb!' thundered Mam. 'I'll not stand here and be fibbed at! You were playing football, I'd bet my own life on it.'

'Well, what if I was? It's the first time in weeks,' blustered Polly, though she felt a sharp stab of guilt as Queenie started to bawl with hunger, they'd been gone so long. Mam grabbed the baby from Polly's arms and sat down on the back step, unbuttoning her dress to feed her.

'I'll hang the laundry now . . .' said Polly sheepishly.

'And what's the use in that?' barked Mam. 'It'll never dry in time today . . . not to mention having to wash those filthy sheets again.'

Polly didn't have an answer to that.

'Perhaps that vicar was right. It's time you learned a thing or two.' Mam sighed. 'You'll have to do better than this when you get a job.'

Polly froze. So the idea hadn't been forgotten after all.

'I saw my friend Vera today,' said Mam. 'She's heard of a scullery maid's position in a fancy place up on Lilac Hill. It might suit you just right.'

'But . . .' Polly felt panic rising inside her. If she was sent out to work in some big house, there'd be endless chores to do – scrubbing and washing and carrying – even worse than at home, and she'd never have any time to play football. 'What will you do for help around here if I'm away all day?' she pleaded desperately.

'You're no help to me anyway,' Mam snapped. 'Not if you're sloping off every five minutes to kick a ball about.'

'That's not fair!' cried Polly.

'You'd be bringing home a decent wage.' Mam stared at Polly over the top of the baby's head, sucking air through her teeth. Polly had seen that look before. It scared her. It was the look Mam got down at the butcher's shop if there was a pound of tripe going cheap because it was on the turn – a deal too good to resist.

'You could start on half days,' she said, light flashing in her eyes. 'Then help me with the cooking and whatnot when you get back.'

'What about the little ones?' said Polly desperately, as the boys chased a piglet across the yard. 'Who'd look after them if you had to go out and do the coal.'

'We'll work round it!' said Mam decisively. She buttoned her dress and passed Queenie up to Polly to hold. 'We can always pay a neighbour a penny or two out of your wages to watch them if we must.'

Polly growled with fury. All this just because she'd sloped off to play a bit of football?

'Peel the spuds. I'll be back in a bit.' Mam was already heading out the gate.

'Where are you going?' asked Polly.

'To get the details from Vera,' said Mam. 'With any luck, you can start this week.'

So that's it, thought Polly. It was all decided.

'Don't I get any say in this?' she cried.

But Mam was already gone.

CHAPTER NINE

Mam was gone for so long, Polly was just poking her nose out of the back door to see if Frank was free for another quick kick-about, when she burst through the gate, triumphantly waving an envelope in the air.

For a moment, Polly forgot all about the horrible servant's job Mam had gone to find out about. 'Is that a letter from Joe?' she cried, excitement leaping in her chest.

'Better than that,' said Mam, still grinning – though Polly couldn't think of anything better than a letter from Joe, even if it was only saying how cold his feet were and how he wished he had more dry socks.

'This is a reference from the vicar saying how you're a girl of good character,' Mam said, putting the kettle on the stove to boil. 'You'll need it. Vera says you're to go up to Lilac Hill first thing in the morning and if the housekeeper likes what she sees, she'll take you on.'

Polly's heart sank. The last thing she wanted was to be a scullery maid.

'The job's only daily, so you'll come back here every night,' Mam prattled on. 'I don't want you living out yet. I know what some of these servant girls get up to. It's not decent, a lass living away from home before she's married.'

Polly sighed. Why did everyone always talk about getting married as if it was the same as losing your baby teeth or your monthlies starting? Something that just happened to girls, whether they chose it or not.

'You might at least try and look pleased,' said Mam. 'It's a big fine house by all accounts. You're lucky to have a chance like this, Polly.'

Lucky? Polly raised an eyebrow. Surely even Mam didn't believe that. She'd be up to her elbows in freezing water, washing dirty dishes all day. Polly knew from other girls what a scullery maid's job was like, shoved away in a dark, damp cubbyhole behind the kitchen somewhere, so lowly that even the other servants wouldn't speak to you. She was about to say as much, when she noticed Mam was holding the envelope over the plume of steam rising from the kettle.

'What are you doing?' she asked.

'Finding out what the vicar has to say about

you,' Mam explained. 'We can't be sure he's been complimentary, can we? Not after that business at our Queenie's christening.'

'Oh dear!' Polly let out a snort of laughter. Perhaps Mr Graves's reference would be so awful she wouldn't be given the job after all.

Mam slipped her little finger under the edge of the envelope as the glue started to come away in the heat of the steam, then she gently eased the letter out from inside. She opened it up on the table, smoothing out the thick folded paper, and standing back so that Polly could read the vicar's scratchy handwriting too.

To Whom It May Concern:
Polly Nabb is the 15-year-old daughter of a general labourer . . .

'I'm not fifteen!' cried Polly. 'I don't even turn thirteen till the end of the month.'

'I told him you were fifteen,' said Mam simply. 'You're tall enough that no one will question it and the old fool was too lazy to check the parish records.' She grinned. 'It'll mean you can work more hours and there won't be any nonsense about how you should still be in school.'

Just like that, thought Polly. She'd grown up in a single stroke.

She looked back at the page and found her place again.

The girl is one of a large and chaotic brood, which the mother struggles to feed, clothe and maintain.

Mam stiffened beside her, but they both read on.

Young Polly herself is, I fervently believe, on the very edge of running wild. Lacking the niceties of the female sex, she is most often to be found playing out on the waste ground; pushing, shoving and brawling with half the youths of the neighbourhood.

'Rubbish!' cried Polly. 'I'm only playing football.'
Mam tapped her finger firmly on the page.

Physically strong, it is high time this excess of energy was put to better use, with Miss Nabb acquiring the womanly skills she may one day need to become a homemaker herself.

There it was again, the idea that all she should wish for was to make a home of her own. It was more than Polly could stand. 'He means I should learn to scrub pots and pans, because I'm a girl! I can do that already . . .'

'Just read, can't you?' growled Mam.

Polly scanned the last few lines through narrowed eyes.

An additional income for the household, as could be earned by a young girl, would be of enormous benefit in avoiding the crushing poverty this kind of shambolic family so often sink to.

I urge you to take on this Christian challenge. Employ the girl in simple, honest women's work as befits her status.

Yours, etc.

Reverend Christopher Graves

St Saviour's Parish, Lowcross.

'Well,' said Mam, rocking back on her heels. 'That'll do nicely.'

'What?' Polly was stunned. 'How can you say that? It's an awful letter, Mam. Horrible! He calls our family . . . What was it?' Polly searched the bottom of the page for the spiteful phrase. 'Shambolic! That's a posh way of saying we're a mess, Mam. How dare he?' Fury bubbled up inside her. 'Just because we don't have a nice, big, cosy vicarage like he does. He says I'm running wild.'

'What did you expect?' Mam laughed, but not unkindly. 'He was hardly going to call you an angel, Pol.'

'True,' said Polly with a small smile. After all, it was her fault he'd got pig poo all over his shiny shoes. It was a miracle he hadn't mentioned that. 'At least he says I'm strong.'

She couldn't understand why Mam was looking so happy, though. Surely no fine fancy house would want a servant who was 'wild' or 'lacking the niceties of the female sex', whatever they were.

'I suppose there's no point going for the job any more? Not with that reference,' she said hopefully.

'Nonsense!' Mam was still grinning. 'Don't you see? It'll be impossible for anyone to refuse a letter like this. Especially from a vicar.' She was almost clapping her hands she was so excited. 'It says you're in desperate need of good guidance and a steady wage. It would be ungodly of the housekeeper to turn you away.'

'Oh,' Polly growled. So yet again she was a problem to be straightened out. 'I still think it's blooming rude!'

Mam folded the letter, slipped it back into the envelope and licked the edge of the flap to make the glue stick down. 'Good as new!' she said, popping it up on the mantelpiece behind the pewter clock. 'Now put another kettle on. We need to fill a bath and scrub behind your ears, Polly Nabb!'

'Why?' said Polly in horror. 'Do you think the bossy old housekeeper will check to see they're clean?'

This job was getting worse and worse.

Early next morning, with her hair combed and ears scrubbed pink, Polly set out wearing a fresh blouse, her long Sunday skirt and Mam's best bonnet. She had the vicar's letter slipped in her pocket.

It was still dark outside and Mam walked with her as far as Duke's.

'Head on past the railway station,' she said as they stood under the gas lamp at the top of the street. 'Then follow the Old Mill Road as far you can. You'll see there's a couple of big factories back there. Hold your skirt up to keep it out of the muck and don't tread in any puddles.' Mam prodded her arm sharply. 'Are you listening, Polly?'

'Hold up my skirt. Don't tread in any puddles,' Polly repeated.

'Just mind you remember that,' said Mam, prodding her again for good measure. 'Cross over the canal and you'll see a pretty little park with some smart houses on the other side. That's Lilac Hill. Head to the top and you'll find Fairview. That's the one you're looking for – a big white house with a lawn out the front. Apparently, you can't miss it.'

'Fairview. Lilac Hill.' Polly nodded. The name sounded so swanky that she imagined the people who lived there must walk about with their noses stuck in the air all day.

'Don't knock on the front door,' said Mam firmly. 'Go round the back to the servants' entrance. Mrs Crawford the housekeeper is expecting you. Be polite. No answering back. No cheek. No funny business. Do you hear me, Polly Nabb?'

'I can behave myself if I try, you know.' She gave a mock curtsey. Mam's huge bonnet fell down over Polly's eyes and she pushed it up again.

'Stop clowning about,' said Mam. 'And for goodness' sake, quit fiddling with that hat!'

'It's too big,' said Polly. She wished she didn't have to wear it. It was an enormous, old-fashioned thing, made out of thick black felt and as tall as a policeman's helmet.

'It makes you look presentable,' said Mam. 'Now get going or you'll be late.' She bustled Polly down the street.

'All right. I'm off.' Polly strode away, waving over her shoulder. She knew there was no point in begging Mam to let her stay. Besides, that horrible old vicar was right. They did need the money.

As soon as she was out of sight, Polly stopped and looked around for a moment, wondering if there was somewhere she could stuff the awful hat and pick it up later – perhaps under a bit of fence or behind a wall – but if it got lost or stolen, Mam would skin her alive.

'I suppose I'll just have to wear it!' she muttered as she stomped off through the darkness towards the railway station.

Polly had never been on the far side of the station. There hadn't been any reason to. As Mam said, it was just a couple of big factories tucked away in the back there, before you got out towards the edge of town and the fancy houses up on the hill.

Although it wasn't yet light, it was a lovely crisp morning without any rain, for once. Polly swung her arms, enjoying the walk. If she was going to be cooped up in some little scullery from now on, she might as well make the most of the fresh air while she could – not that it was fresh, exactly. It was full of smoke and steam from the factories, but it still felt good to be out and about and free. She darted forward, dodging round a lamppost and kicking an imaginary ball in the air.

'Blast!' Polly felt a gush of icy water splash up the inside of her legs. Looking down in the gaslight, she saw she'd stepped straight into a big, muddy pothole, right up to her shins. Her skirt was dripping wet and covered in slimy mud all around the hem.

She remembered, too late, that she'd promised Mam to lift her skirt – but what was the point in wearing something you had to hitch up the whole time? As she bent down to inspect the mess, Mam's hat fell off into the puddle too.

'Blinking heck!' Polly cursed, scooping up the soggy hat and putting it on top of a post box for a moment as she leaned against the high brick wall at the side of the road. She clutched the bottom of her skirt and rang it out with both hands. A stream of muddy water splashed on to the ground. Polly was just wondering what she was going to do about the thick brown ring of mud all round her hem, when she heard a familiar sound – the thwack of leather.

She let go of her skirt and pricked up her ears.

Football! There was a game going on. Polly could hear it: the scuff of feet and the thud of the ball, just on the other side of the wall.

Instinctively, she looked up. The brick wall must have been ten or twelve feet high. There was no way she'd ever be able to see over it.

'Here,' someone cried out. 'Pass to me!' Polly smiled. From the sound of the voice, it appeared to be a girl shouting, but she couldn't be sure.

Suddenly, a loud cheer went up – a great whoosh of voices altogether: 'Goal!'

Polly was amazed. That definitely sounded like girls. Lots of them.

She started to run as fast as her legs would carry her, darting along beside the wall, frantically searching for some way to see in.

As she pelted around the corner, she found a pair of high iron gates, with a big yellow sign hanging across them:

LOWCROSS MUNITIONS FACTORY.
AUTHORISED WORKERS ONLY.
KEEP OUT!

Polly skidded to a halt and peered through the iron bars. Even in the grey morning gloom she had a clear view of the factory forecourt, which was lit up by lights all around the side.

Polly held her breath and stared, all thoughts of the big house on Lilac Hill vanishing from her head.

She was right.

Girls were playing football together . . . Lots of them. All running about, shouting and kicking the ball.

CHAPTER TEN

Polly stared at the football players. She was gripping the iron bars of the gate so tightly that her knuckles turned white.

She had never seen girls playing football together like this before. There were so many of them, just girls and women, without a boy or a man to be seen. All of them were wearing trousers – this alone was enough to make Polly gawp, excitement pounding in her chest.

'Hello!' Polly rattled the gates, but they were locked.

'Hello!' she cried louder, leaping up and down and waving her arms. 'Looks like a good game you're having.' She barely knew what she was shouting, but she had to say something. She put her fingers in her mouth and whistled, desperate to attract someone's attention. There must be a way to get through the gates and join in. 'Oi!'

Nobody seemed to hear her.

'Hey!' she tried again, pressing her face to the bars, but just as she spoke, a lanky girl with legs like a stork, scored up at the other end of the forecourt where they had two goalposts painted white.

It was a nice shot too – a thirty-yard screamer!

A great roar went up, but was drowned out suddenly by the clang of the factory bell. Work was starting. The game broke up instantly. The goalie tucked the ball under her arm and hurried off, along with all the other girls, towards a series of sheds and huts around the edge of the forecourt.

'Wait!' cried Polly, but like water draining from a sieve, the players were gone.

Polly stared at the empty lamplit space. She'd have been less surprised if she'd seen a flight of angels land on that factory forecourt than all those girls playing football together.

'Hello!' She rattled the gate again, hoping desperately that there might be some way in. More than she'd ever felt anything in her life, Polly knew she belonged on the other side of those gates – a place where girls played football and ran around and shouted at the top of their lungs.

She stepped back and read the sign above the gates

again. 'Munitions factory,' she mumbled, an idea forming in her head ...

Everyone's so sure I need a job, so why not get one here? She remembered Daph, Joe's secret sweetheart, though she hadn't seen her since that day at the station. This must be the place she worked ... and if Daph worked in the munitions factory, then why shouldn't Polly?

Yet almost as soon as she'd had the thought, Polly knew it was impossible. Her future had already been decided. She had to slog on up the hill to fancy Fairview and make sure she got the rotten, stinking servant's job that Mam and Mam's friend Vera had gone to so much trouble over. A job where she'd scrub someone else's pots and pans all day and peel spuds and scour floors – and be polite about it too.

Polly trudged on towards the bridge over the canal and the nice houses beyond. Not since she'd said goodbye to Joe and watched him heading off to war, had she felt so utterly miserable. Seeing those girls playing football and knowing she couldn't join them made her want to scream.

Polly kicked a stone hard with the edge of her boot. She watched it plop into the canal, disappearing beneath the grey-green stinky water. It wasn't fair, but there was nothing she could do about it. She started to run, tripping over her damp skirt. If she was going to get this stupid job, then the last thing she needed was to be late.

Polly was halfway across the canal when she realised she'd forgotten Mam's hat. She remembered putting it down on the post box when she trod in the puddle. She stood dithering on the bridge for a second, but from the tangle of dark curls whipping round her face in the wind, it was clear her unruly mop was in no condition to be seen without a hat. She turned and pelted back past the factory gate, promising herself she wouldn't even glance in. She didn't have a moment to waste if she was going to be up Lilac Hill before the clocks struck seven.

She grabbed the hat and turned back, but this time Polly couldn't help herself. As she drew level with the entrance, she slowed down. Her eyes darted towards the factory just as a lady wearing a smart blue suit passed by on the other side of the gate.

'Wait! I want to work here,' cried Polly, words flying out of her mouth before she could stop them. She rattled the gate. 'Have you got any jobs?'

'Goodness!' The lady jumped in surprise. Then she heaved the heavy gate open and beckoned Polly in.

'Chop, chop!' she said brightly. 'I suppose you were sent by the Labour Exchange? Follow me.'

'Er ... right!' Polly's stomach flipped over, but she didn't need to be asked twice. She gave a last glance towards Lilac Hill and darted through the gates.

'Welcome to Lowcross Munitions,' said the lady, leading her across the factory forecourt and into a small hut brimming with piles of paper and official-looking documents.

'I'm Lady Gidleigh. I volunteer here in the office,' she said, holding out her hand before Polly even had time to gather her thoughts. 'Everyone just calls me Lady G.'

'Blimey!' spluttered Polly. 'I've never met a Lady before.' She shook hands, wondering if she ought to curtsey.

'Get away with you!' Lady G grinned, revealing the whitest teeth Polly had ever seen. 'We're all girls together these days, right? All mucking in to do our bit and build bombs for our boys.' Her voice was so posh it sounded as if she had a bowl of cherry stones stuck in her mouth.

'Right!' agreed Polly doubtfully. In her smart suit, Lady G didn't look anything like the 'girls' Polly had seen outside playing football. She was young though – perhaps about nineteen or twenty, a year or two older than Joe at the most.

'Do you really have a job going?' Polly shuffled from foot to foot with excitement. Not only would she get to play football in the yard with all those other girls, she'd be making munitions, building shells and bullets to help boys like Joe fight the enemy and win! An image flashed before her eyes of Daph and how her skin had turned bright yellow from working here. Polly didn't care, just as long as she could stay. 'Will I get to use gunpowder?' she asked, delighted.

'Steady on, Guy Fawkes.' Lady G laughed. 'I need to see your paperwork first.'

'*Paperwork?*' Polly froze and her palms turned cold. *Of course!* She should have known it couldn't be this easy. She didn't have any paperwork. Unless … She remembered the vicar's letter. Would that be any good?

She handed over the white envelope with: 'To Whom It May Concern' written across the front.

'Let's have a look.' Lady G ripped the envelope open, clumsily tearing it all down one side. Polly flinched. It was too late to turn back. She couldn't take the letter to Fairview now it was torn open like that, not even if she ran up Lilac Hill like a greyhound. The scullery maid's job was lost forever. Her only chance was to hope Mam was right and that anyone who read the vicar's reference would feel it their duty to take her on.

'Golly!' Lady G raised her eyebrow as she read. 'This sounds worse than my brother Roly's school reports, and he was a right tearaway!'

'I'm not as bad as he says,' said Polly defiantly. She wanted Lady G to understand. 'I'm just ... you know, not much of a one for housework.' Polly felt her cheeks reddening. She hated fancy Lady G reading all the stupid things Mr Graves had said about her.

To her amazement, Lady G threw back her head and laughed. 'He does sound like a rotten old dry stick, your vicar.' As she laughed, Polly was surprised to see tears sparkling in the corner of the young woman's eyes. 'You do remind me of dear Roly,' she said in a shaky voice. 'Always causing mayhem. Cricket-mad, you know. Forever lobbing a ball through the glasshouse roof. Drove Mother potty.' Her lip trembled. 'He died last Christmas. Had his final innings at the Battle of the Somme.'

Polly's hand shot out and she squeezed Lady G's arm, not caring if it was proper to do that to a titled Lady or not. 'I'm so sorry,' she whispered, her own voice quivering too.

'Silly of me!' Lady G flapped her hands in panic. She

swallowed hard, visibly controlling her emotions. Then as if making up her mind, she tossed the vicar's letter on to a lopsided pile of papers. 'You're supposed to have your proper documents from the Labour Exchange, but that'll do for now, Polly.' She smiled again, shakily. 'After all, you can't go in any of the really dangerous sheds. Not till you're eighteen. But we'll find you something useful to do, I'm sure.'

'You mean, I've got a job?' asked Polly, in amazement.

'Of course! We'll get you started right away.' Lady G ushered her towards the door. 'This could be the last big push of this beastly war. We need all the bold, strong hands we can get.'

As Lady G led her back across the empty forecourt, it was all Polly could do not to break into a run, cheering, with her arms thrown up in the air. She had got a job at Lowcross Munitions – and it paid five pence ha'penny an hour, far more than being a rotten scullery maid. Even Mam couldn't argue with that.

CHAPTER ELEVEN

It was the first time Polly had ever worn trousers in her whole life and it felt brilliant.

'Gracious!' said Lady G, poking her head round the cloakroom door just as Polly flicked her legs in the air and did a handstand up against the wall. 'Are you an acrobat?'

'I could be in this outfit, couldn't I?' said Polly, amazed and delighted to have an upside-down conversation without a skirt hanging in her face or her knickers showing. She wobbled suddenly as she remembered she was talking to a Lady – it probably wasn't very polite to do that upside down – and she was meant to be fifteen as well. Polly supposed girls that age didn't do much tumbling about. She quickly turned herself the right way up again and straightened her khaki tunic over the top of the trousers.

'Very smart!' said Lady G encouragingly.

Polly stood tall as a soldier. She felt so important wearing a uniform, and the same colour as Joe's army one too. She didn't care that it was thick and scratchy or that it had obviously already been worn by somebody else as the hems and cuffs were frayed.

'Don't forget your cap,' said Lady G, pointing to the bench behind her. 'It's regulations to wear that at all times on the factory floor, otherwise your hair might get caught in one of the machines and you'd be crushed to death.'

'Crikey!' said Polly. Even she felt a little queasy at the thought of that.

She pulled on the stiff white mob cap and stuffed her hair tightly inside. It was the only part of the uniform that still looked as if it belonged to a girl. It was nothing like Joe's army cap, more the sort of thing a maid might be given.

'At least I won't have to wear a frilly pinny!' joked Polly.

'Certainly not! You're a munitionette now.' Lady G smiled and handed her a small yellow card. 'Here's your pass. It's official.'

Polly felt butterflies in her stomach as she read the serious-sounding printed words and saw her own name added in Lady G's curly handwriting:

LOWCROSS MUNITIONS

This is to certify that *Polly Nabb* is wholly
employed at Lowcross Factory, in connection with
the production of war munitions.

THIS CARD IS NOT TRANSFERABLE
AND IS TO BE RETAINED BY THE
PERSON TO WHOM IT IS ISSUED AND
PRODUCED UPON REQUEST.

Well, thought Polly with a grin, *I wouldn't get that
for being a scullery maid, would I?*

'Don't lose it,' warned Lady G, as Polly slipped the
card into the top pocket of her uniform. 'Now follow me.
I'll take you to B Shed where you're going to be working.'

'You don't happen to know a girl called Daph,
do you?' Polly asked as they hurried back across the
forecourt. 'Daphne Jenkins. She's friends with my
brother Joe. He's away fighting …' Polly trailed off,
hoping she wouldn't make Lady G think of her own
poor brother again.

'Jenkins?' Lady G shook her head. 'What does she
look like?'

'Bright yellow!' said Polly before she could stop
herself, but it really was the very first thing you'd think
of. 'I mean, just a bit. She's really pretty too.'

'Ah!' Lady G didn't bat an eyelid. 'She'll be in the Danger Shed, then.' She pointed towards a tall grey building at the far end of the forecourt. It had big white crosses and netting on all the windows. 'It's the TNT that turns the girls yellow. That's the explosive they put in the shells. You won't be working there, though. We're bending the rules having you here at the factory at all when you're only fifteen. But our manager, Mr Thornbury, doesn't mind a few young ones to take up the slack. All the munitions places do it.'

Polly swallowed hard. What would Lady G think if she knew she wasn't even thirteen for another three weeks.

'I am very grown up,' she said, hoping she sounded it.

'I don't doubt that,' said Lady G kindly as they approached a vast warehouse building. 'Welcome to B Shed.' She slid open the big, rusty door and gestured for Polly to go ahead. 'I have to get back to the office but don't worry, they're expecting you. Someone will tell you what to do.'

'Thank you,' said Polly, a jolt of nerves running through her as the door slid shut.

The heat and noise hit her instantly. The hot, echoey shed was filled with row upon row of giant, juddering machines. Moving belts, hooks and sharp metal teeth all clattered and clanged and whirred at once. Women and girls hurried up and down the rows of machinery, carrying huge metal pipes or wheeling shell cases on carts. Others stood in long lines, so still they barely seemed to move at all, just their hands flicking in a steady rhythm as they turned a bolt with a spanner or shunted a piece of shining metal further along the line.

Deep in the broiling fug, the orange glow of a furnace blinked like a dragon's eye. In spite of the sweltering heat, a shiver ran down Polly's spine. It was a mix of excitement and fear. Lots of the men and women from around Link Street worked in factories, of course. Dad got odd shifts in the glass or chemical plants when his health was good, but Polly herself had never been inside anywhere like this before.

She stood, looking about her and feeling daft. She had no idea where to go or what to do. She didn't like to disturb anyone at the machines in case they lost concentration and cut off all their fingers.

'All right, pet?' A plump middle-aged woman with a warm smiley face came bustling down the aisle between the machines. 'First day today?' she hollered over the din.

'Yes! I'm Polly Nabb,' Polly bellowed back, feeling better at once.

'How do?' said the woman, patting her heartily on the back. 'I'm Norah.' She led Polly up the aisle of clanking machines, past buckets full of dirty rainwater where the roof had clearly leaked. 'You look like the sort of hearty lass we need around here,' she bellowed over her shoulder.

Polly grinned. 'I am,' she promised, still shouting at the top of her voice. 'I want to do my bit to help our boys.'

'That's the spirit,' said Norah as they stopped beside a big lathe at the very end of the row. They could talk a little more easily here. 'You'll need to keep your wits about you,' the older woman warned. 'This rotten old place is falling down around our ears and the management are mean as weasels.'

Polly nodded. She could see the shed was dangerous, loud and dirty, but it still felt like an exciting adventure. The only person in charge she'd met so far was Lady G, and even though she was posh as an empress, she'd been kind and helpful.

'Come on, then! We'll start you off here.' Norah led her round the back of the big, greasy lathe.

Polly's ears were ringing from the noise of the machines, her eyes were stinging and her throat was full of dust. She didn't have a clue what she was expected to do, but she didn't care. Anything was better than being cooped up in a scullery, peeling spuds . . .

And best of all, before long, she'd be able to get out in that yard and play football.

CHAPTER TWELVE

Norah told Polly she was going to prepare metal parts for shells.

'We never get to see the whole weapon put together in this shed,' she explained, showing Polly a pair of heavy steel rings as broad as the rim of Mam's dreadful hat. They had sharp snags of metal inside them which needed flattening out on the lathe. 'Just turn this handle here, like this ... and round the whole thing goes. We have to polish thousands of these beggars till they're smooth as a baby's bum.'

Polly stared down at the big, spinning rings. It was hard to imagine that something that looked as harmless as a church bell could be part of a deadly weapon. For the first time since she'd arrived at the factory, Polly thought about what she was actually making. Proud as she was to be doing her bit for the war effort, she didn't want to think too much about her part in helping to create a shell that might explode and kill an enemy fighter. A lad just like Joe. Except German, of course.

She shook her head and pushed the thoughts away. If she was going to learn to do this job, she'd better learn to do it properly or she'd be sacked and sent home before the day was over.

'Watch out when you get to the end,' Norah was saying. 'Check everything's stopped spinning before you pull this little lever and release the rings. Then you lift them into this crate here ...' She pointed to a shiny pile of finished rings on the right-hand side of the machine. 'And take a new pair from here.' She gestured to the left, where towers of rough rings were waiting to be smoothed down.

'Now you try.' Norah stood back and let Polly have a go on her own.

'You'll be grand,' she said, after watching for a couple of turns and making sure that Polly was careful to slowly release the lever when the heavy rings had finished spinning. 'I'm right here on the next lathe. Holler if you want me.'

'I will!' said Polly, hunching over her machine with more concentration than if it was a page of tough arithmetic.

Her shoulders soon felt stiff. After a while she relaxed a little though, realising it was easy if you just built up a rhythm . . . like running washing through a mangle. She was even keeping pace with Norah on the machine beside her. They both heaved their finished rings down into a crate at the same time with a loud clank, then loaded up another set.

The noise had died down a little in the shed now, or perhaps Polly had just got used to it. She could hear someone singing in the row of machines behind theirs.

> 'Keep the home fires burning,
> While your hearts are yearning . . .'

Suddenly, it seemed as if every girl and woman in the shed had joined in with the well-known song, raising their voices to the leaky roof beams like a choir.

> 'Though your lads are far away
> They dream of home.'

Someone was banging on a hollow shell case like a drum.

'There's a silver lining
Through the dark clouds shining . . .'

Walter always said Polly's singing sounded like a strangled crow, but she didn't care. She joined in and belted out the next lines, which were the most rousing of them all.

'Turn the dark cloud inside out
'Til the boys come home.'

Everyone stamped their feet. They were just starting on 'It's A Long Way To Tipperary' when the singing petered out at the other end of the shed.

'All right, ladies, pipe down,' bellowed a man's voice. 'Get on with your work.'

Polly turned her head to see who was talking but there were too many machines in the way.

'What harm's a little bit of a sing-song?' cried Norah, with a wink at Polly. 'It's the rotten lad who checks on our machines,' she added in a stage whisper. 'Never lifts a finger, just struts round as if he's king of this place. Yet if he was half the man he reckons himself, he'd be off fighting in the war!'

'You can't tell us what to do!' hollered someone else.

'Yeah! Put a sock in it!' bellowed a chorus of outraged voices.

'Go and play with your spanner!' A red-haired girl on the machine opposite blew a giant raspberry as the entire shed let out a roar of laughter.

Polly smiled. She'd never heard a bunch of women stand up to a man like that before ... Quite right too. Why shouldn't they sing if they wanted? If anything, Polly had been working faster as she kept pace with the rhythm of the songs, and was just finishing yet another pair of steel rings. The machine man sounded like a right bully.

Pulling the lever to release the rings with one hand, she turned her head again to try and see him.

Ping! Like a catapult hurling a stone, the giant rings shot out of the machine. They flew across the workshop, spinning through the air ...

'Look out!' screamed Norah.

The girl who'd blown the raspberry ducked just in time. It was lucky her head wasn't sliced clean off.

'Sorry!' cried Polly, dashing forward, as the rings clattered to the ground and slid across the concrete floor.

They came to rest in front of a pair of big brown boots.

The machine man.

Polly looked up. Her jaw dropped. She was staring straight into the oil-smudged face of Don Sharples.

Polly had no idea he even worked here. She hadn't seen him since the day she'd made fun of him on the pitch outside Duke's.

'Blooming idiot!' he roared. 'You could have killed someone.'

'I'm sorry,' said Polly, her cheeks burning with shame. It was true. It was a stupid, dangerous, careless thing to do. And she'd made herself look like a fool in front of Don Sharples.

Perhaps he won't recognise me, she thought, turning her head and pulling her mob cap down over her brow.

'Polly Nabb. I might have known,' he said, his voice cold as steel.

Polly could feel the whole shed watching them – like the moment a player walks up to take a penalty shot, the crowd poised with anticipation to see which way it'll go.

She lifted her head. 'That's right. I work here now,' she said, determined to pull herself together, though her hands were still trembling. She wasn't going to let Don Sharples see that she was shaken up.

'Well, Nabb,' he said, with the sort of smile she

imagined a fox might give a chicken. 'You clearly can't be trusted on these dangerous machines, so I've got another job for you.' He picked up a broom, which was leaning against the wall, and thrust it into her hands. 'You can sweep the floors from now on. Surely even a girl can manage that?'

Polly was still fuming, hours later, when the bell clanged announcing it was time for lunch. She'd had to plough up and down the aisles all morning, sweeping away the metal filings and sawdust that littered the filthy factory floor.

Sweeping? She might as well have been a maid. She leaned the broom up against the wall and gave it a sound kick for good measure.

'Don't let Don Sharples get to you,' said Jessie, the red-haired girl Polly had nearly killed with her flying rings. 'We all make mistakes at first. I'm sure you'll be back on the machines in no time.'

'I hope so,' said Polly as Jessie gave her a wave and headed off to lunch with a gaggle of older girls.

Polly's stomach rumbled as she leaned against a tall bench and watched the shed emptying. She'd expected to be home by now, back from her interview. Mam would be wondering where she'd got to.

Now she'd stopped moving, her legs felt weak with hunger. There was nothing she could do about it. Even if she'd known she'd be out all day she wouldn't have brought any lunch. It was the same at school. The poorer kids, like her and Frank Cogley, would sit on the wall and watch the others eat their bread and dripping. Like tatty pigeons hoping for a crust . . .

'There you are!' A loud, posh voice broke through Polly's thoughts. 'I've come to take you down to the canteen.' Lady G was beaming as if she'd just invited Polly to tea at the Grand Hotel.

'The canteen?' Polly was confused.

'Yes.' Lady G bustled her towards the door. 'You can get a good hot meal there. Nothing fancy, but it'll warm your belly. It comes out of your wages.'

Polly's stomach rumbled so loudly it could have been one of the grinding machines starting up. Lady G must have heard but was too polite to say anything. She led Polly across the big courtyard again. It was teeming with girls and women all streaming out of the other sheds. There was no football game going on, Polly noticed with relief. She'd have hated to choose between a hot meal and a game. She'd have chosen the football, of course, but wasn't sure her shaky legs would have been able to run.

'Will there be time for a game after lunch?' she asked Lady G excitedly.

'If you eat quick,' said Lady G. 'It depends what you want to play, mind you. The Red Cross ladies have set up all sorts of wonderful things to keep you girls out of mischief. There's bridge club in a hut over by the North Gate. Backgammon and chess in the First-Aid Shed ... a sewing club and even a little orchestra. Do you play an instrument, Polly?'

'No.' Polly realised with panic that Lady G had got completely the wrong end of the stick. 'I was thinking more of—'

'Football! Of course you were,' said Lady G with the same girlish laugh Polly was getting to know so well. 'I was only teasing. You should see the look on your face!' She guided Polly through the door of the canteen. 'Get something hot inside you first, then you can go and get your shins kicked by all those other ruffian football girls!' She handed Polly a battered metal tray. 'Though the orchestra is jolly good fun, you know. I play the clarinet, myself.'

Polly smiled. She didn't mind Lady G's teasing. In a strange way, she felt almost as if they were becoming friends. Fancy that! Polly Nabb having lunch with a Lady. She couldn't wait to write and tell Joe.

'Better get some grub, then!' Polly joined the end of the long queue. 'And you can keep your fancy orchestra, Lady G,' she added cheekily.

'Ruffian football girls' sounded just about perfect to Polly.

CHAPTER THIRTEEN

Polly looked down at her plate. She couldn't believe her eyes. Two fat sausages and a mound of mashed potato all for her.

'Two Zeppelins and a cloud,' Lady G called it.

'Blooming brilliant!' was what Polly called it. She couldn't remember the last time she'd seen this much food. Especially not meat – and definitely never at lunchtime. Everyone was always complaining about wartime cutbacks and how difficult it was to get enough to eat these days. It hadn't made any difference to the Nabbs. They'd never had enough in the first place.

Polly was always the last to be served at home. Dad got any little bit of meat there was, followed by the older boys, then Mam because she had to do the coal round or was feeding a baby. Polly even had to wait until after the little ones, as they were growing. Mostly, she got a cup of tea and bit of bread to dip in it. That's just how it was. All the girls she knew were like that.

Not any more, thought Polly, shovelling half a sausage and a forkful of mash into her mouth in one go. *Not now I'm a munitionette.*

Norah, who had joined them, complained that the mashed potato was grey and the sausages were gristly. Polly didn't care. This was better than Christmas. Forget writing to Joe about fancy Lady G, she was going to tell him about the sausages first. She only wished it hadn't taken so long to queue up and be fed.

She glanced at the big clock on the canteen wall. There were only twenty-five minutes of the hour-long lunch break left to play football.

'Sowwy!' she said, her mouth full as she shovelled the last forkful in. 'Got to go.' She would have licked the plate clean too if Lady G hadn't been watching.

'Run along!' Lady G smiled as Polly pushed her chair back and practically hurled her dirty plate into the basin of soapy water by the door.

She ran out on to the forecourt and, without even asking, skidded into the middle of the group of girls playing football.

She recognised Jessie with her red hair, stole the ball from under her foot, and pelted away towards the goal.

There was a rush at defence, but no one could stop her. The girls cheered as Polly smashed the ball into the goal.

'Nice goalposts you've got there,' said Polly, ginning with pride. Peering through the gate in the gloom this morning, she'd thought the posts were a pair of pillars. She saw now that they were huge, empty shell cases painted white.

'And that's a nice shot too, Polly Nabb!' said a voice behind her. 'Your brother always did say you were the best player he knew.'

Polly spun round and saw Daph standing behind her, still yellow as a lemon, her cheeky pixie face grinning from ear to ear.

'Hello!' The game had come to a stop with Polly's goal and everybody watched as the two girls greeted each other. Polly felt suddenly shy. The last time she'd seen this pretty, boyish young woman, Daph had been kissing Joe goodbye. She was her brother's sweetheart, yet Polly didn't even know her.

Daph was friendly as anything, though. 'You really are the spitting image of Joe, bless 'im,' she said, in her cheery accent. She put her hand on Polly's shoulder and gave it a big, warm squeeze. 'Oh, blimey! Look what I've gone and done!' she cried.

Polly squinted at the place where Daph's hand had

been and saw a set of bright yellow fingerprints on the shoulder of her tunic.

'Sorry! It's always like that, even after I've washed my paws,' Daph explained, showing her palms to Polly. 'Everything I touch turns yellow!' She picked up the football, leaving two mustard-coloured handprints on the side.

'It's the same for all us girls in the Danger Shed,' agreed the goalie, who was tinged with yellow too. 'It's dust from the explosives.'

'Isn't it dangerous?' asked Polly. 'I mean . . . you don't glow in the dark do you?'

'No we blinkin' don't!' Daph sounded outraged, but her eyes were twinkling with laughter.

'As for being dangerous . . .' – the goalie shrugged – 'none of us have died of it.'

'Not yet,' said Daph with a wheezy laugh.

'Good!' Polly smiled, guessing she was supposed to make light of it too, though she wasn't convinced the Danger Shed girls wouldn't explode like firecrackers if somebody kicked them too hard.

'Come on! I'm Olive by the way,' said the goalie, taking the ball from Daph and booting it far away across the forecourt. 'We've only got ten minutes till the bell, ladies!'

Polly darted away, weaving through the stream of girls in pursuit of the ball. She had no idea whose team she was on, but she chased down the lanky girl with stork legs who she'd seen score so brilliantly this morning. She had just got the ball off her when Daph piled in and tackled it back before Polly could make another run at goal.

'You're not a bad defender,' said Polly with a rush of joy. No one had called her names, or looked at her like she was crazy, when she'd joined the game. They'd just got on with playing. These were girls like her. Until this morning, Polly had never known there *were* any other girls like her. Girls like Jessie and Olive and Daph. Girls who wanted to play football.

Even Don Sharples couldn't dampen her mood as he thrust the broom at her when she got back to the shed. 'Start again, Nabb. You missed a bit before lunch. Over by the turret lathe,' he barked.

'Right you are!' Polly pushed the broom away, whistling 'Pack Up Your Troubles' as she went. She knew it would drive Don Sharples mad to see her enjoying her work. If he wanted to ruin her mood, he'd have to try a whole lot harder than making her sweep a floor twice.

When the bell finally rang for the end of their shift

at seven that evening, Polly braced herself, ready to go home and face Mam. She couldn't believe it was only this morning she'd set out for the fancy house on Lilac Hill. It seemed like a world away already.

CHAPTER FOURTEEN

Mam was fit to burst when she heard Polly had dodged out of the scullery maid's job and ended up at Lowcross Munitions instead.

'Trust you to go having your own ideas,' she barked, as if that was a terrible thing. But as soon as Polly mentioned how good the pay was, there wasn't much of an argument left.

'Hmm!' said Mam, which Polly knew was as close to an agreement as she'd ever get. 'I suppose a strapping lass like you might as well make herself useful where she can.'

'Exactly, I'm helping with the war effort. I get a meal at lunchtime too,' she said with a grin. 'It was sausage and mash today.'

'Sausages?' said Ernie in disbelief and little Tommy rubbed his belly.

'Lady G – she's the posh lady in the office – calls them Zeppelins because they're as big and fat as airships!' said Polly, with a wink at her younger brothers. 'I'll bring you one home in my hankie tomorrow.'

The little boys clapped their hands.

'I tell you what,' said Polly, proudly. 'I'll buy you a whole string of sausages from the butcher's on Saturday when I get paid.'

The boys cheered with delight, throwing their arms round Polly's waist.

'You'll do no such thing,' snapped Mam. 'You'll come straight home with that money and give every penny to me. I'll be the one says how it gets spent. There's rent to pay and bread to buy, long before you start promising your brothers sausages. Do you hear me, Polly Nabb?'

'Yes,' said Polly, but nothing could dampen her spirits. She'd sneak a ha'penny from the wages and buy the boys a twist of liquorice if nothing else . . . and she'd start saving for a football too.

'It's not right, girls getting paid so much money,' said Walter. 'What do women need with wages like that?'

'To run away with, so they don't have to marry men like you,' muttered Polly under her breath, but for once she couldn't be bothered to start an argument with

Walter-the-know-all. She was too exhausted after her day of hard work – and too happy to bother winding him up.

She lifted little Queenie out of her crib, blew a kiss on to her soft doughy cheek and sunk into a chair. The baby was almost chubby now, she was doing so well. She cooed and wriggled her legs in delight.

But Walter wasn't going to let things go as easily as that.

'What is it you girls are doing up there, anyway?' he said. 'Polishing the shells with feather dusters?' He laughed delightedly at his own joke. Ernie, the traitor, giggled too. Even Mam chuckled.

'No!' said Polly. She wasn't going to admit she'd been sweeping floors all day. 'I was operating a lathe.' That was true – for an hour at least. 'The girls do everything: making shell cases and bullets, adding fuses, putting the explosives in. Some of them even drive cranes.'

'It doesn't seem right,' said Walter, looking serious now. 'Making bombs is men's work.'

'All the men are away at war,' said Polly reasonably.

Walter growled, annoyed by her logic. He always liked to be right. 'You girls'll get used to working. When the war's over, you'll take all the best jobs from our lads,' he said. 'Who's going to look after the homes and raise the babies then? Who's going to get our dinner ready and put food on the table when we get back from work?'

'You won't be at work if the women have taken all your jobs,' said Polly with a grin. 'The men can get their own dinner, can't they?' Even if she was too tired to argue properly, it didn't mean she wasn't enjoying watching Walter tie himself in knots.

She closed her eyes and snuggled little Queenie as he mumbled to himself and thumped around the room.

'I'm off to bed,' she said before Walter could think up a good comeback. Sitting down had made her realise how bone-tired she was. She had an ache across her shoulders and down the back of her neck from pushing the heavy broom all day.

'Not so fast,' said Mam as Polly staggered to her feet. 'I need help with these pans.' She pointed to a pile of washing-up from the dinner Polly had come home too late to eat.

'But ... I've got a twelve-hour shift tomorrow,' said Polly. 'Seven in the morning till seven at night. Can't I just get to bed? Can't Walter help with the dishes?'

'Housework's for girls,' said Walter with a grin. He picked up his cap and headed out the door. 'See you later!' He was so smug he was practically glowing in the dark.

If Polly hadn't been holding little Queenie, she'd have picked up one of the dirty plates and thrown it at his head.

As it was, Mam got her peeling spuds for the next day's dinner too.

'If you're going to be out so long, I'll need all the help I can get when you're home,' she said.

Dad was just as bad as Walter. He was a gentle soul, so he didn't argue with Polly or bully her, but she'd never known him lift a hand to help around the house. He just left her and Mam to it while he pottered about with his chicks.

In the end, when Mam wanted to sweep up round his chair, she sent him out on an errand. That was man's work at least.

'Go down to Duke's and tell old Starkie to wake our Polly at five fifteen every morning from now on,' she told him. None of the families on Link Street could afford alarm clocks so they all relied on Mr Starkie, the knocker-up man, to come along and bang on their windows with his big stick.

'Right you are,' said Dad, ambling out the back gate.

*

Polly was so keen to be at the munitions factory in time for the early morning kick-about, she was out of bed and dressed in her uniform even before her wake-up call.

Stamping her feet into her boots, she ran outside to stop Mr Starkie banging on the upstairs window as she heard him rattling down the street.

'You're up before the larks, lass,' he laughed. 'What is it? Meeting a secret sweetheart on the way?'

'Better than that,' said Polly with a grin. 'I'm going to play football!'

She ran off down the road, stuffing a crust of bread in her mouth as she went.

It was still pitch-black when she arrived at the gates of the munitions factory. Polly was lost in her own thoughts, imagining she was scoring the winning goal for Lowcross United in a nail-biting FA Cup final. The crowd were on their feet cheering her on. She was clear of the defenders, charging towards goal when ...

'Polly!' A voice greeted her from the darkness.

'Who's there?' Polly nearly leaped out of her skin. A small, shadowy figure stood in the gloom by the post box.

''Ello!' The figure stepped forward. 'I didn't mean to make you jump.'

'Daph!' cried Polly, smiling in relief.

The older girl grinned back. 'I bet I know why you're here,' she said.

'Football!' Polly beamed.

'Me too, although we're a bit early,' said Daph, pointing to the closed factory gates. 'Night shift's still on. But the others will be here soon and Olive will bring the ball.'

Polly felt the same thrill of excitement as yesterday. At last she had found other girls like her. Girls who were prepared to get up at the crack of dawn just to knock a ball about.

'Where I was growing up in London, it was only the boys who played football,' said Daph, kicking a pebble towards Polly.

'You grew up in London?' said Polly, automatically kicking the pebble back. That explained Daph's accent. Polly had never met anybody from as far away as London before.

'Down the East End,' said Daph. 'It was just me and my dad.' They began idly kicking the pebble back and forward between them. 'Mum died when I was born. Dad was a docker, until he passed away last year too.'

'You're an orphan,' Polly blurted out. 'Poor you!' It seemed so sad that someone as bright and bubbly as Daph should be all alone in the world, with no brothers or sisters either. Yet, at the same time, Polly was ashamed to feel there might be something exciting about it – like being a kite, up in the sky, with your string let go. Flying high over rooftops, with nobody able to reach you . . .

'The first time I ever kicked a football was with your Joe,' said Daph. 'When I say "kicked" it, I missed actually. My foot whizzed right over the top. Joe said I ought to get lessons from his sister. Then I saw you do that thing at the station, where you shot the ball right into his hands through the window of the moving train, and I knew you were something special.'

Polly grinned so hard she thought her cheeks might split. She wasn't used to people coming right out and saying nice things to her like that.

'It was nothing . . .' she said with a shrug. 'I was just showing off!'

Daph raised an eyebrow, her pixie eyes twinkling in the lamplight. 'It was pretty amazing whatever it was,' she said. 'I was jealous when I saw how impressed Joe was, and all those other soldiers too, and I thought: I wish I could do something like that. Beat the boys at their own game. Something that would make them all sit up and think. Then when the factory girls here started kicking the ball about, remembering you made me want to join in.'

'You're really good,' said Polly 'I can't believe you're so new to the game.' She recalled how Daph had taken the ball away from her yesterday. 'You're so small and fast, everyone would expect you to be a striker, but you're able to just nip round, steal the ball and pass it on before anyone even knows what's happened.'

Now it was Daph's turn to blush.

'By the time Joe comes home we'll be good enough to play for Lowcross United,' said Polly, giving the pebble an excited kick. 'We'll be as good as the men!'

'No!' Daph let the pebble shoot past her. 'No, we won't.' Her face darkened.

'I don't see why not?' Polly sighed, disappointment seeping out of her like air from a punctured ball. Daph had seemed like such a firebrand. She had said all that stuff about beating the boys at their own game. Yet here she was, giving up at the first hurdle, admitting defeat before she'd even tried. Polly turned away, finding a new pebble and kicking it down the street. Daph grabbed her shoulder.

'Listen to me, Pol. We're not going to be as good as the men, because we're going to do better than that,' she said. 'We're going to be as good as ourselves! We're not going to care what the lads think or say, or what their rules are. We're just going to play our own game the best we can, for ourselves and by ourselves!'

'Yes!' said Polly, a burst of fire exploding in her belly. She'd never thought of it like that before, but Daph was right. 'Our own game!'

'Exactly!' Daph grabbed Polly's hands and the two of them spun in circles, going so fast that they didn't dare to let each other go. If they had, they'd have gone flying off in opposite directions, thrown back like the spinning rings from Polly's lathe.

CHAPTER FIFTEEN

As the factory gates opened, Daph and Polly were soon joined by other players who began to gather in the forecourt, waiting for Olive to arrive with the ball.

When she finally appeared, racing into the courtyard, the goalie looked stricken.

'I've forgotten it, girls,' she cried, gasping for breath. 'I'd forget my head if it wasn't screwed on . . .'

'Oh, Olive . . .'

'You forgot your pass last week . . . and your mob cap . . .'

'What are we going to play with . . .?' the girls began to moan.

'Does this mean we won't be able to play for the rest of the day?' said Polly anxiously.

'Don Sharples has got a ball,' said Mary-Anne, the tall girl who had scored yesterday.

'He'd never let us borrow it, though,' said Daph. 'So don't ask him. Don't give him the satisfaction of saying no.'

'But I want to play,' said Polly desperately. She glanced over her shoulder. Don Sharples was leaning against the wall of the Danger Shed, watching them. He had a lit cigarette in his mouth, even though you weren't supposed to smoke near the Danger Shed.

'I've got an idea,' Polly whispered, noticing Lady G had come outside.

'Polly . . .' said Daph.

'You're not going to make trouble, are you?' said Mary-Anne. 'Be careful. That Don's a spiteful beggar.'

'Trouble doesn't worry me!' said Polly, almost truthfully. She threw her shoulders back. Even when she didn't go looking for it, trouble had a habit of coming to find her. She might as well get to play football at the same time.

Before the girls could argue, she strode off across the forecourt. Every second they wasted, was a second they could be playing.

'Excuse me, Lady G?' she called, raising her voice as she got near to Don Sharples. 'Could I ask you something . . .?'

Out the corner of her eye she saw Don hastily stub out his cigarette, eager not to be caught smoking by anyone from the office.

'Hello, Polly!' Lady G turned and smiled at her. 'How are you settling in?'

'Very nicely, thank you,' said Polly, still speaking louder than she needed to. Even without turning to look, she could feel Don Sharples listening to them. Just as she knew he would. He was a nosy so-and-so.

'There's just one tiny problem, Lady G. Me and the ruffian football girls have hit a bit of snag,' said Polly, purposefully using the teasing name for the team which the posh young woman had come up with herself. 'We want to have a quick kick-about before our shift starts, but we haven't got a ball.'

'Oh!' Lady G looked sorry but raised her hands, ready to shrug. Polly knew she was about to say she couldn't help them, but Polly was too quick for her.

'Thing is, Lady G, we wondered if one of the chaps might have a football we could borrow.' Polly felt daft as a brush, saying 'chaps' like a posh lady would, but hoped it might make Lady G see the solution more clearly. 'We're just a little shy to ask, that's all,' she said, trying to look as helpless as she could and stepping back so Lady G would have a direct line of vision to Don

Sharples eavesdropping a couple of feet away. 'We'd love to have a quick kick-about if we could.'

'Of course you would,' said Lady G kindly. 'Mr Sharples.' She raised her voice and called to him, although he was already skulking away. 'Mr Sharples, I think I've seen you and some of the men playing soccer. I'm sure you have a ball the girls could borrow, don't you?'

'Er...' Don looked like a rabbit caught in the glow of a poacher's lantern. Polly knew the last thing he wanted was to lend them his ball – but he wouldn't dare refuse Lady G.

'Go on, Mr Sharples,' she urged in her cut-glass voice. 'Be a sport, old chap.'

'Fine!' Don sighed. 'I'll go and fetch it, Lady Gidleigh.'

Polly practically punched the air as she watched him head off sulkily towards the locker room.

The girls cheered.

'Skilfully played, Polly!' whispered Daph.

Polly grinned. 'And there wasn't even any trouble!'

At least, not yet, she thought, but Don Sharples would not like being out-foxed like that.

By the time they finally started, the morning kick-about was too short by far.

Polly helped Lady G persuade Don to lend them the ball for the rest of the day, so at least they could make the most of lunchtime, though he scowled horribly as he agreed to it.

The minute the bell rang, Polly charged to the canteen, so she'd be at the front of the queue today. Some of the volunteer servers looked like very grand ladies indeed. The one who served Polly was wearing a huge, fluffy ostrich feather in her hat. Polly held up her plate for a mound of boiled potatoes and a thick slice of chicken pie. 'Thank you very much,' she said politely, thinking how odd it was to be served by someone so grand. Girls like Polly would normally be employed as maids, emptying the bedpans of well-to-do ladies like this. Now, because she was a munitionette, things were the other way round. The war had made everything so strange.

The slowest queue of all was run by a very elderly lady dressed in fountains of lavender lace. Polly heard somebody whisper that this was the Duchess of Downmead and nobody dared to tell her to hurry up. Polly made a note never to get in that line.

As soon as she had her food, she skidded into a seat, peeled the pastry lid off her pie, wrapped it in her napkin and popped it in her pocket. There hadn't been any sausages today, but her little brothers would be thrilled enough with the pastry crust.

In what seemed like only a matter of minutes, Polly had scoffed everything on her plate. Her tummy was full of warm food and hot sweet tea, which she had to keep blowing on and adding extra milk to so that she could drink it faster. Then she was out the door again, with the whole lunch break free to play football.

The Ruffian Girls – as they had all proudly begun to call themselves – came out of the canteen in dribs and drabs. Soon there were enough of them to make two sides.

'Anyone who wants to be on my team, take your hat off,' shouted Polly boldly, tossing her own stiff mob cap on to a pile of sacks. She glanced around and spotted Mary-Anne, the tall striker. 'Anyone on Mary-Anne's team, keep your caps on.'

'Who made Nabb queen of the pitch?' said someone.

'She looks younger than my kid sister,' added someone else.

'She's the one who got us the ball,' said Mary-Anne, fairly. 'And a pretty decent player from what I've seen.'

'Someone has to take charge of us. Polly's certainly bossy enough,' said Jessie, giving her a wink.

There was a little more muttering but, for the most

part, the girls obediently began to sort themselves into two teams.

Polly tried not to tap her foot or be too impatient as the girls milled around. Some were worrying whether they were on the same team as their friends. A few were refusing to take off their caps, fretting that their hair looked messy.

Over at the edge of the pitch Polly could see Don Sharples, a sneering smile on his face, his arms folded, as if he was all set to have a good laugh.

'Let's shift!' she barked, frustration spilling over – she was so desperate to get the girls moving and make the most of the lunch break.

'All right! Keep your knickers on!' someone laughed, as the teams were finally sorted.

Polly tossed the ball to Mary-Anne. 'You can kick off,' she said.

'Hold on a minute, ladies!' Don Sharples strode into the middle of the pitch, his arms held up like a policeman directing traffic. 'You'll need an umpire if you're going to play a proper game. I'm a fully trained linesman as it happens. I used to work up at Lowcross United, before they stopped having matches for the war.'

'We don't need your help, thank you,' said Polly,

grinding her teeth. She knew he was more interested in causing trouble than ensuring fair play. 'Get out of our way.' Without thinking, she gave Don Sharples a little shove.

'Oi!' he roared, but a great cheer went up from the girls.

'Yeah, Don. Get out of the way,' cried Olive.

'Go and find something useful to do, you get paid enough money for it,' shouted someone else. The few men at the factory were paid almost double what the women were.

'You could always go and check on our machines,' hollered Jessie. She'd told Polly earlier that men like Don were only employed at the factory because the male unions insisted on it. That way, they could claim women had never worked entirely by themselves and so were not as qualified as the men. It was a trick really, to make sure women wouldn't be able to take jobs away from men once the war was over – the thing Walter was so afraid of.

'How about doing something really useful, like going off to fight?' bellowed Mary-Anne. 'My fiancé Peter would swap places with you no trouble.'

'Yeah, Don? Why don't you join up?' bellowed someone else.

'Cow-ard! Cow-ard! Cow-ard!' A rumbling chant had started, beginning with the goalkeeper down the far end and spreading across the pitch.

Polly looked at Don's face and saw the panic rising in his eyes. She hadn't meant for this to start.

'Cow-ard! Cow-ard!'

Don bit his lip and shrugged, as if he didn't care what a lot of lasses thought. But Polly could see that his hands were shaking. He caught her eye and glared at her across the pitch.

Polly lowered her eyes. The women were right, Don Sharples probably was hiding away here in his soft job at the factory, while the rest of the young men – men like Joe, lads Don had played football with – were sent away to fight in the horrible, terrifying trenches. She couldn't bring herself to taunt him along with the others, though. Not when she'd seen his hands shaking like that.

'You lasses will never be able to play football properly,' he bellowed, shouting over the noise and jeering. 'I bet you don't even know the rules.' He strode off the pitch, then stopped suddenly and spun back round.

He marched up to Mary-Anne and snatched the ball from her hands.

'This is mine, remember.' He grinned. 'And you girls can't use it!'

He stormed off the pitch again and this time he kept on walking, away down the side of the Danger Shed, taking his ball with him.

'Wait!' Polly chased after him, furiously waving her arms. 'Please!' But she knew it was hopeless.

She sagged down in a heap, clutching her head in her hands. Their game was over and the whole lunch break was wasted now. 'Why do they always do that?' she roared. 'Why do the lads always take the ball?'

Chapter Sixteen

After their confrontation with Don Sharples, Daph started being the one to bring the ball each day so that poor Olive wouldn't forget and leave it at the hostel where they lived. The Ruffian Girls played every morning before work and every lunchtime too, dividing themselves into teams of 'On'ers' or 'Off'ers' depending on whether or not they wore their caps. Polly was always the first to fling her stiff, tight mob cap to the ground.

'I wish you'd play on the same side as me sometimes,' said Mary-Anne admiringly one day. 'You really are a brilliant striker. By far the best player we've ever had.'

Polly smiled, but it didn't stop her stealing the ball and slamming in another goal.

'I just wish someone else would try and stop you scoring,' laughed Olive picking herself up from the ground. It was Polly's fourth goal that lunchtime. A little cheer went up from a few girls who'd come to watch from the sidelines.

Don Sharples made himself scarce and didn't bother coming to sneer at their games. Polly began to hope he might leave the Ruffian Girls alone for good. He even seemed to have stopped picking on her in particular.

He sniffed furiously, but didn't complain out loud, when Norah told Polly to 'quit sweeping like a skivvy' and come and operate the lathe with the rings again. Polly was thrilled and always careful to watch the spinning steel hoops at every turn now. It was heavy, bone-aching, repetitive work, but at least she felt like she was doing something useful.

As Christmas drew nearer, Polly slept like a log each night, not noticing if Queenie howled, Tommy wet the mattress, Ernie stole the blankets or Bob wriggled. But exhausted as she was from the hard work at the factory, she felt she'd never had as much spark inside her either. Well fed each day and refreshed after a good night's sleep, she leaped up in the freezing dark long before dawn, never needing to be woken by Mr Starkie, and raced through the empty streets to get to the factory.

It was often she and Daph who arrived first. The two girls would practise passing the ball, zigzagging along obstacle courses of rings from Polly's lathe, and raced each other round the sheds. Polly was stronger and could run for longer, but Daph was faster – like a whippet. She always won their sprint races, though she would often have to clutch her chest for minutes afterwards, bent double, unable to speak.

'Dust!' she'd pant at last, shaking her yellow fist at the Danger Shed. 'There's more gunpowder inside me than in a shell!'

One particularly frosty morning, Daph's chest was rasping harder than usual in the cold. They sat on the steps of the Danger Shed so she could catch her breath. As Daph wheezed in and out, Polly blew on her chilly fingers and watched her own deep breaths make clouds of steam in the freezing air.

'What are you doing for Christmas?' asked Daph, lifting her head at last. It was only a week away now and everyone at the factory would have the day off.

Polly shrugged. There was never much of a fuss in their house. The children all got an orange each, sometimes a twist of sherbet or some liquorice too. The piglets, now fully grown, had been sold to the butcher and there'd be a leg of ham left over for their lunch with roast potatoes and carrots – sponge pudding for afters too if Mam had enough for a tin of treacle. The thing Polly usually loved about Christmas Day was that she and Joe would play football once dinner was done. That wouldn't happen this year, of course, and she couldn't get too excited about anything else.

'Do you want to come to ours?' she asked, feeling guilty she hadn't invited Daph before. She didn't know if it was her place. Joe had kept his sweetheart secret from the family – perhaps he was ashamed of them all. Perhaps he didn't want Daph to see how they lived, with the muddy yard and the dark, cramped room. Or perhaps it was all the shouting and bickering that Joe had wanted to save Daph from. Even on Christmas Day there was always an argument of some kind, Mam clipping someone round the ear … She might be furious with Polly for inviting Daph. Every slice of Christmas ham was precious, and with so many mouths to feed it had to last long into the new year.

None of that mattered, though. It was Christmas. Surely Joe wouldn't want Daph to be alone. Lots of the other girls from the hostel were arranging to see family, but Daph had no family left.

'You'd be welcome!' said Polly decisively. She knew she'd like to spend Christmas with her new friend too. If Mam complained about the food, Polly could remind her she was earning a decent wage. Mam had taken every penny of it, not even allowing Polly to save up a little each week to buy a ball.

'No thanks.' Daph's breath had steadied and her eyes were alight like advent candles. 'It's kind of you, Pol, but I've got something even better planned.' She grinned, never taking her eyes from Polly's face. 'Something incredible as it happens!'

'What?' cried Polly, desperate to know. 'You're not meeting Joe are you?' She suddenly hoped – wildly, desperately – there might be some way he was coming home from the Front. But that couldn't be true. He wouldn't be given leave for months yet. Not even for Christmas. He'd only be coming home if . . .

'He's not wounded is he?' she asked, clutching Daph's arm. 'Has he been injured in a battle? Have you heard something? Tell me!'

'No!' Daph laid her hand over Polly's. 'This has nothing to do with Joe, I promise. But it is something you'd love . . .'

'What?' said Polly, leaping to her feet. 'What is it? Just tell me.'

'It's football!' said Daph in a great gush of breath. 'There's going to be a match on Christmas Day. In the afternoon. Over in Kerston. On the proper pitch at Kerston FC.'

'Oh.' Polly felt a twist of jealousy. She wished she could be free to go along and see the lads play too. She'd gone to a couple of matches at Lowcross United with Joe, but Kerston was over twenty miles away. It was a far bigger town and their football club was one of the best in the country. They had even won the FA Cup. Mam would never let her miss Christmas dinner to go to a football match, though. 'I'd thought they'd stopped all the matches for the war,' she said. 'Have they gathered together enough men to play?'

Daph shook her head.

'It's not men,' she said with a grin. 'It's women. Two whole teams of them, Pol.'

'Girls?' Polly could hardly believe her ears. 'They're going to have a proper football match with girls?'

'Yes!' said Daph simply. 'The munitions factory over there have challenged a rival women's team.'

'Then I'm coming with you,' said Polly, her heart leaping into her chest. She didn't need to think about it for a moment more. Never mind what Mam would have to say about it. 'Christmas or no Christmas, I have to be at that match.'

CHAPTER SEVENTEEN

On Christmas morning, Polly was up earlier than ever. She slipped out of the bedroom and sneaked downstairs to get dressed, pulling on her tunic and work trousers as usual. Polly wondered if she'd ever choose to wear a skirt again. She didn't bother with the silly mob cap of course, but tied an old scarf around her head to keep her hair out of her face.

She peeled a huge basin of spuds, going so fast she cut her fingers twice, then scraped and washed the carrots and heated the range so it was ready for Mam – all the time trying not to make a sound. Then she carved two slivers of cooked ham, made a couple of sandwiches, wrapped them in greaseproof paper and popped them in the old cloth bag Mam took to market. She looked longingly at the bowl of juicy oranges on the table, one for each of the children, even little Queenie. She hesitated for a moment, then grabbed the biggest one off the top of the pile and popped it in the bag. She found a pencil and scribbled a note on the back of an old envelope:

Happy Christmas.
Gone out for day. Home later.
Polly.
P.S. Hope the chores help.

She put the note on the mantelpiece, leaning it against the pewter clock next to a Christmas card that had come from Joe. *'Joyeux Noël'* it said, with layers of daft paper lace sticking out all around the edge of a picture of an old French church in the snow. Polly rolled her eyes. Whatever had made Joe choose something so frilly and fancy-looking? She opened the card and read the message inside for the hundredth time:

Have a merry, safe and splendid Christmas!
Wish I was home with you all.
Your loving son and brother, Joe

It didn't even sound like him – it was so stiff and polite, nothing like the real Joe who would have caught her round the legs and rugby tackled her to the ground on Christmas morning as they play-fought over their oranges.

'I wish you were with us too, Joe!' she whispered, putting the card back. If he was here, they could have gone to the football match together, all three of them – her and Daph and Joe. Polly smiled at that idea. They'd have larked about on the journey, shouted themselves hoarse at the match and talked for hours afterwards about the game. Maybe one of Joe's mates would have given them a lift over in a cart or van. Joe always knew someone. As it was, Polly and Daph were going to have to set off on foot over the wind-blown moors to Kerston and just hope someone took pity on them along the way. Polly had never been there before – she had never left Lowcross, even – but she knew it was up hill and down dale all the way. They'd be lucky to reach the football ground in time for kick-off. Then, of course, they'd have to come all the way home again too. Polly didn't care. She just wanted to get going.

She heard the rafters creak above her head. Mam was getting up. She grabbed the cloth bag and darted for the door. She was halfway across the yard when she heard Queenie start to bawl.

'Polly!' roared Mam. 'See to the baby, can't you. Polly? Where are you?'

'Keep it down!' bellowed someone from the house next door. 'It's Christmas morning for goodness' sake!'

'Pipe down yourself,' hollered someone from the next house down. A dog started to bark.

'Polly?' roared Mam again, crashing out into the yard.

But Polly was already haring down the alleyway. There was no turning back now. Mam wouldn't hear of her dashing off to a football match on Christmas morning. She'd have her standing over a basin, mixing suet for the pudding before Polly could say 'Ding Dong Merrily on High!'

As she reached the station, she glanced at the clock and saw in panic that she was ten minutes late.

'All those blasted spuds!' she groaned, looking round desperately for Daph. They'd agreed to meet opposite the statue of the big fat fellow on the horse – General Whatever-his-name-was from some other stupid war.

Polly paced up and down. She was so excited she hadn't even been able to drink a cup of tea this morning, let alone eat anything. Her tummy was all a-flutter. She had to see this match: women playing against each other on a real pitch, with white lines and goalposts and a referee and everything. Spectators too, although Polly wondered how many would bother to turn out ...

There was no sign of Daph anywhere. Surely she wouldn't have set off without her already. Polly was only ten minutes late.

'Ten minutes!' Polly cursed herself. How could she have managed to get so delayed? Daph wouldn't have gone without her, would she? Polly glanced over her shoulder towards the station. Should she check inside? No. Daph had definitely said to meet out on the road. There wouldn't be any reason to go inside. As far as Polly knew, they were walking to Kerston not taking the train.

When another ten minutes passed, though, she did dart in and run up and down the platforms just in case.

There was no sign of Daph anywhere. No sign outside either and a full half hour had gone by now.

'Come on!' said Polly, pacing again and growling out loud as her cold breath came out in clouds. She stamped her feet to keep warm and stuffed her hands deep in her pockets.

Had Daph overslept? Had she changed her mind and decided not to go to the match after all?

Polly circled round the fat general on his horse. She

tried not to look at the clock every five minutes but threw her hands in the air and wailed when a full hour had passed. They'd be so late now they'd miss kick-off for sure. Half-time too unless they ran all the way.

Polly had decided to wait just five minutes more before she set off alone, when a spluttering motorbike came hammering down the quiet Christmas street.

It skidded to a halt just beside her. Some stupid lad showing off. Polly leaped backwards.

'Watch it!' she barked. 'You nearly had me over!'

'Nonsense! I was nowhere near you,' said the driver.

'Yes you blooming were . . .' Polly's words trailed away.

Daph was grinning up at her from behind the handlebars of the bike. She was dressed in a long, brown leather coat and the sort of goggles an airman might wear.

'Sorry I'm late. Spot of engine trouble,' she said. 'Hop on!'

Polly couldn't believe her eyes.

'W-we're going to Kerston on a motorbike?' she stammered, almost dropping the bag of sandwiches.

Daph pushed the goggles up on to her head. 'You're not scared are you?' she said kindly.

'Scared?' Polly nearly bit her head off. 'Of course I'm not scared, you daft cow! I'm excited,' she said

156

truthfully, a smile spreading over her face. Polly was about to leave Lowcross for the first time in her life. Until now, she had never driven in a motorcar and had only ridden a bicycle once, yet here she was about to ride all the way over the moors on a motorbike ... and there'd be football waiting for her at the other end.

'Quit dithering,' she cried. 'Let's go!'

Polly climbed on to the back of the spluttering motorbike and put her arms round Daph's waist.

'Hold on tight!' Daph warned as they roared out of town.

Polly couldn't believe how fast they were going – her heart leaped into her mouth and the ground whooshed away under her feet.

This is what flying an aeroplane must be like, she thought as the wind whipped her hair across her face. She felt the old, tattered scarf she'd tied around her head blow away and her bun come loose at the back.

'Whoopee!' she cheered, as they shot over a hump-backed bridge at the edge of the moors and her tummy seemed to get left behind. Up and down they went, flying along the empty roads between the high, dark hills, speckled with white frost, which looked like icing sugar on a pile of buns. Polly had no gloves and her fingers were numb from gripping Daph's waist. Her cheeks stung with cold and her eyes were watering, but she didn't care.

'Faster!' she begged, bellowing in Daph's ear.

No sooner was the cry out of her mouth, than the motorbike made a funny choking noise and Daph swore.

'Come on, Green Dragon!' she coaxed as the bike slowed and coughed like a sick old man. 'Blast!' Daph steered it towards the edge of the road as the engine gave one final splutter and died.

'Sounds like I need to do a bit of tinkering,' she said, and the girls climbed down from the bike.

Polly's legs felt wobbly beneath her as she touched firm ground. Daph opened her long leather coat and pulled out a collection of wrenches, spanners and screwdrivers from the inside pockets.

'Can you fix it?' asked Polly, pacing up and down in panic. She had no idea what time it was now or how far they had come. 'I don't want to miss the game.'

'You won't,' said Daph calmly. 'The old Green Dragon can be a little cranky but we'll get her going again in no time.'

'How long will it take?' asked Polly desperately. All she could see for miles around were the dark moors and a couple of scraggy sheep. She kept glancing down the road in the direction of Kerston, wondering how much further there was to go.

'It'll be much quicker if you help. Hold this spanner tight there while I give it a good thump!' Daph whacked a wrench down hard on something in the middle of the engine, which looked like a small, round, greasy cooking pot. 'That sometimes does the trick.' She grinned.

At that moment, a flat-bed truck came into view roaring along the road from Lowcross.

'Merry Christmas!' A gang of lads standing up in the back called out to them as the truck drew near. They jostled together, a group of pals home on leave it seemed, as most were wearing uniform.

'All right, mate?' called a sailor standing in the middle of them all.

'Fine thanks!' Daph turned away quickly and carried on working on the engine as the truck slowed down, then stopped completely.

'Blinkin' heck!' said the driver, clattering the gears and reversing a little to draw level with them again. 'It's a girl fiddling with that engine . . .'

'It's one of those canary lasses from munitions,' cried someone else and they all stared at Daph's bright yellow skin.

'Do you need a hand with that spanner, love?' asked the sailor. 'Or are you ladies going to knit the engine a little tea cosy...'

That did it. Polly stepped forward with her hands on her hips. 'We're fine, thank you. My friend can get on very well without the help of any lads.'

'How do, Polly? Merry Christmas. I thought it was you,' said a quiet voice from the front seat in the cab.

Polly saw that it was Alfie, his scarred face smiling shyly out at her. 'Don't mind the boys, they're just in high spirits. We're all off to see the football.'

'The munition workers?' said Polly. 'In Kerston?'

Alfie nodded. 'The ladies' game. I only heard about it yesterday but I guessed you might be coming. Exciting isn't it?'

'Too right it's exciting! All those ladies,' said the sailor. His wide grin showed a big gap where both his front teeth should have been. He made a low comment under his breath that Polly didn't hear but it made the others snort with laughter, so she guessed it must be something smutty.

'I wish Joe was here to come along too,' she said, talking only to Alfie. Most of the others weren't paying any attention to her anyway – they were busy gawping at Daph who was wearing a pretty red dress underneath the long leather coat. She was gathering up her tools and stuffing them back into her inside pockets.

'Tell you what,' said the sailor with a stupid wink at Daph, 'if we're all going the same way, why don't you throw that broken motorbike on the truck and hop up beside me. I'll hold you tight and make sure you don't fall off!'

For a moment, in spite of the horrible way the sailor was leering at her, Polly wondered if Daph might say yes to his offer. She hated the idea of having to accept their help, even if Alfie was there to make sure the lads behaved themselves … but she didn't want to miss the game.

Daph smiled at them. 'No thanks,' she said brightly, buttoning her coat. She gave Polly a quick nod, gesturing for her to get on the back of the Green Dragon. 'Thing is,' she said coolly, 'this motorbike isn't broken. Not any more. I just fixed it.'

With a kick of her heel on the pedals, the engine roared into life.

'See you at the game, lads!' cried Polly with a wave.

They swerved around the side of the truck and sped away, leaving the boys far behind them on the frosty road.

Chapter Eighteen

The pitch where the men of the famous cup-winning Kerston FC had always played was on the edge of the town at a place called Steepside, looking out towards the towering grey hills and the ring of coal mines all around.

Daph and Polly parked the motorbike in a side street and set off towards the ground on foot.

'There's no mistaking which way we need go. Just follow the crowd,' said Daph in astonishment as they passed under a huge banner reading: 'MERRY CHRISTMAS, 1917'.

'Do you really think all these people are here for the match?' asked Polly as they were swept along the road by an ever-growing bustle of men, women and children spread out three and four deep across the lane. They were all wearing their Sunday best, red-faced and jolly from eating Christmas dinner.

For those who'd missed their meal, there was a barrow selling hot meat pies and a man roasting chestnuts on a roaring brazier. Polly's tummy rumbled and for a moment she thought of the ham sandwiches in her bag. She hadn't eaten anything all day, but quickly forgot about food as the crowd in front of her came to a halt and she stood on tiptoe trying to see what the hold-up was.

'You don't think they've cancelled the match, do you?' she asked, jumping in the air to try and see over a tall man's broad shoulders, then crouching on the ground to peer around his legs.

'No, I don't!' Daph laughed at her.

'Excuse me!' Polly tapped the man firmly on the back. 'Can you see what's going on? Why can't we get through?'

'Lot of folk here. That's all,' said the man flatly.

Polly grabbed Daph by the sleeve. 'What if the stands are full? Will they turn us away?' She had never dreamed so many people would come to see two teams of women play a friendly – not even with all the men's matches stopped for the war.

'It's just the turnstiles, that's all,' Daph reassured her. 'Everyone has to show their tickets or hand over their money.'

'Blast!' Polly froze, not even taking a step when the tall man in front suddenly moved on.

'Shove up!' said a couple of lads behind her, trying to squeeze past.

'Watch it!' Polly came to her senses and pushed forward too. There seemed to be a sudden surge now, with everyone moving towards the gates at the same time.

'What's the matter, Pol?' said Daph. 'You look like you've lost a pound and found sixpence.'

'That's just it!' Polly could see the turnstiles up ahead, like the arms of a metal spider, slowly letting one person through at a time. Official-looking men in brown overalls stood beside them, checking tickets. 'I don't have a blinking sixpence . . . and I certainly don't have a pound.' She groaned. 'I forgot we'd need to pay to get in.'

She couldn't believe how stupid she'd been and she didn't like to admit to Daph she wouldn't have been able to pay even if she had thought of it. Not with Mam still taking all her wages.

'Don't worry. My treat,' said Daph.

'No!' Polly blushed. She couldn't take the money off Daph – it wouldn't be right. Perhaps there'd be a way to sneak in under a fence somewhere or hop over the turnstiles once the game had started.

'I might have known you'd be all proud about it,' said Daph with a sigh. 'Think of it as a Christmas present. I don't have anyone else to give a gift to, not with Joe away, and I don't have any family left. You can be my sister for the day if you like!'

Polly opened her mouth to argue again, but she didn't know what to say. The thought of being Daph's sister – even if it was only pretend and just for Christmas Day – made her feel warm and happy inside.

'Football sisters!' said Daph. 'That's family, right?'

Polly nodded.

'You've only just started working and I know you have to help your mum out,' said Daph with a wave of her hand. 'They pay us more money in the Danger Shed too, remember?' She guided Polly forward. 'I wanted to come and see this game and I can't think of anyone better to be here with …'

'Thank you!' Polly gave Daph a playful shove. 'I mean it,' she said, clearing her throat. Nobody had ever given her such a generous and wonderful present before.

She dug around in the cloth bag and pulled out her orange. 'You can have this if you like.' She thrust it into Daph's hand just as a brass band marched by playing 'We Wish You a Merry Christmas' and bashing a drum.

She knew it was only a bit of fruit but it was the best she could do.

Then Daph paid for two tickets and they squeezed through the turnstiles and into the stands, already chock-a-block with spectators.

'I can't see anything from back here,' said Daph standing on tiptoe.

'Hold on!' Polly, who was much taller, spotted a gap at the front. 'Follow me!' She shoved her way forward, dragging Daph behind her, paying no attention to anyone who swore or shouted at them as she wriggled her way through to a space against the railings, right beside the pitch.

It was the least she could do after Daph had bought the tickets.

'We've come all this way and you've paid good money. We might as well be up close to the action.' She beamed.

Ten minutes later, the two teams marched on to the frost-speckled pitch as the brass band played and a gasp went up from the stands.

The munitionettes from Kerston Electric Manufacturing Company were playing against their neighbouring factory, Wardour Munitions. The team from Kerston Electric wore black-and-white striped jerseys and Wardour wore red, but that wasn't what had got the crowd in a fluster.

The players were wearing shorts.

Polly had never seen a grown woman show her knees in public before.

'Blimey! Look at their legs!' hollered a man behind her.

Polly glanced back and saw the group of lads from the truck they had met on the road. There was no sign of Alfie, but the others were all whistling and cheering, nudging each other like fools. Polly suddenly realised why so many men and lads had turned out to see the match – they weren't interested in watching women play football. They'd just come along to ogle a lot of lasses in their knickers! The women were just as bad. They seemed to be there to judge.

'Shame on those girls!' said a plump lady on Polly's left, dabbing her lips with a hankie. 'I'm glad no daughter of mine is flaunting herself like that.' She shook her head and tutted.

Polly couldn't understand it.

'What does it matter what they're wearing?' she barked. No one had ever discussed the kit when she and Joe had gone to games at Lowcross United and the lads' big muddy knees had been on display for everyone to see.

The crowd were whooping and laughing as if they were at the palais watching a music-hall show. Polly couldn't bear the event being treated as a joke; all she wanted was to see a proper game.

The two captains had stepped forward now and the male referee was tossing a coin. The girls on both teams looked terrified and some of them were giggling.

After the first five minutes of play, Polly's heart sank.

'This is no good,' she said to Daph. 'They're not taking it seriously.'

'Give them a chance. It's their first big match,' said Daph.

One Wardour defender actually stopped and apologised for taking the ball from a Kerston forward. Most of the others were barely even watching the pitch because they were so busy looking at the crowd for approval.

'Play up!' screamed Polly at the top of her lungs – she didn't care which side won, just as long as it was a real match.

Slowly, as the crowd quieted a little, play settled down and the munitionettes from the Kerston Electric Manufacturing Company began to push forward. It was finally starting to look like a half-decent game, but none of their new supporters seemed to know what to shout.

'Come on, Kerston Ladies!' boomed some of the fans.

'Come on Kerston Electrics!' cheered some of the others.

'Come on Electric Manufacturing Company,' cried a few, though that was definitely too much of a mouthful.

'If they're so good at making electrics in this factory, they should bring a spark of it to the pitch!' Polly shouted in Daph's ear as their striker missed an open goal. 'That was a blooming sitter! I could have scored with my eyes closed,' she roared. 'Come on, you Sparks!'

In an instant, the lads behind them had taken up the cry and half the stands joined in ...

'COME ON, YOU SPARKS!'

Like electricity running down a wire, the chant seemed to travel on to the pitch and set it alight. The striker ran clear of the Wardour defence again, and this time she smashed the ball into the back of the net.

'I think they've got you to thank for that one, Pol!' said Daph, slapping Polly on the back.

The Sparks really did seem to come alight after that.

As their nerves settled, it was clear they were a far better team than Wardour. By the half-time whistle, they were up three-nil.

'The blonde striker who scored that first one looks pretty good,' said Daph as the players ran off the pitch

'She looks pretty tasty, I'll tell you that!' said a voice behind them.

Without even turning her head, Polly knew it was the sailor with the missing teeth.

'Ignore him!' hissed Daph, unwrapping the sandwich Polly had just offered her.

But Polly had already spun round, only to be greeted by a dirty laugh.

'*This,*' she said, pointing to her own ham sandwich, 'is tasty.' Her heart was thumping with fury as she pointed to the pitch. '*That* is a game of football. If you don't know the difference, then shove off.'

'Whoa!' The sailor's pals erupted in a cheer of laughter.

'She told you, matey!' jeered one of them.

Without waiting to hear more, Polly turned back to Daph and continued to discuss the game excitedly. 'The Sparks are making good use of the wings,' she said through a bite of sandwich. 'That's why they're getting forward all the time . . .'

As she spoke, she felt a sudden sharp ache for Joe. It was Christmas Day ... She hoped he was getting to play football in no man's land, just as they'd talked about all those months ago. Ever since he'd gone, Polly had a constant gnawing feeling in her tummy of missing him and the dread of bad news – but sometimes it stabbed at her like this, with a sharper pain, when her guard was suddenly let down. She wished more strongly than ever that he could be here with them now. He wouldn't have wolf-whistled stupidly or made rude comments, she was sure of that. He'd have been too interested in the game.

They're a tidy squad, he'd have said about the Sparks.

'You should play for a team like that, Pol!'

For a moment Polly thought she was still in her daydream, imagining Joe's voice inside her head. With a start, she realised it was Daph who had spoken aloud.

'You're as good as any of those Sparks,' she said, her bright green eyes staring steadily into Polly's face. 'I know we've only been kicking about and playing rough games at the factory, but even I can see you've got real talent. And all the other girls agree.'

Polly grinned. She'd give anything to be out on that pitch.

'Think how proud Joe would be if he came home to find his sister playing in a real team,' said Daph.

'A girls' team,' whispered Polly. Joe would never believe such a thing could be possible.

'We should do it together,' she said, grabbing Daph's arm. 'You, me, Olive and everyone. We should make the Ruffians into a proper team.'

Daph nodded thoughtfully. 'Why not! If anyone can make it happen, you can, Pol.'

Before Polly could answer, the two sides ran back on to the pitch and the stands erupted in spontaneous applause. This time there was less wolf-whistling or cat-calling silly names – just the roar of spectators eager to see the outcome of a game. Even the lads behind them joined in with a heartfelt cheer.

'COME ON, YOU SPARKS!'

Polly's blood raced with excitement.

'Can you hear me, Joe Nabb?' she roared, bellowing over the noise of the crowd. 'By the time you come home, we'll be proper footballers too, just like those lasses out there.'

Daph smiled. 'You're barmy,' she said.

But Polly meant her promise with all her heart.

Chapter Nineteen

It was only when the thrill of the match was over that Polly noticed how cold she was. Her feet were like blocks of ice and her freezing hands were red and stinging, she'd clapped so hard.

An official-looking army gent with a megaphone strode out to the middle of the pitch and announced in a plummy voice that ticket sales had raised a whopping six hundred pounds for Kerston hospital to help wounded soldiers returning from the war.

'Six hundred pounds? The girls can be proud of that,' said the lady who'd complained about the players showing their knees.

'They can be proud they played well too, shorts and all!' said Polly with a cheeky grin, though she had to admit six hundred quid was an awful lot of money. You could buy up every house on Link Street with cash like that.

'It was a grand day, wasn't it?' she said to Daph, beginning to feel her freezing toes again as they followed the crowds out of the stands.

The final score was five-nil to the munitionettes from Kerston Electric – or the Sparks as everyone was now calling them. Wardour missed an easy penalty in the last five minutes, but other than that they never really got a look at goal.

'It was cracking!' agreed Daph, as they squeezed towards the exit. 'See that fellow talking to the referee? I think he must be the Sparks manager.' She pointed to a roly-poly man with a big moustache. He was wearing a tweed suit with a yellow bow tie and matching pocket handkerchief so bright that Polly could see the splash of colour from halfway across the pitch. It wasn't the handkerchief she was staring at, though. He was holding a big net bag full of shiny footballs.

'Blimey!' Polly whistled through her teeth. The bag was the size of one of Mam's sacks of coal. Imagine having all that lot.

'That's the Sparks manager, all right,' agreed a lass who must have overheard them. 'I work at the munitions factory with him. His name's Mr Tweedale, but everyone calls him Tweedy because of those fancy suits he wears. He's the one who rented this swanky pitch to make a big Christmas Day attraction for the girls.'

'My sister's the goalie,' said a lad beside her. 'Tweedy's promised he's going to recruit the best lasses he can find and make the Sparks the greatest women's football team in the country.'

The lad laughed as if it was the daftest thing he'd ever heard, but Polly smiled.

Imagine playing for a team like the Sparks. A tingle of excitement ran from her freezing toes right up to her fingers.

A flash of guilt shot through her too. She'd only just had the idea of getting the Ruffians together and already she was thinking of moving on ... But it was clear that there was something special about this team Tweedy was building. He was right to have high hopes ...

'Come on,' said Daph, pulling her through the turnstiles.

It was dark now, but people were still milling about outside, discussing the game. Polly spotted the lads from the truck gathered round a battered cart where a man was selling beer.

'You've got to hand it to those lasses, they played well,' said a solider, lifting his pint.

The toothless sailor grunted as Daph and Polly passed by. 'They weren't bad, I suppose. For girls!' Polly had the feeling he was raising his voice deliberately to make sure they heard him. 'Of course, once the war's over, we'll put a stop to this sort of rubbish. Women can get back to their kitchens and football can be a proper game ... played by men!'

'Ignore him. He's a stupid fool,' said a voice from the shadows.

Polly blinked through the gloom and saw a hunched figure sitting on a bench by the bus stop.

'Alfie!' she cried, dashing forward. 'I didn't see you at the game. The Wardour defence was woeful but ...' Her words trailed off.

Alfie was trembling. 'I couldn't go in,' he said, clutching his hair and letting out a whimpering noise like a dog.

Daph crouched down, placing a hand on Alfie's shaking knee. 'It's all right. It's over now,' she whispered.

'It was the drums.' Alfie trembled. 'They wouldn't stop. Boom! Boom! Boom!' He was hugging his knees with his one good arm and rocking back and forward on the bench.

'Like guns?' said Polly quietly, remembering the brass band marching by with their cheering Christmas carols. For poor Alfie it had sounded like the blast of shells.

What terrible things he must have seen, she thought.

'Folk were pushing at the turnstiles,' Alfie quivered. 'Some fellow blew a whistle and bellowed at us to calm down ... like being back in the trenches ... like the moment we have to go over the top. The moment they slaughter us,' he said, his eyes wide, staring up at Polly, but looking through her at the same time, as if she wasn't there. As if he was watching ghosts instead.

'Shh!' said Daph, drawing Alfie into a tight hug and rubbing his back like he was a little boy. 'It's over now!'

'Not for me!' Alfie stood up so quickly that Daph toppled backwards and nearly knocked Polly over as well. 'I wish I'd died out there in the mud.' He clutched hold of Polly's shoulder to steady himself, trembling so hard that a shudder ran through her too.

'You don't mean that,' said Polly trying to grab at Alfie's sleeve.

'Yes, I do.' He pushed past her. 'You should wish the same for your Joe ... any of us who've gone out there, we'd all be better off dead.'

'Don't say that!' Polly's stomach flipped over. 'Take it back!'

Alfie shrugged and limped away towards his pals.

'None of us even know what we're fighting for. We're led by idiots and the whole thing's a stupid mess!'

'Alfie?'

'Best leave him,' whispered Daph.

But Alfie turned back for a moment, the pain on his scarred face caught in the lamplight. 'Sorry, Pol,' he called, his voice cracking. 'Pay no heed to me. Merry Christmas, lass. Just a rotten awful day, that's all.'

'Merry Christmas, Alfie!' Polly waved, trying to sound bright and cheerful. Inside, her nerves were jangling. Only a minute ago she'd been so happy – now all her excitement had turned to tingling dread. It was as if she'd walked under a ladder, broken a mirror or seen a lone magpie – one for sorrow – staring at her with a beady eye. She felt Alfie had tempted fate, saying those terrible things about her Joe and how he would be better off dead.

CHAPTER TWENTY

The ride home over the moors cleared Polly's mind. It was even more exhilarating to be on the bike in the dark than it had been in the daylight.

As the wind whipped through her hair, she peered over Daph's shoulder and watched the beam from the headlight dancing on the empty road ahead. She ran her mind back through every detail of the match.

Polly thought of her dreams of making a team with the Ruffians and imagined stepping out in front of a cheering crowd like that herself. She thought of playing for the Sparks one day too and imagined lifting a big silver cup. Despite poor Alfie, and the constant nagging worry about Joe, this had been the best Christmas Day ever.

As the bike sped on, Polly tried not to think about arriving home and the rage Mam might be in.

She was pleased when they stopped halfway in the thick winter darkness on the side of the road. The cold air blasting against the front of the bike had made Daph's wheezy chest ache and she needed to catch her breath.

'That's better!' she said, breathing in and out slowly in long deep puffs. Then she pulled the orange out of her pocket and offered it to Polly.

'Let's go halves!'

'No,' said Polly, although her mouth was watering. 'It's all yours. It's your Christmas present.'

'Nonsense!' Daph wouldn't hear of it. 'I've sat on it anyway so we'd better eat it quick!'

She was right – the orange was squashed but delicious and juicy all the same. They ate it sitting on a big, flat stone starring up at the starry sky. Polly had never seen so many stars before. The sky in Lowcross was always thick with fog and factory fumes.

'That's the North Star,' said Daph, pointing to the brightest one of all, like something on a Christmas card. 'Let's make a wish.'

'Get away!' Polly laughed. Walter and Ernie would have teased her rotten if she'd suggested something daft like that.

'Close your eyes and think of something special,' urged Daph. 'You don't have to tell me what it is.'

'All right.' Polly closed her eyes and made a wish.

'I bet I know what you wished for,' said Daph.

Polly smiled in the darkness. 'I reckon you might!' It wasn't hard to guess.

'Maybe we wished for the same thing!' said Daph.

'Maybe ...'

It was only later Polly realised that Daph would have wished for Joe to come home safely. Polly had forgotten about him. Just for a moment. She'd wished to play football in a proper match instead.

Perhaps if there'd been two wishes for Joe on that Christmas star it might have been enough.

Perhaps Polly's wish would have made a difference.

'Come on!' said Daph after they'd rested on the side of the road for a while more. She took a last deep breath and climbed to her feet. 'We'd better get you home before Boxing Day. We've got work in the morning, remember.'

'No hurry!' said Polly, chewing a piece of orange peel. She'd happily have stayed out there on the moors all night ... anything to avoid the fuss there was bound to be about her sloping off.

Yet all too soon the Green Dragon roared over the bridge into Lowcross and Daph came to a stop outside Duke's.

'I hope your ma's not too furious,' she said.

Polly shrugged. 'It's been worth it!'

Even so, her heart was pounding a little as she tiptoed into the yard and saw from the flickering shadows in the window that a lamp was still lit. She'd be for it now. Mam must be up, waiting for her, wanting to know where she'd been. Polly sighed and braced herself as she bashed open the back door.

'Listen, here,' she said, ready to fight first . . . but the words drained away.

Polly stood in the doorway and stared.

Mam and Dad were sitting at the table together, their heads bent, holding hands. The defiance in Polly's chest turned to panic. Something was wrong. She didn't think she'd ever seen Mam and Dad hold hands before.

Everyone else seemed to have gone to bed.

The only sound was the ticking of the pewter clock.

'What is it?' Polly whispered, and a gasp caught in her throat as she saw an envelope with a blood-red stamp smudged across the front. Beside it, a typewritten letter lay open in the pool of lamplight. Polly shook her head. This couldn't be true. Yet even on Christmas Day the dreaded post still came, bringing not just cards and packages, but bad news too.

'Is it from the army?' she asked, bursting into the room, letting the door slam shut behind her. 'Is it about Joe?'

Dad looked up, seeming surprised to see her there.

Mam snatched the letter and held it to her chest as if she could somehow shield Polly from the terrible news it contained.

'Tell me!' Polly raged, ready to rip the paper from Mam's grasp if she had to. 'What does it say?'

'He's missing,' said Mam gently. 'Our Joe's missing.'

CHAPTER TWENTY-ONE

'Missing?' Polly rolled the word around her mouth. She knew no one could hear her as she stood at her bench in the munitions factory, watching the heavy steel rings spinning on the lathe. For the first time since she'd seen the letter, she felt strangely calm. Joe was missing – like a button or a potato knife or a peg doll. The sort of thing that turns up again, quite unexpectedly, under a mattress, behind a barrel, in a forgotten apron pocket. *I'm always losing things, then finding them,* she thought with a flash of relief. *Joe will turn up again too.*

She heaved another pair of rings on to the lathe.

'Missing's not so bad,' she said triumphantly. It was loud enough that old Norah looked up from her machine and glanced at Polly in concern.

Polly flashed her a stupid smile, as if to say, 'Don't worry, nothing's wrong!' Yet they all knew, of course.

Somehow word had spread so fast that even Daph had heard before Polly had the chance to come in at dawn and break the news herself.

Waiting for her by the factory gates, Daph had looked tiny and tear-stained and frail; nothing like the fearless aviator-mechanic who had ridden the Green Dragon over the moors the day before.

Polly still hadn't cried a single tear, although she'd thrown up in the coal bucket the moment Mam broke the news – a sour mix of orange juice and bile – her stomach aching all night as the acrid taste stung her mouth and throat. Beside her, Queenie had fretted and bawled, picking up on the panic hovering like gas above the crowded bed. Polly cuddled the baby tightly, trying to soothe her, trying to make sense of it all and trying, hopelessly, to believe somehow that it might not be true...

Now, as she stared down at the heavy steel rings spinning beneath her, she seemed able to gather her thoughts at last.

Joe's always going missing. Wandering off. Disappearing for hours on end. He'll turn up again. He always does.

She clanked a finished pair of heavy rings into the crate and automatically loaded up another set.

As the steel spun, she could almost see the typewritten words of the letter blurring in front of her eyes: 'Private Joseph Nabb …' It wasn't even a proper letter really, more of an official form.

She blinked furiously, but the bold, black words still spun in front of her eyes. 'Missing…'

'Missing's fine,' she whispered.

But she knew the letter had more to say. 'Missing… presumed killed.'

'Aaargh!' Polly leaped backwards, reeling in pain as the sharp edge of the spinning steel caught her finger and sliced the skin. She thrust her hand between her knees and sucked in her breath.

'All right, duck!' Norah was at her side in a second. 'They ought to have given you the day off! Rotten swines,' she cursed. 'It's always the same. No matter what sort of news has come, they expect us to turn up and work.'

'I'm fine,' said Polly through gritted teeth. She was glad to be at work. Anything was better than being at home, staring at the mantelpiece with that dreadful letter and Joe's fancy Christmas card side by side. She'd never known their house so quiet. Just the wretched ticking of that pewter clock.

'You'll need to get that to the First-Aid Shed,' said Norah, gently taking the hand from between Polly's knees. 'Nurse'll fix you up.' She pulled a clean hankie from her overalls and wrapped it around Polly's fingers, the white turning instantly red. 'There's Lady G. She'll take you.'

Norah beckoned her over.

'What's happened here, then?' Lady G put a reassuring arm round Polly's shoulder. 'I was so sorry to hear about your brother,' she said, guiding her towards the door. 'I remember the afternoon the telegram came with news of poor Roly . . .'

'Telegram?' Polly stopped walking. 'They sent you a telegram?'

'Yes,' said Lady G. 'The same dreadful day. Whenever it's an officer they . . . Oh . . . how rotten . . .' She trailed off and Polly growled.

Of course! When officers were missing or killed, their families were sent telegrams right away. Not so for ordinary soldiers like Joe.

'We got a letter,' she said, realising with a jolt that the words about Joe might have been written a week ago already. He could have been missing for five or six days before Polly and her family even heard the news.

Five or six days . . .

'All that time, and you never knew,' said Lady G, stricken.

But Polly shook her head, a fresh burst of hope rising

inside her. 'Don't you see? It's good,' she said. 'Perhaps they've found him again already and we just haven't heard. Perhaps another letter's already on its way.'

'That's the spirit. Chin up!' Lady G squeezed her shoulder. 'Let's get you to the nurse.'

Polly was aware of everyone's pitying eyes on her as she was bustled along between the machines. 'I'm fine!' she called out defiantly.

And Joe will be fine too . . . No matter what they want to presume about him . . . Missing things, and missing people, they turn up again. They do!

When they reached the First-Aid Shed, Polly found Daph was there too, doubled over, fighting for breath. Her yellow skin looked damp and grey.

'I can't breathe,' she wheezed, a halo of sweat across her forehead.

'Oh dear,' said Lady G. 'Is it asthma?'

'Fumes . . .' Daph rasped.

'Nonsense!' said the nurse. 'It's purely psychological!'

'She *has* had a spot of bad news,' said Lady G.

'Well, there you go!' said the nurse, sourly. She was built like Polly, tall and wide-faced, but with eyes so narrow it was impossible to see what colour they were. Her lips were narrow too and she sucked them tightly together as she glared at Daph. 'Breathe into that paper bag, Jenkins, and don't be so silly.'

'Silly?' said Polly, snapping out of herself. She leaped to defend Daph, who didn't seem to have enough breath to blow into the brown paper bag, let alone fight back. 'It's not silly if the fumes in the Danger Shed make her . . . Ouch!'

The nurse grabbed her roughly by the wrist. She undid Norah's handkerchief and plunged Polly's injured hand into a bowl of stinging yellow iodine. 'You should be more careful around the machines. Sometimes I think you girls have these little accidents just to get time away from the factory floor.'

'No,' Polly began to protest, but the nurse pulled her hand from the iodine and peered at the deep wound on the end of Polly's index finger.

'This is going to need stitches. Sit still and don't fuss.'

'I wasn't going to fuss,' said Polly, although her head swum strangely as the nurse set about sterilising a needle and finding some thread. Was she going to sew Polly up like an old sock?

While the nurse prepared her instruments, the only sounds were the clinking of metal trays, the hiss of steam and Daph's rasping breaths as she breathed into the paper bag.

'Actually,' said Lady G suddenly, as if to break the tension, 'I'm glad I'm here. I wanted a word with you, Nurse.'

'Oh!' The nurse raised an eyebrow. Polly guessed she would like to be as rude to Lady G as she was to the rest of them but didn't quite dare. 'What can I do for you, Lady Gidleigh?'

'It's about all the wounded boys coming home from the war,' said Lady G. 'Nobody seems to look after them once the army has no further need of their services. They have to pay for their own medical treatment, as I'm sure you know . . . The ones with no legs even have to buy their own wheelchairs and crutches . . . and that's just the wounds we can see. Some of those poor chaps are so damaged in their minds . . .'

Polly thought of poor, terrified Alfie, so frightened by the noise and crowds at the match. Lady G was right. It wasn't just wounds to skin and bone which needed healing.

'I don't know what people expect,' said the nurse, sighing almost as loud as her steaming kettle. 'We can't go around giving free medical treatment to everybody, you know.'

Why not? thought Polly. *Especially if those people have been wounded fighting for their country.* But Lady G nodded.

'Of course,' she said. 'That's why I was thinking of organising a little fundraiser for the wounded men. I thought, as a nurse, perhaps you might be able to advise on how the funds could best be—'

'A fundraiser?' Polly cut across her.

'Shh!' said the nurse furiously. 'Don't interrupt when your betters are speaking.'

She grabbed Polly's hand and held it tightly, but Polly would not be stopped. 'What sort of fundraiser were you thinking of, Lady G?' She caught Daph's eye over the top of the rippling paper bag.

'Now Christmas is out of the way, I thought perhaps a little concert of jolly spring music. You know the sort of thing,' said Lady G. 'fresh, hopeful tunes we can all sing along to.'

'Sounds very pleasant,' said the nurse.

'All the girls in the factory orchestra are terribly excited.' Lady G smiled brightly at Daph and Polly. 'My cousin organised something similar down in Worthing and they raised . . .' – she gave a little drum roll with her hands on the side of the nurse's metal trolley – 'seventy-eight pounds!' She announced the figure with such awe it suggested it should be written out in bold capital letters and posted around the town.

'Seventy-eight pounds?' Polly spluttered.

'I know. It's an awful lot of money, isn't it?' said Lady G. 'And for such a good cause too.'

It was true, seventy-eight pounds was a lot of money – a small fortune. Polly would have been impressed herself if she'd heard the figure yesterday. Now she stared at Lady G and said, 'How about raising six hundred pounds? Wouldn't that be even better ...?'

'Well, yes, of course ...' Lady G giggled. 'But ...'

'Don't be silly,' snapped the nurse. 'How would anybody raise money like that?'

'Easy,' said Polly, and she looked over at Daph who had lifted her face from the paper bag at last. 'Football!' she said.

This was the perfect opportunity for Polly and the other Ruffians to play in a proper match of their own. Polly had shouted out her promise to Joe from the terraces at Steepside – now she had the chance to keep that promise. It seemed more important than ever.

She explained to Lady G all about the women's game between the Sparks and the Wardour Munitionettes.

'It's unnatural.' A flush of anger came to the nurse's cheeks. 'Girls' bodies aren't designed for football. It'll be nurses like me who have to pick up the pieces.'

'Can't be any worse than twelve-hour shifts at this

factory, six days a week,' said Daph bitterly with a fresh bout of coughing.

'Now listen to me, Jenkins ...' The nurse spun round, but Lady G leaped in.

'Do you really think we could raise six hundred pounds just from a ladies' football match?'

'Well, maybe not six hundred,' said Daph. 'The Sparks did have the famous Steepside pitch and it was Christmas Day ...'

'But definitely more than seventy-eight pounds. Definitely in the hundreds,' said Polly, hopefully. 'What do you say, Lady G? Let's invite the Sparks to come and play against our team of Ruffian Girls.'

'Oh goodness ...' A shadow of doubt passed across Lady G's usually smooth, unruffled face. For a moment Polly thought she was going to refuse. Then she smiled and her face lit up with girlish excitement. 'Oh, go on then, Polly. I'm sure you and those Ruffians can do anything you put your minds to.'

'You won't regret it!' promised Polly. Somewhere deep below her grinding worry she felt a flash of excitement. This was the right thing to do. The right way to keep hope alive for Joe and to help lads like Alfie too.

Daph was smiling as well, her eyes still red from

crying … but this would help. Bringing the team together and playing in a match would be the best thing they could do while they waited for Joe to be found safely and come home.

'Now get back to work and next time be more careful,' growled the nurse, letting go of Polly's hand.

'What? Already?' Polly looked down at her finger in disbelief. 'It's done?' She had been so busy persuading Lady G to let them host the football match, she hadn't even felt the stitches being put in.

Chapter Twenty-Two

When Polly and Daph told the Ruffians their plan to play in a public match, some of the girls were so horrified they refused to even consider it.

'My dad would kill me if I went out on a pitch with my knees on show,' said Florrie, a midfielder.

'So would my three brothers,' echoed her friend Minnie. 'Even if it is for charity.'

But a core of players were excited and Polly was instantly chosen as their captain.

'You may be the youngest,' said Mary-Anne, 'but you know more about football and play better than the rest of us put together.'

'She's got more energy too! I'm surprised she doesn't explode, she's so full of it,' said Jessie with a grin.

Polly *was* energetic. Wild almost. Desperate to blot out her fears for Joe and hoping they would soon hear news that he was safe and well, she thought of little else but the team.

It was sometimes hard to keep the other girls excited though, with cold morning practice in the dawn light every day.

'When's this match even going to be?' they asked.

'Are these fancy Sparks too stuck up to play us?'

But then, one Wednesday morning in early February, there was news. Lady G had spoken directly to Mr Tweedale at the Kerston Electric Manufacturing Company and had finally managed to arrange a game. True to his word, Tweedy had kept the Sparks busy. They'd been playing – and beating – other teams of girls ever since their success on Christmas Day, but there'd been a sudden cancellation as a team in Manchester had gone down with flu.

'They're coming here on Saturday,' cried Polly bursting out of the office. Lady G had spoken to the local committee at Lowcross United too and they'd reluctantly agreed to let the women's match go ahead on their pitch. She was already busy telephoning the newspapers to place advertisements and sell tickets.

A cheer went up from the team, but Mary-Anne looked worried.

'You don't mean *this* Saturday do you?'

'Yes,' said Polly. 'In the afternoon. Lady G's organised time off for anyone in the team and . . .'

'That's no good. I can't play this Saturday,' said Mary-Anne.

'What?' Polly threw her arms in the air. Was she the only one who took this game seriously? With so many girls refusing to take part, there were barely enough of them to make up a full side as it was. Mary-Anne was one of their very best players. Other than Polly herself, she offered the Ruffians their greatest chance of scoring any goals. 'You'll just have to cancel whatever it is you're doing,' said Polly firmly. Surely nothing could be more important than playing football.

'Cancel it?' Mary-Anne laughed. 'I can't cancel it, Polly. I'm getting married.'

'Married?' Polly's shoulders sagged. Was a wedding more important than a football match? She supposed it probably was. To most people.

'My Peter's only got a few days' leave, then he's back to the Front,' said Mary-Anne. 'We've booked St Saviour's for eleven o'clock this Saturday morning, then I'll be Mrs Dutson . . .'

She clutched her heart and the rest of the girls cooed with delight.

'Eleven?' Polly punched the air. 'That's fine, then.

Kick-off's not till after lunch. You can pelt round and join us as soon as the wedding business is out the way.'

'Pelt round and join you?' Mary-Anne looked stunned. 'Shall I keep my wedding dress on an' all?' she asked sarcastically.

'If you like.' Polly shrugged. She couldn't waste any more time arguing about this. Practice time was precious and the match was only three days away.

Before she could move, a voice boomed across the factory forecourt. 'You're living in cloud cuckoo land, you lot.' Don Sharples was leaning up against the side of the Danger Shed, smoking a cigarette as usual. 'Dutson's never going to let his wife play football once she's a married woman.'

'Yes he blooming will. If I tell him to,' said Mary-Anne, her hands on her hips. 'You know what, Polly? I might make it to the match, after all.'

'Good!' Polly hoped Mary-Anne wasn't just saying it to wind Don up. 'Now can we please get on and practise?'

The following morning there was yet another hold-up when scatterbrained Olive forgot her yellow pass.

None of the girls were ever allowed inside the factory

gates without them, especially not workers like Olive from the Danger Shed.

'You'll just have to run back to the hostel to fetch it,' said Daph.

'Sorry!' cried the goalie, barrelling away down the street. 'I'd—'

'Forget my head if it wasn't screwed on!' sang the rest of the team, collapsing in laughter.

Polly growled under her breath. More precious practice time was being thrown away, yet she knew Olive didn't mean to have her head in the clouds any more than Polly meant to be sharp-tongued sometimes. It was just the way she was. She'd forget to bring her pass, or her mob cap, or the football, but once she was standing in goal, between the giant empty shell cases, she became a different person. She leaned forward, her muscles tensed, her eyes focused on every player – watching and waiting for the ball to come towards her, like a cat tracking a fly. Other than Joe, she was the best goalkeeper Polly had ever known.

'Don't forget to turn up to the match on Saturday, that's all,' shouted Polly as Olive disappeared around the corner.

Then she split everyone into pairs and got them running up and down the forecourt.

'I wish we had more footballs,' she groaned. They still only had a couple between them. She sighed, recalling the bulging net she'd seen Tweedy holding at Steepside. The Sparks wouldn't be running up and down their pitch tackling each other for imaginary balls, that was for sure.

'Come on, Betsy. Keep your knees up,' she bellowed to one of the defenders. Unfortunately, it wasn't necessarily the very best of the players who had volunteered for the match, and although Betsy was keen to join in, she liked to sit down and have a little rest in the middle of the pitch whenever she got tired.

'Yeah, come on, Betsy! Waddle like a duck!' cheered Don from the sidelines.

'Get lost!' said Daph, who had drawn level with him. 'And put that cigarette out. You know you're not supposed to smoke anywhere near the Danger Shed!' The girls working there got sacked if they so much as forgot they were wearing jewellery or a stray hairpin, in case the metal caused a spark.

Don smirked and Polly knew he had more to say. He stamped out his fag and walked deliberately into the middle of the path of players running up and down the forecourt.

'I told you I was trained as a linesman, didn't I? Well,

with so many of the boys away, it looks like I've just got a promotion,' he said, staring directly at Polly. 'I heard last night. I'm going to be the referee for your match up at Lowcross United.'

A gasp went up from the team. Polly wanted to roar with frustration but she refused to let him see she was riled.

Don grinned and sauntered off. 'They may let you girls play, but you still need us men to make sure you follow the rules!' he called back over his shoulder.

'That's all we need!' Polly groaned. Don Sharples was never going to judge them fairly. He would do everything he could to make sure the Sparks won.

'Keep running!' she bellowed furiously, seeing that all the players had stopped. Betsy and her partner had even sat down on the ground and were sharing a bar of chocolate.

'How's this team ever going to be ready by Saturday?' Polly wondered.

It wasn't only the Sparks they would have to prove themselves against now, it was Don Sharples too.

Chapter Twenty-Three

Polly was never one to feel downhearted for long.

'Don Sharples can't do anything if we win the match fair and square,' she declared on Friday at the end of what had been a great lunchtime practice. Polly knew most of the girls were only playing for a bit of a laugh. They didn't love football the way she did, and the Ruffians might never be a high-flying team like the Sparks had become, but everyone was doing their best.

Even Betsy had managed to get the ball away from someone once – although she did lose it again almost immediately when she stopped, mid-kick, to bend down and tie her laces.

Daph was making up for it though, darting up and down, tackling anyone whose toe so much as made contact with the ball.

'I'm doing this for Joe,' she'd explained to Polly as

they'd waited for the others that morning. 'Maybe you're right. Maybe there is a chance he'll be found safely somehow and come home to us. If he does, I want to be able to tell him about this. About the day we played the Sparks and won!'

Mary-Anne was on top form too, scoring a lovely goal and only missing the chance of two more because Olive saved them so well. Polly just hoped the young bride really would turn up after her wedding. The whole team had been invited to go along to the church before the match. Polly tried to schedule an extra practice instead, but the other girls said they wouldn't miss the wedding for the world.

Polly herself had scored one good goal that morning too, but Olive was playing better than all of them. The few goals she did let in couldn't have been stopped by anyone, but there were plenty more she saved. Polly was amazed by her skill, especially as the big gentle goalie always seemed so scatty when she wasn't standing at her post.

'Just remember to bring your kit tomorrow, Olive,' said Polly cheekily. Lady G had arranged to have shorts made for them all by a local cotton mill. There wasn't time or money for tops as well so they were going to have to wear their own sweaters, but Lady G had made yellow sashes for the eleven members of the team and an extra one for the reserve. A substitute player couldn't be used once the match had started, of course; that was against the rules, even if one of the team got injured during the game. However, it was good to have a reserve for the start at least, in case someone didn't turn up.

'Listen,' hollered Polly, desperate to grab one last chance to speak to everyone before the match. 'Just remember—'

'Too late, Miss Bossyboots!' said Mary-Anne, as the bell clanged. 'Time to get back to work.'

'Be quick if you're in the Danger Shed,' cried one of Daph's friends from across the courtyard. 'There's an inspector in.'

'Oh no!' Olive looked panicked, but Daph grabbed her hand.

'Come on!'

'Wait!' cried Polly. She wanted to remind them one last time about keeping the Sparks defenders away from goalscorers like her and Mary-Anne . . .

But it was no good. The team had scattered, heading back to work.

Desperate not to be in trouble with the inspector, the girls in the Danger Shed ran fastest of all.

*

Polly's shift finished at seven o'clock and as soon as she stepped outside she knew that something was wrong.

Normally, the girls all hurried off at the end of the day, keen to get home. This evening, a crowd had gathered in front of the Danger Shed, their voices raised and agitated.

'What is it?' said Polly, pushing her way through to where she could see some of the Ruffians huddled together, their heads bent.

'It's Olive,' said Mary-Anne, stepping back to let Polly into the circle. 'She's been sent to prison.'

'Prison?' gasped Polly. That was the last thing she had expected to hear.

'She had a matchstick in her pocket and the inspector found it,' said Mary-Anne. 'We're not allowed anything which might cause a spark in the Danger Shed.'

'It's partly my fault,' Daph explained, looking stricken. 'The gaslights had gone out at our hostel last night. They're always on the blink. I gave Olive two matches to light a candle. She must have used one, then put the spare match in her pocket and forgotten all about it.'

'Poor Olive,' interjected Jessie. 'She'd—'

'Forget her head if it wasn't screwed on!' chanted the little group, but no one was laughing this time.

'They marched Olive straight off to court this

afternoon,' said a girl Polly didn't know. It was clear she worked in the Danger Shed too, as the front of her hair had turned bright green from the chemicals. 'The judge sentenced her to twenty-eight days in prison just for having an unlit match in her pocket.'

'That's not fair,' cried Polly, thinking how Don Sharples always stood smoking right outside the Danger Shed and was not punished at all.

'Surely a warning would have been enough,' agreed Mary-Anne.

'Or they could have docked Olive's wages,' added Daph. 'Lady G offered to pay a fine and they refused. She thinks the War Office are making an example of the case so the rest of us will be more careful. Now Olive's lost her job and her lodgings and been thrown into jail . . . all for a stupid matchstick.'

'Wait!' Polly's mind was spinning. A terrible thought had struck her. 'This means Olive won't be able to play tomorrow!' she cried. 'We won't have a goalie!'

'Polly!' Even Daph sounded shocked.

'Olive's been thrown into prison,' cried Jessie. 'She's going to be there for nearly a whole month and all you can think about is football!'

'There are more important things than kicking a blooming ball about!' snapped Mary-Anne.

'I know . . . of course!' said Polly, her cheeks flaming. 'But . . .'

'No!' Mary-Anne held up her hand. 'Don't you dare mention the game again! Your precious team might not have a goalie, but Olive's whole life has been ruined.'

'You only want to play so you can show off and score lots of goals,' added Betsy, with her hands on her hips. 'You don't really care about the Ruffians at all.'

'You're ruthless, Polly Nabb. That's what you are!' said Mary-Anne, turning on her heel.

CHAPTER TWENTY-FOUR

Polly barely slept a wink that night. The boys had stolen the blanket, Ernie's foot was shoved in her face and Tommy had wet the bed as usual.

As she lay there shivering, she thought about poor Olive and tried to imagine what it would be like to be locked up in a dark, cold cell. It wasn't right. Would the gentle-hearted goalie be imprisoned with thieves and murders just for forgetting she had a matchstick in her pocket? Would they let her out for exercise? The idea of not being able to stretch her legs – or run and kick a ball – made Polly feel tight and panicked as she lay in the cramped bed.

She felt prickly and restless as she remembered how cross everyone had been with her, even Daph. She hated the thought of Daph being cross. But they were wrong. All of them. Polly felt anger rising inside her. She did care about more than just football. She cared about Olive, of course she did. She cared about Joe too. But there was nothing she could do to help either of them. They were both goalies ... and now poor Olive was in prison, and Joe ...

Polly tried not to think about Joe. She thumped the mattress and Ernie kicked her soundly in his sleep. She wished for the hundredth time that she had a space of her own somewhere in this house, somewhere she could roar with anger or pace about. Everything was all mixed up in a gnawing worry inside her – like having a rat in her gut.

Polly thought about the match too, of course, fretting over who she could put in goal now poor Olive was gone. How would the Ruffians field an even halfway decent team if Mary-Anne didn't turn up either? Which she probably wouldn't now, she'd been so cross ... calling Polly ruthless.

Mary-Anne was right. Polly was ruthless, if that's what wanting to play well tomorrow meant, and she didn't care what anyone thought.

But there was more to it. Ever since the Christmas game, when she had heard that Tweedy was scouting for new talent, Polly had held a secret dream that he might spot her and ask her to be a striker for the

Sparks. This match tomorrow was her one and only chance . . .

At last, she slipped into a light and fitful sleep.

It seemed like only moments later that she woke to Walter bursting into the room. 'Ready for this so-called match of yours?' he said with a sneer.

Polly sat up and nearly punched him in the head. Instead she scrambled out of bed and pulled on her work trousers, even though the Ruffians had all been given a rare Saturday morning off.

Mam looked her up and down. 'You can't wear that to this fancy wedding.'

'I'm not going,' said Polly, making up her mind for certain.

'In that case, you can help me,' said Mam, stripping the bed and thrusting the wet sheet into Polly's arms. 'Get that washed and . . .'

'I can't. Not this morning.' Polly dropped the sheet in a soggy heap, grabbed the bundle of shorts and shin pads Lady G had given her for the game and dashed out of the room.

'Wait,' cried Mam. 'Come back here, Polly Nabb.'

'Where are you going?' whined Ernie as she almost tripped over him on the stairs.

'Out!' said Polly. Before anyone could ask her any

more questions, or find her a thousand jobs to do, she fled across the yard and turned left down Link Street, towards Frank Cogley's house.

Nobody would miss her at the wedding. Not even Daph. They'd said it themselves – all she ever cared about was football, so she'd prove them right. She'd stay away and practise shooting goals instead.

'Frank!' she yelled, battering on the Cogleys' back gate. 'Frank! Have you still got that soggy ball you found in the canal?'

Outside Duke's, Polly shot a tenth goal past Frank Cogley's ear. The battered football was too squashy and flat to fly far, but she still managed to fire it just above his right shoulder.

'This is no fun,' Frank moaned. 'Can't you let me try and save a few?'

'No,' said Polly, retrieving the ball and practising a corner kick. 'What would be the point in that?' She ran back down the gravel chasing the lopsided ball, although the wretched thing had already practically stopped rolling.

'Can't you go in goal for a bit, then?' said Frank.

'No! I'm the one who's got a match today,' said Polly. 'I need the practice.'

'You're so selfish when you play,' whined Frank, running out of the goalmouth to tackle her. 'If you don't let me have a go at shooting, I'll—'

'Take your ball away?' said Polly, dodging round him and thwacking another shot into the empty goal. 'Why do boys always threaten to do that whenever I'm beating them?'

Before Frank could answer, she heard the unmistakable roar of a motorbike – *The Green Dragon,* she thought ... and a second later, Daph skidded to a halt in front of Duke's.

Frank opened and closed his mouth like a fish.

'Blimey, is that a lass?' he gulped. 'Is that her motorbike?' Anyone would have thought a mermaid had just flopped out of the canal, he sounded so amazed.

Polly ignored him. She busied herself with collecting the ball from behind the goal. The last thing she'd expected was to see anyone from the team this morning and she certainly wasn't ready to face Daph.

'How do?' said Frank, still gawping as he edged closer to the bike. 'Can I have a look?'

'Go ahead.' Daph nodded. 'Hello, Pol. I thought I might find you here. Are you sulking?'

'No,' said Polly, balancing Frank's soggy football on

the toe of her boot. 'I'm just practising. Someone on this team needs to take it seriously!'

She dribbled the battered ball around Daph and furiously kicked it hard and aimlessly away across the pitch.

Splosh!

The ball landed with a wet plop in the canal.

'Polly!' cried Frank, and they charged to the edge of the bank. Too late. With one last sad sucking sound the battered football sank beneath the greasy water, back where it had come from all those weeks ago.

'It's a goner this time,' groaned Frank, lying flat on his belly and peering into the slimy black depths. 'It's too deep. Trust you, Polly!'

'I'm sorry!' She really hadn't meant for that to happen. 'I'll get you another ball. A brand-new one,' she said, though she had no idea how, of course.

'Don't fret.' Frank clambered to his feet. Whether he was showing off for Daph or just being decent, Polly couldn't tell, but he shrugged and strolled back to the motorbike. 'Just score a couple of goals for the Lowcross lasses today,' he said. 'Show Kerston what for, and we'll call it quits.'

Polly smiled. He was all right, Frank Cogley.

'Good. That's sorted,' said Daph brightly. 'Now

you've got no excuse not to come with me. Hurry up, Pol. The girls are waiting.'

'Waiting for me?' said Polly. 'Why?' The last she'd seen of them, everyone had turned their backs on her and walked away. The match wasn't for hours yet.

'To go to the wedding, of course,' said Daph. 'We're all bridesmaids ... the whole team. You included.'

Polly froze. 'I am not going to be a blinking bridesmaid,' she said, digging her feet into the gravel. 'No way!'

Frank was laughing like a loon.

Polly had never been to a wedding before, but she'd seen pictures in the papers – little apple-cheeked girls with baskets of petals and frilly dresses. That might be all right for someone as pretty as Daph, or as elegant as Jessie, or soft plump Betsy with her golden ringlet hair. Not big, tall Polly the size of a lad. 'I'd look ridiculous!' she cried, panic shooting through her tummy in long, cold spears.

'It's not what you think.' Daph tapped the seat of the bike and smiled. 'Come on! You never know, even *you* might approve, if you try.'

Chapter Twenty-Five

There were ten 'bridesmaids' in all. The group was made up of the entire remaining football team, including the reserve, but without poor Olive and of course Mary-Anne.

'Isn't this fun!' cried Betsy, swinging a little basket festooned with pink bows and filled to the brim with dried rose petals. 'I'm going to toss these over the happy couple when the ceremony is done.'

Polly glanced around. Other than Betsy's basket, she was relieved to see there was barely a frill in sight.

Instead, the girls were all dressed in their factory overalls.

'We're the Guard of Honour,' Daph explained, passing Polly a long-handled spanner. 'It's like the Tommies do, when a soldier gets married. They wear their uniforms to show how proud they are, and make an archway of swords or rifles for the groom to walk through.'

'Like this,' said Betsy, ushering them into two lines either side of the church doorway.

'We don't have rifles or swords, of course,' said Jessie. 'That's where our spanners and wrenches come in.'

Polly glanced down at the heavy tool in her hand. Someone, probably Betsy, had wiped it clean of oil and grease and tied a pink ribbon around the handle. Yes, that would definitely have been Betsy!

Polly smiled. Daph was right. She really didn't mind being a bridesmaid like this. She was proud of her work uniform, of being of munitionette, and of all her friends from the team gathered together to wish Mary-Anne luck and happiness in her future.

'Quick. Hold up your tools,' squealed Betsy. 'She's coming!'

Mary-Anne stepped through the gate, on the arm of an elderly gentleman who must have been her father. She looked beautiful in a long white dress, with just the toes of her black boots peeping out below the hem. Her hair was piled up on top of her head, under a veil of lace, with tiny white snowdrops dotted amongst her curls.

Mary-Anne blushed when she saw her teammates and passed under their archway of tools into the church.

The team followed and took their places in the back pews.

Mary-Anne's Peter was standing at the altar in his army uniform. He turned, and when he saw his bride, his cheeks grew pink and he grinned at her as if he was marrying a queen. Even from the back of the church, Polly could see he was blinking tears from his eyes.

She felt a sudden rush of unexpected happiness, so strong that she had to swallow hard for a moment to catch her breath. *Joe will come back, and he'll marry Daph, and it will be a day like this,* she thought.

She was glad now she had come.

'We have gathered here together,' began Mr Graves in his usual slow, pompous voice . . . Polly let the words wash over her. She always found it hard to concentrate in church. She wished there were cushions for a start. She wasn't used to sitting down much – it was like being back at school – and the hard wooden pews made her bottom feel numb. It was chilly too.

She tried not to fidget, though, as Daph and the other girls sat as still as statues. Instead, she watched the smiling faces of Peter and Mary-Anne's families and looked up at the high arched beams as pale sunlight speckled through the stained-glass windows. The old church felt so peaceful and unchanged, it was hard to believe there was a war raging on the other side of the English Channel.

Polly enjoyed the hymns and not just because it was a chance to stand up and stretch her legs. She loved the way the voices swelled together, rising up into the roof beams. She joined in, belting out the words she knew, singing so loud at one point that Daph, standing beside her, got the giggles.

Then Mr Graves got up into the pulpit and Polly's heart sank. She hadn't realised the vicar would give a sermon. She was just drifting off again, thinking about the match this afternoon, when something the vicar said caught her attention.

'... football.'

Polly sat up.

Why was Mr Graves talking about football? In church? At a wedding?

'I have become aware of a fixture taking place today, to be played by ladies ...'

The team glanced at one another along the pews.

'For young men and boys,' said Mr Graves, 'I believe that soccer is the finest outdoor game invented ...'

'Can't argue with that!' Polly whispered, yet she had a feeling there was a 'but' coming ...

'But,' said the vicar, glaring at the girls in the back pews, 'it is highly unsuitable for ladies.'

Here we go! thought Polly.

'I am sure, as a new husband you will agree with me, Mr Dutson,' said the vicar, leaning over the pulpit to stare at the groom. There was a titter of laughter as if this might be a joke. Peter looked flustered and Mary-Anne blushed, but Mr Graves carried on. 'We men do not want our wives, sisters or daughters running all over a football pitch, dressed in scanty costumes which are neither graceful nor becoming.'

There was a murmur of approval now, some of the men in the church nodding vigorously.

'I would urge you not to attend this vulgar spectacle,' said the vicar. 'Not as spectators, as you will only encourage this foolishness, and certainly not as players.' He glared at the team again, seeming to look longest and hardest at Polly, but she refused to drop her gaze.

'All this fuss about a few girls running up and down a pitch,' hissed Daph furiously, as the vicar raised his eyes heavenwards at last. 'While over in Europe those poor boys are being blown to smithereens night and day.'

'Exactly,' hissed Jessie on the other side of Daph, but some of the rest of the team were shifting uncomfortably, as if they really did believe they might be doing something wrong. At the altar, Mary-Anne looked the most anxious of all. Polly was more convinced than ever that the bride wouldn't turn up to play.

And the vicar was still going...

'I don't even think it will be a good game,' he said, laughing now and leaning on the edge of the pulpit as if sharing football wisdom in the pub. 'I've never seen a match played entirely by women myself, but do not think lady footballers will ever be able to 'shoot' properly. They'll probably charge the enemy's goal like geese and all hustle the ball into the net together!'

He chuckled delightedly but Polly wasn't going to stand for this.

'That's just not true!' she cried. The words were out of her mouth and flying across the echoey church almost before she realised it.

People turned and stared. Polly felt colour rising to her cheeks, but she didn't care. The anger that had been bubbling away inside her for weeks, came surging back.

'Come and see the match for yourself, Mr Graves!' she hollered. 'We'll show you!'

'Shh!' hissed Betsy. 'We're in church for goodness' sake!'

But Polly wouldn't be stopped, church or no church. The vicar was wrong. He was talking rubbish and he knew it! He'd seen Polly play often enough at Duke's to know she could shoot a decent a goal.

There was an uneasy rustle in the church as people

coughed and shuffled at Polly's interruption – even Mr Graves looked a little flustered at being heckled. Then he raised a finger to point at Polly and said, 'That outburst demonstrates the point of my sermon perfectly. No ladylike young woman can ever be involved in playing football. Leave it to the men, I pray!'

Polly bristled. There it was, the same old argument. Women must be like *this*. Men must be like *that*. Yet nobody ever said *why* it had to be that way ... It was all decided by smug fellows like the vicar, up there in his pulpit.

Mr Graves glared at Polly one last time, his face flushed with anger as he called for the final hymn and the congregation rose to their feet.

'Oh, Pol,' Daph whispered under the sound of the wheezing organ music. 'You are terrible.' Polly tensed, thinking she was going to be in for another lecture, but Daph elbowed her playfully in the ribs. 'Who'd want to be ladylike if they could be like you?'

Polly chuckled, feeling the tension escape from her neck and shoulders almost instantly. She should have known Daph would be on her side. She felt a tap on her back and looked round to see Louisa, the team reserve.

'Well spoken,' she whispered with a shy smile. 'By the way, I don't mind being goalie, if no one else will.'

'Really?' Polly spun right round in the pew.

'I've got seven brothers so I'm used to it,' Louisa whispered. 'It's the only position they let me play.'

'Perfect!' Polly mouthed, relief flooding over her. Although Louisa was quiet and had only recently joined the team, Polly sensed she had a gentle calmness about her. None of the other players had even come close to volunteering for the nerve-racking goalkeeper role.

Now they had their team in place, at last.

Polly turned round again and took a deep breath. As the organ music swelled she belted out the words of the hymn. It was one of her favourites:

> 'Dear Lord and Father of mankind,
> Forgive our foolish ways . . .'

It didn't matter what the spiteful old vicar thought. The Ruffian Girls were going to play their first match this afternoon and nobody could stop them.

As the service ended, the 'bridesmaids' dashed outside to form their Guard of Honour. They held their wrenches and spanners high and clinked them together like gleaming swords as the happy newly-weds passed underneath. Betsy threw handfuls of petals and the girls cheered at the tops of their voices.

'Thank you! That's a lovely touch,' said Peter, blushing. 'And … er, good luck with the game this afternoon.' He glanced round as if to check that Mr Graves wasn't leaning over him. 'I bet my Mary-Anne scores at least three goals.' He beamed with pride as Mary-Anne kissed him on the cheek.

'You mean, you're going to come along?' cried Polly.

'Too right, I am,' said Mary-Anne. 'How dare that old vicar call us geese.'

The team honked with delight and flapped their arms like wings.

'It's the same with us boys in the trenches,' said Peter seriously. 'Toffs are always trying to tell us what to do. But the war's changing all that. Us working men and women have had enough of being pushed about.'

A whoop of agreement rose up from the girls and Peter's soldier pals too.

Polly was amazed. Peter looked so timid, but she saw there was a fire in him after all. Perhaps he was right. Perhaps this long, horrible war would change what they were prepared to put up with.

Peter drew Mary-Anne close to him, blushing with

love and pride again as he put his arm round her waist. 'Just as soon as the new Mrs Dutson here has had her photograph taken with me, she's all yours,' he said.

'See you at the pitch, girls,' agreed Mary-Anne.

Polly cheered with relief. She grabbed a last handful of petals from Betsy's basket and tossed them over the bride and groom.

CHAPTER TWENTY-SIX

It was a rush to get away from the church and over to the Lowcross United pitch on the other side of town. When the team finally arrived, it was already starting to get busy around the ground. Polly's heart leaped. This was what she had been waiting for, her chance to play a real match in front of a proper crowd. No more scuffling about for Frank Cogley's condensed-milk can outside Duke's or dodging piglets in the yard.

The only thing that dampened Polly's excitement was the sight of Don Sharples coming to let them in to the ground. She had almost forgotten he was going to be the referee.

'Just the team for now, ladies and gentlemen,' he barked at the spectators, giving a great show of rattling his keys and making clear to everyone that he was in charge.

He was still jangling his keys as he led the Ruffians through the clubhouse, pointing to the glass trophies full of team photographs and silver cups.

'You've got big boots to fill. Great *men* have played here,' he said, stopping in front of one of the glass cases. 'I hope this little charity event won't be too overwhelming for you.'

'We'll be fine,' said Polly. She'd had enough of chatter and time-wasting. 'Just show us where to get changed.'

In truth, though, the rows of glass cases and pictures of past teams did make her feel a little unsettled. There was a photograph of young defender George Coombes, who had done a brilliant job the last time she and Joe came to see a match here at Lowcross. Also a huge painting of the legendary striker Ned Shorrock. Probably Lowcross United's greatest ever player, people in the town called Shorrock a traitor as he had transferred to Kerston FC and won them the FA Cup in 1910.

Polly held her chin high and winked at the picture. 'All right, Ned,' she muttered, thinking of her own hopes to be a striker for the Sparks one day. If he could quit his small, local team to dream big, then why shouldn't she?

'Change here,' barked Don, pushing open a door to

the dressing room. 'Then there's some photographer fellow waiting for you on the pitch.'

He rolled his eyes as if he had no idea why anyone would want to take a picture of a team of girls, then left them to it at last.

'Good riddance!' said Jessie and everybody cheered, even though they'd have to face him again soon enough as referee.

The girls had grown used to getting undressed in front of one another from changing at the factory, but Betsy still tried to hide behind a locker door.

'Don't look,' she squealed, turning pink as piglet. 'I'm only wearing my second-best smalls!'

Everyone giggled but paid no real notice. Polly quickly pulled on her shorts and sweater, adding her mob cap and Lady G's yellow sash. For the first time in her life, there were shin pads too.

She felt a flush of pride. It wasn't the striking black-and-white kit of the Sparks, but it was something. She was glad there wasn't a mirror though, as glancing down at what appeared to be acres of bare leg between her shorts and socks, she felt taller and more ungainly than ever.

Jessie, usually so strong and confident, looked suddenly panicked. 'I can't go out like this with my legs on show,' she said, crouching behind a shoe rack.

'Me neither!' wailed Betsy. 'It's just not decent.'

'It's too late to worry about that now.' Daph stepped out into the middle of the room, looking as if she had worn skimpy shorts every day of her life. 'The crowd will soon forget about looking at our legs when they see how well we kick the ball.'

'Exactly!' Polly could have thrown her arms round Daph's neck and hugged her for her good sense. 'Let's just get out there, shall we? The Sparks will be here soon.'

As the Ruffians emerged from the clubhouse, cheers and wolf whistles erupted from the stands.

'I'm guessing that's at the sight of our knees, not the thrill of the game ahead,' said Daph with a sigh.

'Don't worry, we'll soon show them!' Polly threw her shoulders back. She remembered how the big, raucous crowd at Kerston had been won round by the skill of the Sparks at the Christmas Day match.

'Oh, Lord!' squealed Betsy as a man with a bushy moustache leaned right over the low wooden barrier and blew her a kiss.

'Look at her! That little blonde's a peach!' he bellowed to his friend.

'Just ignore them,' said Daph.

'Pretend they're not even there,' agreed Polly. She put her hand firmly on Betsy's back and manoeuvred her towards the pitch, terrified she might make a run for it and retreat to the dressing room to hide. They had no reserve left now Louisa had taken Olive's place, and there was still no sign of Mary-Anne. They couldn't afford to lose any more players before the match even began.

'Blooming heck!' Polly opened her mouth and stared at the enormous, wide pitch.

'What is it?' said Betsy, in panic. 'Polly? What?'

'This!' Polly crouched down and pulled up a bunch of the short mown grass. 'Smell it!' she said, thrusting the green shoots under Betsy's nose.

'Smells like grass to me,' said Betsy, sniffing.

'Isn't it brilliant?' said Polly, sinking to her knees and putting her nose flat to the ground.

'It's just grass,' said Betsy again. 'You're mad, you are, Polly Nabb.'

But Daph had knelt down beside her and some of the other players too.

The crowd behind them roared with laughter, but the girls took no notice.

'Better than the concrete we play on at the factory,' said Jessie with a grin.

'And the gravel at Duke's,' said Polly, thinking how often her knees had been filled with grit. The only time she ever got to play on grass was down the back of the canal where it was full of rabbit holes and broken bottles, or in the park where they were always chased out after ten minutes when the park keepers found them. Now here she was on a flat, mown, perfect surface.

Just as she stood up, a new roar rose from the crowd, with a fresh burst of wolf whistles.

The Sparks had arrived.

The Ruffians turned and stared as their opponents sprinted on to the pitch in their black-and-white jerseys.

'Oh, dear!' Betsy swallowed as if she might be sick.

'Bring on the battle!' whispered Polly with a fresh leap of excitement.

Chapter Twenty-Seven

With just ten minutes until the start of the match, the two teams lined up in front of one of the goals to have their photographs taken. Polly kept glancing towards the clubhouse, looking out for Mary-Anne.

'I hope she hasn't run off on her blooming honeymoon!' Polly hissed, making the photographer bellow at her to keep still.

'She'll be here,' said Daph calmly.

But there was no sign of the bride when the photographs were finally done.

It had started to drizzle and Lady G dashed on to the pitch with a newspaper over her head. 'Best of luck! The stands are not jam-packed, but we've raised at least two hundred pounds for our wounded soldiers.' She smiled delightedly, patting Polly on the back.

'That's good,' said Polly, pacing up and down as she

looked for Mary-Anne. There was still no sign of her, though Polly spotted Dad, Ernie and Walter amongst the spectators behind the goal. Dad gave a shy wave and she could hear Ernie screeching her name. 'Come on, our Pol!'

Walter was pretending he couldn't even see her, of course.

Polly gave a quick wave over her shoulder as she turned towards the clubhouse again. If Mary-Anne wasn't here soon, the game would start without her and they'd have to make do with just ten players for the whole match.

Don Sharples strode into the middle of the field.

'Captains, please!' he bellowed.

Polly's heart pounded as she stood alongside Joyce Shaw, the athletic blonde striker for the Sparks.

'Welcome to Lowcross, Miss Shaw. I hope you have a good game,' Don said, smiling. To Polly, he narrowed his eyes and the smile turned to a sneer.

'Heads or tails, ladies?' he asked, taking a silver shilling from his pocket.

'Wait!' begged Polly. 'We're still one player down.'

The shiny coin spun in the air. 'Better call it!' Don laughed.

'Heads,' cried Joyce.

'Heads it is, Miss Shaw.' Don smirked at Polly though he never showed them the coin.

'We'll start, then,' said Joyce, grabbing the ball.

'Wait,' begged Polly. 'Please.'

'Too late. It's time for kick-off.' Don raised the whistle to his lips.

'Stop! She's here,' Polly cried as Mary-Anne appeared suddenly in the doorway of the clubhouse. She leaped forward and grabbed Don's arm before he could blow the whistle.

'Don't touch me! I'm the ref,' he hissed, but Mary-Anne was safely on the pitch at last.

She'd changed into her kit but still had her wedding veil pinned on her head instead of a mob cap like the rest of the players. The white lace flew out behind her as she ran.

A huge cheer went up from the Ruffians. The delighted crowd began to sing 'Here Comes the Bride'.

Don scowled, then blew his whistle and the Sparks kicked off.

'Come on, Ruffians, let's show 'em what we can do,' roared Polly, racing the length of the pitch to help her team out at the back. A Sparks defender shadowed her all the way.

'We heard you might be trouble,' she said, panting

for breath. 'Our delivery driver saw you playing at the factory and reported back to Tweedy. He likes to keep an eye on rival teams.'

Polly flushed with pride. So Tweedy had heard of her already! Perhaps her plan would work. If she played well today, he really would invite her to join the Sparks. She darted forward, nicked the ball off Joyce Shaw and sped away up the pitch.

She had a clear shot on goal. Behind her, she heard the breath of the defender catching up. Polly smashed the ball hard, aiming for the top right-hand corner of the net. The goalie wouldn't stand a chance. But as the ball left her foot, the Spark's defender jumped in the air, threw out her hand and deflected it.

'Oi!' cried Polly. 'You can't do that!'

It was a handball. She looked desperately to Don, who had run along level with her and must have seen the whole thing.

Surely it would be a penalty.

Don grinned – a smile so sly and narrow that only Polly would see it. It was the same mean grin he'd given her that day she'd mocked him on the pitch at Duke's. He'd warned her then to be careful. Don held her eye for a moment longer, then denied the penalty.

'What? You must be mad!' roared Polly. She'd known

Don might pick on them ... on her in particular, but this was outrageous. It was a blatant foul.

'Goal kick to the Sparks!' said Don calmly.

'No!' Polly threw her arms in the air. The team shouted. The home crowd booed. But it made no difference.

Don's spiteful decision was made.

The Sparks goalie was fast. She booted the ball down the other end.

A moment later Joyce Shaw scored.

After that nothing seemed to go Polly's way again. She was so closely marked she couldn't get an inch of space, let alone another chance at goal.

The Ruffians kept giving away the ball. As the drizzle turned to rain, even the local crowd seemed to turn against them, and when the half-time whistle finally blew, the Sparks were three-nil up.

'Chin up, girls!' said Lady G, popping her head round the dressing-room door. 'Don't look so glum. I remember when we played hockey once against St Augusta's at school. They were absolutely slaughtering us until the second half. These things can turn around ...'

The team made a grumbling sort of acknowledgement. They all blamed Don that things had turned against them, but Polly knew it was more than his spite that was losing them the game. The Sparks were brilliant. The Ruffians were just not good enough to beat them. *Like racing the milkman's ponies against a field of thoroughbreds,* Polly thought.

'Come on! Time to go back out there,' said Lady G and the disheartened players shuffled back towards the pitch.

Lady G put a hand on Polly's shoulder.

'It's up to you,' she whispered. 'You're the only one who can change this game.'

Polly almost shrugged Lady G away. Then she stopped for a minute and took a deep breath.

'Yes!' She'd been so riled by Don, and so hemmed in by the defenders ever since, she had lost all her fight, but it didn't have to be like that. Even if it was just one good goal, the team could still do something to save their pride. *She* could still do something . . .

'Come on!' Polly roared, charging out into the rain. 'Let's show 'em what we're made of, Ruffians! Lady G's right – we're not beaten yet!'

If anything, the second half was harder than the first – a boxed-in, scrappy fight – but Polly refused to give up. She was doggedly determined to keep playing her best, even if it was a futile battle.

The grass was soft to fall on at least, but horribly slippery in the pelting rain. Polly wasn't used to the way the mud clagged on her boots, making her feet feel heavy. She and the rest of the Ruffians were playing in their leather work boots – not proper football studs like the Sparks – and they slipped and slid around like newborn calves.

Half the spectators seemed to have gone home, too wet or unimpressed with their local team to bother staying until the end.

But Polly was relentless. She just kept on going, ploughing up and down the muddy field, slipping and sliding and slithering her way to the ball.

Once she got almost close enough to shoot before the defenders ganged up and got the ball away again. They passed it straight back to Joyce who sent a thundering shot right past Louisa's shins.

Four-nil against Polly's Ruffians.

'Play up!' Polly screamed, pushing on. Her legs grew heavy as cramp bit into her right calf.

Then suddenly, out of nowhere, Daph slid forward across the mud and passed her the ball.

There was space at last.

The defenders were finally tiring.

Polly spun towards the goal and charged forward.

The defenders were on her tail like hounds on a fox.

Out of the corner of her eye she saw Mary-Anne – in her pinned-up veil with wet snowdrop petals still in her hair – running up the right-hand side. Alone. Unmarked.

Polly knew she should pass the ball.

But this was her big chance to prove what she could do. The Ruffians might not have a hope of winning, but at least Polly could show Tweedy her true skill.

The defenders were gaining on her fast. The noise from the crowd swelled.

Polly skidded sideways and swung her left foot. Her right leg slipped in the mud underneath her ... a complete mishit. The ball flew high over the bar.

Stupid! She had rushed it. She had messed up. She had missed. Polly clutched her head, her cheeks burning.

She could see Dad, Ernie and Walter leaning forward in the stands behind the goal. Dad and Ernie's eyes were wide with disappointment. Walter's were crinkled up in glee.

She sunk to her knees.

'What were you doing? I was completely unmarked!' cried Mary-Anne furiously. 'You should have passed to me.'

Polly scrambled to her feet as the keeper took a

quick goal kick and the ball was down the other end again. She couldn't give up. The rain was pelting down so hard, she could barely see, but she chased away again. Spotting Joyce undefended, she slid in and stole the ball.

There were only minutes left.

Once more, Polly was running back up the pitch, pursued by defenders.

Mary-Anne was still up their end, unmarked.

This time, Polly passed the ball, leaving it to the very last minute and letting it fly like a magnet to Mary-Anne's feet.

'Go on!'

The young bride charged forward and scored a beautiful, smooth-as-butter goal!

The home crowd went wild. It was as if the Ruffians had won the match, not scored a solitary goal in a resounding four-one thrashing.

Mary-Anne flung her arms round Polly's neck and screamed with delight. As she let go, Polly's shoulders were covered with damp petals falling from Mary-Anne's hair.

'Well done!' croaked Polly, forcing herself to smile. She was pleased the Ruffians had scored at last, of course, but her mouth felt sour with jealousy. The team were still losing the match and it was Mary-Anne who had got the only goal, not Polly.

She charged back down the field as fast as her aching legs would carry her. Too late. Don Sharples blew the final whistle. Polly sunk to the ground, exhausted. She had given everything she had, and it was nowhere near enough.

Joyce Shaw and a bunch of Sparks almost tripped over her as they ran past, cheering.

Polly lay breathless on her back. The match had been a disaster. The Ruffians had been thrashed and any secret dreams Polly had of impressing Tweedy were surely trampled in the mud.

CHAPTER TWENTY-EIGHT

The rain had finally stopped now the match was over.

'Come on!' called the photographer, beckoning to both teams. 'Let's get another picture of you plucky ladies. A load of muddy lasses like you might just make the front page of the *Lowcross Herald*.'

He ushered them all into the goalmouth, right in front of where Dad, Ernie and Walter were still standing. Lady G and Don Sharples were there too, as well as Tweedy in his smart suit and hat.

Polly hung back, squishing a divot of mud with her boot. She couldn't face having to grin like a monkey, all bunched with the others while they chattered. They didn't even seem to care about the final result any more. Polly cared. She was supposed to be a striker but she had messed up and hadn't managed to score even once. Never mind impressing Tweedy, Joyce Shaw and the rest of the Sparks were probably laughing their heads off at her.

Don Sharples was grinning like a wolf. 'Not your day, eh, Nabb?'

That did it.

'I-I've got to go!' cried Polly. 'I ... er ... bad tummy!' Her stomach really didn't feel good. Her insides were all stirred up with disappointment, shame and jealousy too.

She started to run.

'I'll need to take a special picture of the beautiful goal-scoring bride,' Polly heard the photographer say to Mary-Anne, still dressed in her football kit and veil.

Polly belted away across the pitch, not looking back, desperate to be alone. She bashed open the door of the dressing room, grabbed her bundle of clothes and barged out again, not stopping to change. She just wanted to get away. She needed to roar, and run, and kick something, all by herself, without having to talk to anyone.

Storming down the corridor, Polly passed under the painting of Ned Shorrock staring down at her in his Lowcross United colours. 'Clear off!' she snapped. The legend's friendly smile now just seemed smug.

Two steps later, Polly skidded to a halt.

Leaning up against a cabinet of trophies was a bulging net of footballs, just like the one she'd seen at the Christmas Day match. Tweedy must have brought them with him.

Polly glanced both ways up and down the long, polished corridor. There was nobody about. She stared at the net, her heart thumping as she counted in a whisper, '. . . five, six, seven . . .' Eight footballs. All shiny as chestnuts and brand new.

Polly's palms were damp. Her head scanned the long, echoey corridor again. Still nobody there. Just the eyes of Ned Shorrock, staring down.

'What are you looking at?' said Polly scowling at the picture.

She picked up the net of balls and ran.

As Polly fled from the football ground, the pavements were still thick with spectators milling about. She put her head down, and smashed through the crush, running flat out with her bundle of clothes under one arm and the net of stolen footballs flung over her shoulder.

'Watch it!' cried a man pushing a bicycle as she nearly barged him into the gutter.

At last, when the streets grew quiet, she slipped into

a dark doorway, dropped the footballs at her feet and leaned up against the wall catching her breath. She looked down at the stolen net, not quite able to believe what she had done. There was no going back now. She thought for a moment of leaving the balls there in the doorway for someone else to find. But she couldn't. Eight beautiful footballs ... She would be in trouble enough just for stealing them – she might as well keep them too.

What did it even matter? Nothing seemed to matter any more. She'd promised Joe she'd play in this match – she'd hoped to make him proud – but it had all come to nothing. She was almost glad he wasn't here to see it. Almost ... though of course, if he was here, she would know where he was.

Polly pulled her work clothes on over her kit, picked up the net and stepped out of the doorway again, trying to look as if she always carried a bag of brand-new footballs home.

She took the long way round so that she wouldn't bump into Dad and her brothers coming back from the match. She couldn't face Walter's smart remarks about the way she'd played. Dad most likely wouldn't say anything at all but slump a little further as the weight of another disappointment bore down on all the rest.

She dawdled on home as dusk fell, passing along behind the prison.

'Olive!' she shouted up at the high stone wall. 'Olive, we missed you today!' Not that the goalie could have saved them from defeat. Louisa had done her best but the Sparks were just too good. There was no reply from over the high dark prison wall, of course. Polly shuddered. It was a horrible place. Poor Olive.

Suddenly her heart leaped into her mouth. Could she be thrown into prison for stealing the balls? She certainly shouldn't be standing outside, shouting at the top of her voice with the net slung over her shoulder like a bag of robber's swag.

Polly darted away down a side street. When the prison was far behind and she couldn't resist it any longer, she took a shiny new ball out of the net and dribbled it along the gas-lit pavements, circling lampposts, until she finally reached the top of Link Street.

It had started to drizzle again but Polly still wasn't ready to go home. She didn't want to have to explain the footballs – Mam would have Ernie down the back of the market selling them by morning – and she definitely didn't want to talk about the match. She didn't want to go up to Duke's either. The men would be drinking in the pub by now, getting in as many rounds as they could before the early-closing time which they all had to put up with because of the war. Some of them might have seen the game. Don Sharples could even be there, regaling all his mates with how awful Polly and the Ruffians had been.

Polly darted down Link Street before anyone noticed her.

As soon as she was round the corner she stopped. She couldn't be seen from Duke's here, or from the house. She dropped the net on the edge of the pavement and, keeping one ball out, she kicked it up against a lamppost. She bounced it on the side of her foot and kicked it back again. It felt calming. She liked the precision, the way she had to hit the narrow post exactly in the middle, for the ball to come back to her.

Standing in the pool of lamplight she began to count, seeing how long she could keep on kicking without dropping a shot.

'. . . three, four . . .'

The streets were quiet. There was no sound except hard leather hitting the iron post.

'. . . eight, nine . . .'

She threw in a header.

'. . . eleven, twelve . . .'

Polly pushed on towards twenty, lost in the game, focusing on nothing but the skill.

'... eighteen, nineteen ...'

'Hello, there.' Someone was right behind her.

Polly jumped, missing her next shot. The ball bounced and she grabbed it, clutching it to her chest as she spun round, blinking in the lamplight.

'Tweedy! I mean, Mr Tweedale, sir!' Polly gasped. The Sparks manager was the last person in the world she had expected to see there.

But she knew why he had come ...

The bag of shiny stolen footballs was lying right beside his feet. Polly's cheeks burned with shame. He'd come to find the thief and she'd been caught red-handed by the man she most wanted to impress.

'I'm sorry,' she said. There was no point in even trying to hide the ball she was holding. 'I was just leaving the dressing room and—'

'Goodness me, Miss Nabb, you're a hard woman to find,' said the manager cutting across her. 'Nobody I met seemed to have a clue where Link Street was.'

'No. I suppose not,' said Polly slowly. No one ever had any reason to come to this grimy, rundown area behind Duke's pub unless they lived here or were chasing a bad debt. In a poor part of town, this was the poorest of all with whole families crushed into single rooms. As darkness fell, the narrow alleyways were a haunt for drunks and pickpockets, and girls not much older than Polly heading out to work the night.

'Well, I've found you now,' he said, clearing his throat.

'Yes. You've found me, all right.' Polly sighed, bracing herself for trouble.

'I'll need to speak to your parents,' said Tweedy firmly. 'Are they home?'

Polly nodded and her shoulders slumped. Things were going from bad to worse. She should have guessed Tweedy would involve Mam and Dad. One of them would have to come along to the police station when the manager turned her in.

'Mam's going to skin me alive!' she groaned. Trouble with the police was the last thing the Nabbs needed.

'Really?' Tweedy looked surprised. 'I suppose she'll miss you if you go, of course!'

'Go?' Polly swallowed. Did Tweedy think she'd be sent to prison? 'I know you must be very cross about the footballs, sir. But . . .'

'Oh, those! What are they doing here?' Tweedy glanced down, as if seeing the net of balls beside him for the first time. He smiled and shook his head as if it didn't matter in the slightest. 'I believe I must have left them in the corridor at the clubhouse. How careless. It was kind of you to look after them for me.'

'But ...' Polly opened and closed her mouth like a fish. She was sure Tweedy didn't believe for one minute she was keeping the footballs safe. 'Are you not going to have me arrested?' she asked.

'Arrested?' Tweedy scratched his chin. 'Of course I don't want you arrested, lass. I want you to come and play for the Sparks,' he said.

'You ... What?' Polly stammered. This didn't make any sense. She had a tight feeling in her chest, almost as if she couldn't breathe.

'You heard me, lass,' said Tweedy, his eyes twinkling in the lamplight. 'You're being scouted! I want you to join my team.'

'Blinking heck!' The words shot out of Polly's mouth. For a moment that was all she could say. She held the lamppost to steady herself. 'But I played so badly,' she whispered at last. 'That dreadful shot which hit the bar ... and I didn't even score.'

Tweedy smiled. 'I don't care a jot about that. What I liked was your determination, lass. I instructed my best defenders to stick to you like glue, especially in the second half, and yet you never gave up.' He picked up the net of balls and slung them over his shoulder. 'I'm building the greatest women's team there's ever been, Miss Nabb. You've got just the sort of gusto I'm looking for.'

'Gusto …' repeated Polly. She hugged the last football tightly to her chest, breathing in its leather scent, now mixed with mud and grit.

'I'm going to play for the Sparks!' she cried.

Tweedy laughed. 'So is that a yes, lass? Would you like to join my team?'

Polly threw the football high in the air. 'Yes, I blooming would!' she whooped.

CHAPTER TWENTY-NINE

'Let me get this straight, Mr Tweedale,' said Mam. 'You want to offer my Polly a job making munitions at your factory over in Kerston?' Her eyes were boring into him, looking for some sort of trick. 'And she'll be playing football with a lot of lasses too?' Mam was rocking Queenie on her lap, while Bob and Tommy pulled at her skirts.

'That's right, Mrs Nabb.' Tweedy nodded.

He wasn't stuck-up or posh at all. He spoke with the same broad Lancashire accent as the Nabbs, yet he seemed like a real gent all dressed up in his fancy suit with bow tie and matching pocket handkerchief.

Polly wondered what he must think of them all. She thought how poky and cluttered their dark little house must seem. For a family who didn't own much, they'd certainly crammed enough junk into this tiny room: there was laundry drying over the back of chairs, two bulging sacks of coal waiting for Mam's delivery round in the morning – you couldn't leave it in the yard or someone might nick it – a pail of Queenie's dirty nappies soaking by the range and another pail filled with potato peelings to be taken out to the pig. There was a smell of pig too. Polly cringed.

'Thing is,' said Mam, picking at her teeth with a chewed matchstick, 'our Walter says Polly played rotten.'

'Well, our Walter's wrong, isn't he!' snapped Polly before she could stop herself. Ten minutes ago, she would have agreed with her brother, but now she was enjoying watching him stand halfway up the stairs, staring at the football manager with his mouth wide open.

'You want to shut that big gob of yours, Walter, or you might catch flies!' She laughed, forgetting to be on her best behaviour. Tweedy shot her a look. Even in the dim light Polly could see that his eyes were smiling.

'The wages will be better than what Polly earns at Lowcross, Mrs Nabb,' he explained. 'Plus she'll get a ten-shilling bonus every time she plays in a match for the Sparks. Our bosses at the factory are very proud of the team. And I'll organise somewhere for Polly to live in Kerston too, of course.'

'Live?' Mam sat up so quickly that Queenie started to bawl. 'What'll she need to live there for?'

'The factory's over in Kerston,' said Walter. 'She can't exactly walk there every day, can she?'

'I hadn't thought of that,' said Mam as Polly grabbed the howling baby from her arms and jiggled her up and down.

'I'll not have her staying in one of those hostels full of wild lasses.' Mam heaved herself out of her chair and stood eye to eye with Tweedy across the fireplace. 'It's not decent for a girl to leave home before she's married.'

Not this again, thought Polly, but a sense of panic was rising in her. Was Mam going to stop her going away?

'I understand your concern, Mrs Nabb,' said Tweedy calmly. He didn't seem in the slightest bit daunted by Mam growling at him like a wild bear. 'I can arrange for Polly to lodge with a very respectable family. Probably someone who also has a daughter in the team ...'

Mam folded her arms. 'It's out of the question.'

Polly groaned. 'Mam ... Please ...'

There was a movement in the shadows and a voice spoke up from the corner.

'She should go.'

Everyone jumped. As usual, Dad had been so quiet they had almost forgotten him, but he got out of his chair and came and stood in the pool of pale light around the table.

'Polly should go,' he repeated. 'Mr Tweedbottom here, is right.'

'Tweedale,' hissed Mam. 'The man's name is Tweedale.'

'How do.' Dad nodded, without looking over at the manager at all. 'The fellow knows what he's talking about,' he said. 'Our Pol was really something on that pitch today. Like a terrier she was.' He stretched out his hand and stroked the top of Polly's head. 'I was that proud of you, lass . . .'

He trailed off as if the words had caught in his throat.

Polly swallowed hard and found that she couldn't speak either. Instead, she buried her head in Queenie's hair. The baby was quiet now, all soft and sleepy.

'There we are, then,' said Mam, as Dad slunk back to the shadows. 'The man of the house has spoken.' It was that rare Dad said anything at all, Polly knew it had taken everyone by surprise. Yet it would still be Mam who had the final say.

'The extra money will certainly come in handy,' she said at last and Polly realised she'd been holding her breath. 'When will our Polly have to go?'

'Straight away on Monday,' said Tweedy. 'She'll need

to sign some paperwork to release her ⋮
here, then Lady Gidleigh's offered ⋮
Kerston. She has a delivery to bring ⋮
He smiled at Polly. 'I'm keen to get y⋮
as we can.'

Training . . . with a team like the Sparks. Polly's heart leaped. *Just wait till Joe hears about this.*

Mam grunted as if she had something more to say.

'I want my own room!' Polly blurted out. It was the only thing she could think of to stop Mam finding another argument.

'Polly Nabb!' Mam spun round in shock. 'You're getting ideas above your station. All girls your age have to share a bedroom.'

'My own room with my own bed,' said Polly holding her ground. If the Sparks wanted her that badly, perhaps it wouldn't be too much to ask.

'I'll see what I can do.' Tweedy smiled at her as if she'd requested something as simple as a cup of water.

And just like that it was arranged. Polly was going to make munitions at the giant Kerston Electric Manufacturing Company and play football for the Sparks. She hugged Queenie tightly, realising how much she would miss her baby sister when she moved away.

ll see you on Monday, Miss Nabb.' Tweedy lifted
ne stolen bag of footballs without another word. Then
he raised his hat to them politely and strode off across
the yard.

It was only long after he was gone, and Polly was
drifting off to sleep in the cramped bed she was sharing
for almost the very last time, that she remembered the
eighth football had never been put back in the bag.

She had kicked it somewhere behind Dad's chair
when they first came into the house.

She sat up in panic ... then sighed, snuggled down
again and smiled.

'I know exactly what I'll do with that ball,' she
murmured to herself.

It was perfect.

CHAPTER THIRTY

'For me?' It was Monday morning and Frank Cogley stared at the brand-new football as if his eyes were going to pop out of his head.

'I can always take it away if you don't want it,' Polly teased.

'No!' Frank ripped the ball from her hands. 'Thanks, Pol.' The blush went right up to the tips of his sticky-out ears.

'You're welcome. I owed you,' said Polly truthfully. Giving him the last of the stolen footballs felt like the right thing to do – a sort of justice for kicking his ball in the canal.

'Anyway,' she said with a grin, 'I'll have so many footballs where I'm going, I can learn to be a juggler if I want.' She couldn't help showing off. 'Tweedy plans to make the Sparks the best girls' side in the country, you know.'

'Aren't they the only team of lasses?' said Frank. 'Other than your soppy lot of Ruffians over at the factory.'

'That shows what you know,' said Polly, although it was only since she'd started building the Ruffians that she'd learned how many other women's teams there really were. 'There's girls playing down in London, up in Scotland. Everywhere.'

Frank wasn't interested. 'Remind me again? What was the score on Saturday?' He chuckled.

Polly ignored the jibe. She was used to Frank ribbing her and the less she had to think about that match, the better. It didn't matter, though. Incredibly – somehow – it had worked a miracle and the Sparks manager had decided he wanted her to play for his brilliant team.

'Mr Tweedale says I'm the most determined player he's ever seen,' bragged Polly.

'Yeah!' Frank's smile vanished for a moment and he looked thoughtful. 'I don't doubt that.'

Polly was surprised. She'd expected him to tease her again, to knock her down a peg or two. It was half the reason she'd shown off in the first place, just to wind him up.

'All the same,' he said, still deadly serious, 'this Mr Tweed chap will have his work cut out with you.'

'What do you mean?' said Polly, more rankled than if he'd just plain laughed at her. 'Come on, spit it out?'

'Well, you know ...' Frank edged backwards as if he regretted opening his mouth. 'You just always do your own thing, don't you, Polly? You're used to getting your own way on the pitch.'

'Of course I get my own way. I'm a striker,' said Polly, throwing her hands in the air. 'It's my job to get my own way.'

Frank shrugged. 'If you say so. Thanks for the ball, Polly. It's a beauty.' He turned back down the street. 'Got to dash. Mam has me running errands. Good luck with those Sparks.'

'Thanks, but I won't need it!' Polly called after him. She picked up her sack of clothes, threw it over her shoulder and headed off towards the Lowcross factory for the very last time. She had already said goodbye to her family and given baby Queenie a long cuddle. All she needed to do now was sign the papers with Lady G and she could be off.

Polly hurried across town to the factory. The morning shift had already started, but she was desperate to say goodbye to Daph and the other girls before she left. She would miss them ... more than her family perhaps.

She was just running past the station when she saw Mary-Anne ahead of her.

'Wait up!' she called.

Mary-Anne turned and Polly saw her cheeks were stained with tears.

'Don't mind me.' She sniffed as she linked arms with Polly. 'I was just saying goodbye to my Peter. He's off to the Front again this morning. One day of married bliss and that's it – he's been sent back to the war.'

'Oh … I'm sorry.' Polly looked down at her feet, wishing she knew how to comfort Mary-Anne properly. It seemed so unfair that the young couple couldn't have a little more time together.

'We'll get through,' said Mary-Anne brightly. 'He's got his duty to do and I've got mine. This war will be done soon, then we can start over properly. Mr and Mrs Dutson. Peter's got his eye on a little tenant farm the other side of the moors. I'm a town girl through and through, but I suppose I'll give it a go. Cutting hay and rearing lambs in a little thatched cottage. Doesn't it sound romantic?'

'As long as you like muck.' said Polly with a laugh. If raising piglets in the back yard was anything to go by, farming would be a lot of hard work, and smelly too, but Mary-Anne was smiling. The last of the tears were still caught in her lashes, yet her whole face seemed set alight with love and future promise.

'I'm bloody terrified of cows,' she said with a giggle. 'But I'll milk one if I have to, because I'd do anything for him, Polly. I hope one day you find someone special and get to feel this way. Like there's nothing that matters in the world but the two of you ... and the plans you make. It's the best feeling ever, Polly.'

'Right.' Polly laughed awkwardly and scuffed her feet along the ground. For a moment though, she did think how wonderful it would be to fall in love like Mary-Anne and Peter. But it was daft ... a great hefty lass like her. No one would ever feel that way about Polly. She knew she was still young, but she'd never thought of any fellow in that way either. Not even a crush, like some of the girls at school.

'I don't suppose you'll ever love anyone more than you love football, Polly,' said Mary-Anne with a laugh. 'Isn't it exciting you're off to join the Sparks?' she cried. 'Everyone was talking about it after the match. How Tweedy went on a mission to seek you out. You're so lucky to have such a talent and now you'll get to show it off to all of Lancashire ... all of England ... all the world!' She squeezed Polly's arm as they turned the corner at the end of the lane. 'We knew you were something special from the first time we saw you kick a ball! The rest of us like football, Polly, but you live it.'

Polly blushed hard and had to clear her throat. 'You don't mind me going then?' she said, remembering how the young bride had called her ruthless. Polly was worried the Ruffians would hate her for leaving them behind.

'Of course not. None of us do. We're chuffed to bits! You'll do us proud, Polly Nabb,' said Mary-Anne, as they arrived at the factory gates. 'As long as you don't forget us . . .'

'I'd never do that,' promised Polly. She meant it too. The Ruffians had changed her life forever. She smiled, feeling warm and happy inside.

'Look who it is,' Mary-Anne tutted as they walked through the factory gates. 'Over there. Leaning against the Danger Shed, smoking as usual. Our referee!'

The smile fell from Polly's face as she saw Don Sharples grinning at them both.

She had hoped she might have been able to escape without ever having to see him again.

'Polly Nabb!' he called, shouting across the forecourt. 'Mr Tweedale's hiring thugs and thieves now is he?'

'He's hiring footballers if that's what you mean?' said Polly, smashing her answer back at him.

'Quite right!' said Mary-Anne.

'You are a thief though, aren't you, Polly?' Don grinned. 'I heard about all those shiny footballs going missing. Some fellows might be prepared to believe you took them home to be helpful. Not me, though.'

Polly squirmed and her cheeks flared scarlet as Mary-Anne walked beside her across the yard. If she hadn't heard about Polly stealing the balls before, she had now. All the Ruffians would know.

Mary-Anne just shook her head and smiled. 'You can't bear anyone having good news, that's your trouble, Don.'

'Actually, I've had a bit of news of my own,' he said. 'I finally got my call-up papers last week.'

'Oh.' Polly stopped, shocked. Even if Don was her worst enemy, it was still a terrible thing to be told you had to go off and fight.

'About time too,' snapped Mary-Anne.

But for some reason, Don Sharples didn't look in the slightest bit worried. He was smiling.

'I was all set to go,' he said triumphantly, as he pushed himself off from of the Danger Shed wall and hobbled towards them on a stick. 'Turns out I did my back in running around at your match on Saturday. It's going to take a long, long time to mend.'

'Liar!' cried Mary-Anne. 'I saw you walk away from that pitch no trouble.'

'Tricky thing, backs.' Don sucked air through his teeth. 'By the time they find what's wrong, this war might be over.'

Polly stared at him, speechless. She wouldn't wish the trenches on anyone, but all because he'd refereed their match, a brute like Don Sharples had found a way to escape it, leaving better men – men like Joe and Alfie and Peter – to play their part while he skived off in his cosy job at home.

'Looks like I'm going to be here keeping you ladies in line for a while yet,' he said with a sickening grin. He clapped his hands and shooed Mary-Anne towards the Danger Shed. 'Chop! Chop! Time for work. You're late already.'

'We don't do our jobs because you tell us, Don,' Mary-Anne shouted after him, as he hobbled away, making a great show of using his stick. 'We do it to help our brave boys, fighting out there on the Front. I'd pick up a gun and stand beside them all if I could …' She shook her fist.

Don took no notice, of course. Mary-Anne turned back to Polly and rolled her eyes. 'Let's have a last kick-about at lunchtime, if you're still here.'

'Oh yes,' said Polly. 'I'd love that.' A farewell game with the Ruffians would be the perfect way to say a proper goodbye to Daph and Mary-Anne and the whole team together.

'Can't miss a last chance to play with our very own football star,' said Mary-Anne as she stepped into the Danger Shed and waved.

Polly headed across the forecourt, grinning at the thought of a final game of footie before she went on her way.

'There you are,' said Lady G, beckoning her into the little office. 'Come and sign these papers. Isn't it exciting!' She grinned as Polly stepped inside. 'You and those Sparks are going to show the world just what us girls are capable of.'

'I hope so!' Polly smiled back, her tummy fizzing with excitement as Lady G rummaged around on the desk. 'How soon do we need to leave?' she asked. 'Only I was hoping—'

Before Polly could finish, there was a deafening bang, like the sound of thunder – only ten times louder – as if the sky was being split open with an axe.

Time seemed to slow down as the tiny hut shook like jelly on a plate.

Glass from the windows flew across the room. Polly

was thrown backwards too, landing in a heap by the door. She realised, dully, through her panic, that a pile of Lady's G's papers may have saved her life – breaking her fall.

'The Danger Shed!' screamed Lady G, who was lying on the floor too, halfway under her upturned desk, blood gushing from a wound in her head.

Polly's ears were ringing. Her throat was clogged with smoke. She couldn't make sense of anything.

'The Danger Shed!' said Lady G again, crawling towards the door. 'There's been an explosion.'

Suddenly, Polly understood.

She pulled herself to her feet and staggered through the door, on to the forecourt.

The heat hit her the moment she stepped out. The doorway of the Danger Shed was a wall of blazing flames. Polly heard screams coming from inside. She started to run forward, pushing through crowds of people, all streaming from the other sheds at once.

'Mind out! I've got to help them!' she cried. Daph and Mary-Anne … Louisa too … they all worked in the Danger Shed. 'I have to help my friends!'

CHAPTER THIRTY-ONE

'Daph . . .' Polly's one thought was to save her friends.

She stumbled forward, heading blindly towards the bright red fire of the Danger Shed. The high, mesh-covered windows had been blown out all along the side and thick black smoke was pouring from them.

Polly's ears were ringing as if she'd been hit around the head with a cricket bat, but she could still hear the terrified, screaming voices coming from inside.

'Out of the way!' bellowed a woman from the factory fire squad. Her team was already thundering forward with pumps on a handcart and a great hose on wheels. She shoved Polly backwards as jets of water spurted into the burning doorway.

'Daph!' cried Polly, stumbling forward again.

'I told you, stand back!' barked the fire officer.

'But I can help,' said Polly. 'I'm strong.' She lurched

towards the door, heat scalding her face. A firm grip grabbed her arm.

'That's enough, Polly! Let the firefighters do their work.' She looked down and saw Lady G's blood-stained hand. 'Come away!'

Polly tried to wrestle herself free, but Lady G held on. The fire officer pushed them both aside.

'If you want to save lives, you'll get out of the way and let us do our job!' she bellowed.

At last Polly stepped back, coughing and shaking all over.

'Are you all right?' she rasped, turning to Lady G who had blood pouring from a wound in her head.

'I think so.' Lady G touched her scalp and winced. 'Bleeding like a stuck pig, but it's just a bit of a knock.'

As water from the hose quashed the flames, billows of acrid black smoke filled the air and dark figures stumbled out of the charred doorway.

Louisa came first, her mousey hair black with soot. She lurched towards Lady G and Polly, then collapsed in a heap on the floor, throwing up between her knees and wheezing heavily.

Polly rushed to help her sit up, never taking her eyes form the smoky doorway. 'Did you see Daph?' she asked. 'Or Mary-Anne?'

Louisa didn't seem to hear her.

'There now, breathe deeply.' Lady G rubbed the goalie's back.

Polly paced up and down. A minute passed. Another. She couldn't bear just waiting like this.

The nurse arrived and began to check Louisa over.

'Can you count to ten for me?' she asked.

'One, two . . .' began Louisa quietly.

'Good!' The nurse hurried on, checking each person as they stumbled out of the smouldering building.

Polly ran amongst them, scanning their soot-blackened faces. 'Did you see Daph or Mary-Anne?' she asked, but they just stared blankly at her, lost in shock.

She sprinted back to Louisa. 'Can you hear me? Did you see them? Did they get out?'

'I don't know. I'm sorry.' Louisa put her head between her knees again. 'It was so sudden. I . . .'

She trailed off and Polly's stomach tightened. What if Daph was trapped in there? What if she was dead? Daph was the best friend Polly had ever had – more than that, she was like a big sister. Polly had never even got to say goodbye. What if Joe came home now and Daph was gone . . .?

She tore round the forecourt, pushing through

269

crowds to peer down at wounded faces. None of them were the one she was looking for.

'Daph?' Polly bellowed at the top of her lungs. 'Daph Jenkins?'

Polly couldn't stand it any longer. She swerved between the fire officers as if escaping defenders on a pitch and plunged into the smoke-filled building.

'Daph!' she cried, before her throat was clogged with fumes and she bent double, coughing. Instinctively, she fell to her knees. It was almost pitch-black, but there was a gap of air and light just below the smoke and she began to crawl along the floor.

'Pol?' A wheezing voice called out and a figure stumbled through the smoky darkness.

Polly's heart leaped for joy. It was Daph. Her friend was alive. She was safe.

'Here,' she cried, scrambling to her feet and holding out her hand.

Daph staggered through the smoke towards her.

Polly froze. Daph was carrying someone in her arms.

'Help me!' she choked.

Polly plunged forward, taking half the weight of the body and together they blundered to the dim light of the doorway.

'Mary-Anne!' Polly gasped, her lungs filling with air as she stumbled out into the yard.

They laid the body gently on the ground, beside the giant shell case goalposts.

Mary-Anne's soft face was as still and grey as stone. Her eyes were wide open and staring up at the sky.

'Is she . . .?'

'I don't know,' said Daph, her voice thick with smoke.

'Nurse!' Polly roared.

The nurse came running, pushing Polly roughly aside as she knelt on the ground and pressed her ear to Mary-Anne's chest.

She shook her head, then rolled back the sleeve of Mary-Anne's charred overalls, revealing a white wrist like a line of untouched snow. She searched for a pulse.

'I'm sorry.' The nurse stood up briskly. 'She's gone. There's nothing more I can do.' She hurried away, running to help a woman with a deep gash in her leg.

'Wait! No!' Polly waved her arms furiously. That couldn't be it. 'Come back!' Surely the nurse was wrong.

'Mary-Anne?' Polly crouched down. She wanted to shake her old teammate. 'You promised to play football with me today. Wake up, Mary-Anne.'

'Shh!' said Daph softly, crouching beside her.

Polly stared at the young bride's ash-grey face . . .

How was it possible? Mary-Anne had been so full of life and hope this morning ... not an hour ago ... not half an hour, even ... Now she was lying on the ground, dead – the force of it hit Polly in the guts like a punch.

'Look,' whispered Daph, laying a hand on Polly's arm. 'She's smiling. Perhaps she was thinking about her Peter.'

Polly's throat tightened as she remembered Mary-Anne's dream of the little farm across the moors. She would never get to live in that thatched cottage now or find out if she was brave enough to milk a cow.

'It's not fair,' said Daph, shaking her head. 'She barely got to be married at all ...'

'Will they write to him?' asked Polly. Peter would be halfway to the Front by now. 'Will he get the letter in the trenches?'

'I suppose so,' said Daph.

Polly hugged her knees. It was awful to think of bad news from home reaching that terrible place. It was the soldiers who everyone expected to die, not their loved ones waiting for them back home.

'Poor thing.' Jessie and Betsy had come to stand behind them. Louisa too, still shaking from the blast.

'Has anyone got a handkerchief?' the shy goalie whispered. 'We ought to cover her face.'

'I have!' Betsy unfolded a freshly pressed white square.

'Wait!' cried Polly. She leaned forward and lifted something from the singed curls of Mary-Anne's hair.

It was a tiny snowdrop. The last sign of the bride's beautiful wedding day.

CHAPTER THIRTY-TWO

An hour later, the women from most of the huts had already been ushered back to work. Some had bandages covering burns or cuts from flying glass, but they stepped up to their benches determined not to let production slip for the day.

'We have to keep up our efforts for the boys!' said Jessie. 'Think of Mary-Anne's Peter. We can't let them down. We have to carry on.'

'She's right. We should all get back,' said one of the older women from the Danger Shed after the fire crew had passed the building as safe. 'It's only the area nearest the door that's totally out of action. Let's carry on and see what we can do.'

'We're lucky the whole place didn't go up with all the explosives in there,' said Daph, her voice still wheezing as if her chest was full of smoke. As it was, three other young women besides Mary-Anne had lost their lives in the blast. Two more were seriously injured – it seemed likely neither would ever walk again – and another looked as if she would be blind.

'What do you think caused the explosion?' asked Polly as she sat leaning against the goalposts, waiting for Daph to catch her breath before she would have to go back to work too.

'A dud fuse going off by mistake.' Daph coughed. 'Happens all the time. Unless it was Don Sharples and his blasted cigarette.'

Polly gasped. 'Do you think it might have been?'

'Who knows.' Daph held her chest and tried to breathe in gulps of air. 'I don't suppose we'll ever know. The government always do their best to hush these things up, so people living nearby don't panic.'

'It wouldn't surprise me if it was Don's fault,' said Polly furiously. She hated him more deeply than ever in that moment . . . The careless, arrogant way he always stood there puffing on his fag as if he was above the rules, while girls like Olive were thrown into jail simply for having an unlit match . . . And now Mary-Anne and three other poor lasses were dead.

There'd been no sign of Don during the chaos following the explosion. At one point a fire officer had gone back into the smouldering shed to check he wasn't trapped inside. But he'd turned up safe and sound, bossing everyone around, once any real danger was over.

'Coward!' as Jessie had said.

He'd gone off now – limping still, of course – to organise a team of women from the canteen to sweep up broken glass.

He won't even help with that – just supervises the girls doing it, Polly thought.

'Are you ready, Polly?' Lady G appeared in the doorway of her windowless office, a bandage wrapped around her head like a turban. 'I've still got that delivery to take over to Kerston if you're quick.'

'Am I still going?' Polly was stunned. Surely she couldn't leave today. Not after everything that had happened here. It was just half an hour since Mary-Anne's body had been taken away in an ambulance, along with the other poor girls who had died. The air was still so thick with smoke it seemed like a fog had fallen over the town.

'Tweedy and the team are expecting you,' said Lady G simply. 'Don't worry, I'll send a message home to let them know you are safe. I expect the whole of Lowcross was rocked by the explosion. The police have put a barricade at the end of the road to keep people away. Your family may be worried.'

'Should I go, do you think?' Polly looked helplessly at Daph.

For once she didn't know what to do. She was usually so decisive, especially where football was concerned. But surely she could wait a day at least and join the Sparks tomorrow.

'There won't be another delivery going that way until the beginning of next week,' said Lady G, sounding almost stern for once. 'If you want to play in a match this Saturday, I suggest you buck up now.'

'Go!' wheezed Daph. 'Mary-Anne would want you to.'

Polly nodded, wishing more than ever that she had got to have that kick-about with the Ruffians all together for one last time. That would never be possible now.

'Come along,' said Lady G softly.

Polly heaved herself up.

'If Joe comes back, you will get me, won't you?' she said, helping Daph to her feet. 'Straight away. On the motorbike . . .'

'Of course,' said Daph. 'But if there is any news, it'll be your family who hear first.'

'I'm not talking about news,' said Polly desperately. She had to make Daph understand. 'News will come in a letter.' She was holding on to Daph's sleeve. 'I don't want to know anything about those.'

Polly was afraid if another letter came from the army it would mean they had discovered Joe's body, somewhere out there in no man's land. 'Presumed killed,' would shrink, becoming 'Killed': one hard, hopeless word, hammered in like a nail. Polly wasn't going to think about that.

She fixed on the hope that one afternoon Joe would walk up to Duke's, kicking his old football along the road. Then Daph would jump on the Green Dragon and race to tell Polly he was home.

'I'll come!' promised Daph.

'Thank you!' whispered Polly, then they hugged goodbye. Daph took a big gulp of air and headed back towards her duties in the Danger Shed.

Polly stood still for a moment and took a deep breath too.

There was nothing she could do now . . . nothing to change what had happened here. She couldn't bring Mary-Anne back any more than she could break poor Olive out of prison or find out what had really happened to Joe on the battlefield.

The only thing Polly could do was move forward. She could honour Mary-Anne who had made the same sacrifice at home as the men in the trenches.

Polly would do what she was good at ... She would play football, keep her promise to Mary-Anne and make her proud.

'Ready?' asked Lady G.

Polly nodded.

'Yes,' she said. 'Let's go.'

PART II

CHAPTER THIRTY-THREE

Kerston, Lancashire
February 1918

It was early afternoon when Polly arrived at her new home in Kerston.

'There it is. Number eight,' said Lady G, skidding the van to a halt outside a small, narrow house in a long terrace of similar slice-of-bread white houses.

'I can't come in, I'm already so late with this delivery,' she said apologetically. 'But Tweedy says the girl who lives here plays football too, so you should be all right.'

'I'll be fine,' Polly promised, feeling sick from the journey. She was still so shaken by the explosion that she felt half numb as she climbed out of the van with her sack of clothes and thanked Lady G for the lift.

As the van rattled away, Polly took a deep breath and knocked on the neat blue door.

A plump woman in a flowery pinafore opened it almost straight away. She had a pink scarf tied over her head and a feather duster in her hand.

'Welcome, pet! You must be Polly. I'm Mrs Venne,' she said, ushering her over the threshold. She opened a door on one side of the hallway and showed Polly a cosy snug with a crackling fire and a kitchen behind it. Then, flicking her feather duster at the brass doorknob on the opposite side of the hall, she opened that to reveal a smart little parlour with armchairs and china ornaments on the mantelpiece. 'It's not much, but we call it home.' She smiled proudly, her kind face shining like a rosy apple.

It was true, the house wasn't big or fancy, but Polly had never seen anywhere so clean and tidy in her whole life. She glanced down at her hands. She'd washed thoroughly and changed her clothes before leaving the factory, to get rid of all the soot and ash from the explosion, but her fingers still looked grubby, as usual. She shoved them deep in her pockets, afraid of putting dirty marks on the walls.

'How about a nice cuppa?' said Mrs Venne. 'Or would you rather see your room first?'

'Room, please,' said Polly, relaxing a little under the woman's smiley warmth. 'Isn't it quiet here?' There was no clattering or clanging from the back yard, no hollering neighbours or bickering family like there would have been at Link Street.

'Just you wait till Mr Venne and my daughter Clara get back from the factory,' said Mrs Venne, leading Polly up the stairs. 'There'll be clamour enough then!'

'There's just the three of you?' said Polly amazed. She couldn't imagine a whole family being just three people. Perhaps that explained why the house was so tidy, with no overflowing laundry baskets or unruly piles of kicked-off clogs and boots. Polly was pretty certain there'd be no squealing piglets in the back yard, either.

'We had our Clara fourteen years ago,' said Mrs Venne with a light sigh. 'But we've not been blessed with any other children since. Do you have many brothers and sisters yourself?'

'There's seven of us altogether,' said Polly, determined to still count Joe amongst them. 'Five boys and two girls.'

'Gracious! What a splendid brood,' said Mrs Venne. 'I hope you won't be lonely here without them all.' She opened a little white door at the top of the stairs and squeezed out of the way to let Polly in. 'This is your room.'

Polly stood with her mouth open. There was a soft-looking bed with a white eiderdown, a woven rug covering the floorboards, a chair by the window, and a dressing table with a hairbrush and looking glass on it. A vase of dried flowers stood on a shelf beside the washstand, and above the bed there was a tapestry picture of a black-and-white dog playing with a ball.

'Is this really for me?' Polly gasped. 'All on my own?'

Mrs Venne nodded. 'Of course, pet. It's usually our spare room. It'll be nice to have someone in it.'

'You mean you don't normally use it?' Polly had never heard of anything as flashy as a spare bedroom … but it was hers now. She dropped her ragged sack of clothes on the floor and grinned.

'Is that all you've got with you, pet?' A look of surprise – or perhaps pity – crossed Mrs Venne's kind face for moment.

'Yes …' Polly blushed, kicking the sack under the bed with the back of her heel, though it was too late to hide it.

'Well, I'll leave you to settle in,' said Mrs Venne brightly. 'Come on down if you change you mind about that cup of tea. But I expect you might just want a little nap.' She backed out of the room and gently closed the door behind her.

'A nap?' whispered Polly, smiling as she caught sight of her own shocked face in the looking glass. She hadn't had a nap in the afternoon since she was baby Queenie's age.

She went to the window and peered out between the rose-patterned curtains. Below, there was a neat little yard with an empty washing line strung across it and a broom leaning up against the back fence. Sure enough, there was not a piglet in sight, just spotlessly clean flagstones and a neatly piled scuttle of coal.

Polly sat in the chair and kicked off her boots. They made a loud clattering sound against the varnished floorboards. She scurried after them, placing them neatly side by side under the dressing table. Then she picked up the hairbrush, turned it idly over in her hands and put it down again.

She glanced at the door, checking that it really was closed. Doors were never kept closed at Link Street. Then she leaped into the air and fell backwards on the bed with her arms stretched out behind her. The springs groaned gently and the soft mattress gathered her into a hug.

'Ahhh!' Polly let out a long low breath of utter contentment and smiled up at the ceiling. In spite of everything that had happened today, she felt the sheer bliss of her own room and her own bed.

She closed her eyes and let out another long deep breath, willing the thoughts of poor Mary-Anne and the explosion, which were crowding her head, to stay away. Her ears were still ringing from the blast.

She turned sideways and pulled her knees up tight to her chest. Perhaps Mrs Venne was right. Perhaps she did want a nap . . .

CHAPTER THIRTY-FOUR

'Your tea's on the table!'

Polly was woken by a gentle knock on the door and rolled over to see Mrs Venne popping her head into the little white room.

'Oh!' She sat bolt upright, flustered to be found sleeping.

The moment she was fully awake, Polly could smell the delicious warm scents of rich gravy wafting up the stairs.

'It's only a bit of shepherd's pie,' said Mrs Venne, leading the way back down to the kitchen. 'It's so hard to get good meat with this war on, but I do my best. Mr Venne does like a hot cooked tea after his work, don't you, my dear?'

'I do!' said a broad, red-faced man, sitting at the head of a neat little table covered with a cloth, in front of the stove. He looked Polly up and down as she came into the room and frowned. In spite of changing into clean overalls back at the factory, she wondered if she ought to have worn her Sunday skirt instead.

'I hear you'll be joining us making munitions at Kerston Electric,' Mr Venne grunted. 'I'm one of the foremen and our Clara's on the production line. I expect you'll work alongside her.'

'Hello there, Polly . . .' Clara, who was washing her hands at the sink, turned round and smiled.

Polly felt a funny lurch in the pit of her stomach, as though she had flown too high on a swing. Clara was the prettiest girl she'd ever seen; no, more than pretty – beautiful. Polly stared. She had big blue eyes and dark shiny hair the colour of polished wood on a church pew. There was a sprinkling of freckles on her nose and a little gap between her two front teeth, which showed when she smiled.

'It'll be lovely to have a pal staying,' she said warmly, gliding across the room. Her face lit up as she spoke.

Polly smiled back, feeling suddenly awkward.

'Grab a seat, pet,' said Mrs Venne, and Polly stumbled gratefully to her chair, sending a beaker of water splashing across the little table as she tried to sit down.

'Blast! I mean … sorry …' She mopped madly at the spreading pool on the tablecloth with a rolled-up napkin still in its ring.

Clara giggled, sinking into her seat opposite Polly. Mr Venne sighed. Mrs Venne came to the rescue, tea towel in hand.

'Worse things happen at sea,' she said, mopping up the mess. Then she handed round four steaming plates piled high with meat and buttery mashed potatoes.

Polly pulled herself together and dived in. She hadn't eaten all day, she realised, except for a heel of bread and a cup of tea at breakfast.

'Oh, Mrs Venne,' she cried, looking up from her empty plate and licking the back of her fork where gravy had dribbled down it. 'That was blooming marvellous!'

'Glad you liked it,' said Mrs Venne, beaming. 'It's always a pleasure to feed a keen eater.'

Clara giggled so that her eyes crinkled up. Mr Venne frowned.

It was only then that Polly realised everybody else's plates were still half full. She'd bolted hers, elbows on the table, like a piglet at a trough. What must they think of her? Her cheeks burned and she sat jiggling her legs under the table while the others finished up. Clara neatly prepared each mouthful with her knife and fork, instead of shovelling with her fork like a trowel as Polly had done.

It wasn't Polly's fault. They never all sat down to eat like this at Link Street; there weren't enough chairs for a start. She always scoffed her tea one-handed, standing up against the range.

As they ate, Mr Venne told them at great length about an article he'd read in the newspaper detailing King George's latest visit to the troops at the Front. There seemed to be a lot of information about exactly how many machine guns, rifles and tanks His Majesty had seen. Polly fidgeted, rolling and unrolling her napkin. Clara winked at her across the narrow table.

'A slither of jam sponge?' asked Mrs Venne when the family had finally finished their shepherd's pie. 'It's a day or two old now, but still fresh enough.'

'Yes please,' said Polly, astounded that sponge cake could stay in a house without being eaten the moment it was made.

She grabbed her slice with her fingers, before realising the Vennes were all using spoons to eat theirs.

'Sowwy!' she said through the huge mouthful she had crammed in.

'You are funny,' Clara giggled, but not unkindly, as Polly gulped a glass of water to wash down the cake.

'You're on the football team, aren't you,' she said to Clara as soon as her mouth was empty – though she hadn't seen her at either of the games. Polly would have remembered that. She was desperate to find out more about the Sparks and take advantage of a pause in Mr Venne's list of guns. 'How many times a week do we get to practise?'

The smile vanished from Clara's face. She shook her head, her bright blue eyes boring into Polly as if warning her to change the subject, but it was too late. Mr Venne pushed his chair back from the table with a growl and stood up.

'I'll go and smoke my pipe in the yard,' he said gruffly. 'I've had enough of women's chatter for one night.'

Polly raised an eyebrow. What did he mean? The three women had barely spoken a word between them all meal.

'Pay no heed, pet,' whispered Mrs Venne as her husband stomped outside. 'He doesn't like our Clara kicking a ball about that's all. Doesn't think it's ladylike.'

'He made me stay home to see my auntie from Blackpool when we played your lot on Saturday, the same auntie I had to visit at Christmas, missing that big match too,' said Clara with a sigh.

Ah!' said Polly. That explained it. She knew she would have remembered Clara if she was there.

'Tweedy had to twist his arm to let you lodge here. The factory are proud of the Sparks even if Dad isn't,' hissed Clara, bitterly.

'Oh dear,' said Polly. 'I hope I haven't made trouble for you.'

'Not yet, you haven't!' Clara's warm giggle was back. She leaned across the table and gave Polly's hand a squeeze.

Polly flushed at the touch and her tummy fizzed suddenly as if full of sherbet.

'Thanks for the tea, Mrs Venne.' She stood up so quickly that her chair went flying into the wall behind. She rushed to help clear the plates, grateful not to be penned in by the neat little table any more.

By the time the dishes were dried and put away, Mr Venne was reading his newspaper in the snug and Mrs Venne took out her knitting and joined him.

'Why don't you show Polly your trophies, Clara?' suggested Mr Venne, peering over the top of the front page.

'All right.' Clara skipped away and Polly followed, wondering what it was that an elegant girl like Clara could have won prizes for.

'They're not for football are they?' she whispered, as soon as they were out in the hallway.

'No! Dad would never encourage me to show those off,' said Clara, slipping into the parlour. She pointed to a glass-fronted cabinet with gold and silver medals inside. There was also a fancy crystal swan with Clara's name on a little plaque underneath it, and a brass statue of a girl with long thin legs balanced on one foot.

'Ballet,' said Clara as Polly peered through the glass. 'I used to win all sorts of competitions when I was little. Look.' She put her hands on Polly's shoulders and stuck her leg straight out behind her, just like the dancer in the statue. She was so close, Polly could smell the clean tingle of soap. Then Clara spun away across the room, turning like a spinning top.

'Now you try!' she said, coming to a stop by the mantelpiece.

'Me?' Polly folded her arms across her chest. 'No way!'

'Come on!' coaxed Clara.

'No!' said Polly firmly. 'I'm too tall for dancing.'

'Tall? That's a good thing,' said Clara. 'You're exactly the same height as me.' It was true. The girls were about the same height, but where Clara seemed light and elegant – floating as she moved – Polly felt rooted to the ground like a tree trunk.

'You're strong too.' Clara spun away across the room again. 'Silly thing is,' she said, balancing on one leg, 'ballet's much harder work than football. You have to be twice as fit, if you ask me. Yet everyone makes so much fuss about girls running around with a ball.'

'I suppose ballet's just a bit more ...' Polly tried to think of the right word. She had never seen anything as graceful as Clara spinning across the parlour. '... girlish,' she said, at last.

Clara laughed. 'Men do ballet too, silly,' she said. 'Who do you think lifts the girls up? People like my dad would never think of that, though. In his world, lasses do ballet and lads play football and that's just how it is. Come on.' She grabbed Polly's hand. 'If you're not going to dance with me, let's go up to your room.' She bounded up the stairs, dragging Polly after her. Polly had never been whisked around by anyone like this before. Or bossed around either. She was amazed to find she didn't mind it.

'Here we are!' Clara sat her down in front of the little dressing table. 'I'm going to brush your hair.'

'What? No!' This was going too far. Polly clutched the top of her head. 'My hair's fine.'

Clara was already undoing the pins, her fingers

touching the back of Polly's neck. 'It's like a bird's nest at the back here.'

Polly wriggled.

'You don't get away that easily,' said Clara, smiling at her in the mirror. 'Me and my friend Minnie used to do each other's hair all the time before her dad was killed in the war and she moved to Chorley. Wasn't there ever a pal in your street who popped over . . .?'

'Not exactly.' Polly winced as Clara pulled at a knot. The only person who ever came round was Frank Cogley and all he wanted to do was play football in the back yard or throw rotten chicken's eggs at the wall.

'Well, I think you've got beautiful hair,' said Clara, scooping up a thick bunch of wiry black tresses and wrapping them around her hand.

'Stop that!' Polly tried to squirm free again but there was nothing she could do. Clara wouldn't let her go until she'd twirled every curl and fluffed up Polly's wiry hair into a big black thunder cloud on top of her head. Then she tied a pink ribbon around it all.

'*Voilà!*' she cried in delight. 'You look like a girl from the films.'

Polly had never been to the cinema, but she stared at her reflection in horror for a moment, then burst out laughing. 'I look more like a poodle!' she said, remembering the daft little dog Mr Graves's mother had brought to church last Easter.

Clara collapsed in peels of laughter too. 'Perhaps I did overdo it,' she admitted, as Polly pulled the ribbon out. 'Sleep on it! It might look normal again by morning!' She spun around and skipped out the door. 'Don't let the bed bugs bite.'

After she was gone, the room seemed very quiet – the way a shower of bright rain flashes against a windowpane and then stops suddenly.

Polly washed her face in a big china bowl with water from a jug. Then she climbed into the little white bed and stared up at the ceiling.

She stretched out her hand. Feeling nothing but the smooth cold sheets beside her, she felt suddenly very lonely. Who'd have thought she would miss all the noise and havoc of home?

Polly rolled over and hugged her pillow, wishing she had baby Queenie to cuddle in the night.

CHAPTER THIRTY-FIVE

The clean, bright munitions factory at Kerston was nothing like the rundown old sheds Polly was used to back at Lowcross. It was three times the size for a start and had all been built brand new in the first year of the war.

Clara led Polly across a big, square courtyard with an armoured tank parked in the middle of it.

'We make electrics for the engines of those brutes,' she explained. 'Our job tomorrow will be sorting through buckets of little nuts and bolts looking for any bent ones. Us young ones always get the boring jobs.' She skipped on.

Clara seemed to skip wherever she went.

'Tomorrow?' said Polly, running to catch up. 'What'll we be doing today, then?'

'You'll see.' Clara skipped on round the side of a

low white building marked DANGER and came to a stop in front of a shiny red charabanc parked on the other side.

'Do we make electrics for those as well?' asked Polly, staring at the open-top bus.

'No, silly,' said Clara. 'It's Tuesday. Us girls in the team don't have to work in the factory today. We're off to the pitch for training. The boss thinks the Sparks are a good advertisement for this place. He lets us go three times a week.'

Polly couldn't believe her ears. It was barely nine o'clock in the morning and they were off to play football already . . .

'I love this job!' She grinned, realising for the first time that she truly was here – one of the Sparks.

'Come on. Let's bag the back seats.' Clara pulled Polly behind her as she skipped to the rear of the charabanc and sprang up on to the leather bench. Polly scrambled after her, as the rest of the team began to arrive.

'Hello! We heard you were joining us,' said a few of the girls in a friendly way.

The goalie clapped Polly on the back and congratulated her for her dogged play on Saturday.

'I wish I could have been there instead of sipping tea

with my auntie in Blackpool,' said Clara with a sigh. 'I reckon Dad hopes I'll lose the football bug altogether if I stop away long enough.'

'I don't think it's working, do you?' said Polly, shouting over the babble of noise. To her delight, it seemed as if every girl on the charabanc was suffering from an incurable case of football disease. They were climbing on seats discussing tactics and yelling excited comments to each other up and down the bus.

'I think you should play forward a bit more, Alice.'

'That was a cracker you scored in the second half...'

Polly counted heads. Fourteen. Enough for a whole team and a couple left over. There were a few faces she didn't recognise from the matches as Tweedy was still chopping and changing the side all the time to get it just right. Everyone had said hello to Polly in one way or another by now, even if it was just a quick wave. The only girl to ignore her was the captain, Joyce. She was sitting just two seats away with her nose in the air.

'Don't fret!' whispered Clara, following Polly's gaze. 'Joyce is just jealous because you're a striker too.'

'So that's how it is.' Polly nodded, a spark of competition flashing inside her as the manager appeared. Tweedy was wearing his smart tweed suit as always, with bow tie and matching sunflower yellow handkerchief.

'Morning, team!' He doffed his hat to them.

'Morning, Tweedy!' the Sparks replied in unison. Polly could tell from the way they smiled at him that this softly spoken polite fellow had the respect of every player. He wasn't only the team's manager but their trainer too.

'Welcome aboard, Miss Nabb. Glad to see you're settling in, lass,' he said, doffing his hat again as he climbed into a seat behind the driver. The charabanc juddered into life, heading towards the famous Steepside football ground where Polly had first seen the Sparks play.

Although the journey in Lady G's van had made Polly feel sick, and Daph's motorbike had thrilled her to the core, she barely noticed the ride in the charabanc at all. She was too excited thinking about the day of football skills that lay ahead of her – and at the famous Kerston FC pitch too.

'Again, please, ladies. Quick as you can,' said Tweedy, standing beside the goalposts and barely raising his voice.

He was so polite he sounded as if he was inviting them all to a tea dance, not instructing them to run round a freezing-cold, frost-covered football pitch.

'We've done ten laps already,' panted Polly, her breath making clouds in the icy air and her body dripping with sweat. She was trying to keep up with Mercy, a young forward from Jamaica, who had missed Saturday's match with a twisted ankle. She was certainly better now and seemed to have wings on her feet.

'Ten's nothing.' Mercy slowed for a moment, barely puffing. 'Tweedy made us do twenty last week in the pouring ra ...'

The end of Mercy's words were lost as she sprinted away again.

'Do you need a little sit-down?' asked Joyce sarcastically, overtaking Polly on the next lap.

'No!' Polly redoubled her efforts, though the freezing air made her feel as if her chest might split in two. She'd always thought of herself as fit and strong but was amazed how slow and out of breath she seemed compared to the Sparks. She and Daph had trained hard in their early morning sessions at Lowcross but they had never run like this. Round and round with no end in sight.

'Thank you. That's splendid, lasses! Just splendid,'

said Tweedy at last. Polly had lost count of the laps. She could barely lift her feet off the ground to run the last twenty yards.

The entire team either sank down with their heads buried between their knees or rolled over on their backs, not caring about the freezing ground.

Polly was grateful for the feel of cold grass against her aching neck and shoulders and down the back of her stinging thighs.

'You need to be fit,' said Tweedy, walking amongst them as Polly felt her breath settling and her burning cheeks beginning to cool at last. 'Fitter than you have ever been before. Fitter than any team you'll ever meet. That's how we'll win matches, mark my words. Now on your feet again, please . . .'

A general groan went up from the team.

'Do we get to kick some footballs now?' asked Polly hopefully.

'All in good time, Miss Nabb,' said Tweedy, pointing to a row of long, shiny spears sticking out of the ground. 'These are javelins!' he explained. 'The perfect tool for combining fitness and aim. If you can run up a pitch and hit a marked spot with one of these, then you can kick a football into goal no problem.'

It turned out, for Polly, throwing a pointed metal

spear through the air was far, far harder than whacking a football into the back of a net.

By the time they climbed back on to the charabanc, they'd been training for half the day and she'd never got so much as a peep at a ball.

'Don't look so glum,' said Clara, sliding on to the seat beside her. 'A nice hot shower will sort you out!'

Polly had no idea what her friend was talking about, but when they got back to the munitions factory, all the girls made their way to the smart changing rooms, so different from the old, rat-infested lavatories there'd been at Lowcross. Polly stared in wonder at the gushing streams of steaming water splashing down from a row of showerheads in the ceiling. She had never seen anything like it in her life.

Polly stayed under the warm torrents longer than anyone, letting the water run over her hair and shoulders, all down her face too, catching it in her mouth and spurting it up in the air like a whale.

'Brilliant!' she said when she came out at long last, pink as a slice of ham. She wrapped herself in a soft white factory towel and poked her head round the door of the changing room where the rest of the girls were getting dressed.

'I'll never have a bath again now I know those things exist!' she announced in amazement.

The team collapsed in laughter. Polly joined in, though she hadn't meant to be funny.

Clara was right. The miracle of a shower really did make everything better.

CHAPTER THIRTY-SIX

At training on Wednesday, Tweedy had the charabanc stop just outside the Steepside ground. It was pouring with rain. Instead of going on to the pitch, he sent the girls over the moors on a cross-country run. Polly's limbs were already stiff and aching from the day before and when she returned, third from last, wet through, caked with mud and tired as a dog, she was grateful again to stand under the flowing hot water of the shower.

But she was desperate to kick a ball and show Tweedy what she could really do.

At last, on Thursday, she got her chance. 'We're going to do some actual football today. I know that will please you, Miss Nabb,' he said as she climbed down from the charabanc. 'Make sure you play generously for your side.'

'Right!' said Polly. She could do that. Topping up the scoresheet was the best way to be generous to any team and it was high time Tweedy saw her put something in the net.

As they gathered on the pitch, Tweedy divided the squad of fourteen girls into two teams of seven, handing out red and green sashes. He tapped two girls on the shoulder and told them they would act as the goalkeepers.

'Other than that, I don't want you to discuss your positions at all,' he said. 'Start in the middle of the field and see where you can best place yourselves to assist each other as play unfolds.' He stepped back to the sidelines. 'Build your skills as a squad,' he encouraged them.

Polly was Red. She found herself on the same side as Clara, Mercy and Joyce.

It was quickly obvious that all three were strong, attacking players. Polly was well aware of Joyce's skill. Mercy was fast and determined – a similar player to Polly herself. Clara was swift and agile, darting round the pitch with the same graceful power she'd shown dancing in her parlour at home.

With Tweedy watching every move, Polly knew she was going to have to work hard to prove herself.

She couldn't understand why he had put all his best forwards in the Red team, leaving the Greens strong on defence but without any real chance of scoring goals. One thing was clear though, if she was going to stand out, it wasn't the Greens Polly needed to prove herself against, it was the other Reds.

Joyce scored in the very first minute, off a neat little pass from Clara, and Polly felt a stab of jealousy.

The Greens got the ball down their end and Polly snatched it away. This was her first big chance. She ran the entire length of the pitch, dodging defenders.

'Over here,' shouted Mercy.

'To me!' bellowed Joyce.

Polly ignored calls from her teammates to pass.

'Yes!' She slammed the ball into the back of the net.

'Nice shot!' said Mercy a little grudgingly.

Joyce rolled her eyes.

Clara's right, thought Polly. *The captain's jealous because I'm going to score more goals than her.*

The Greens were on Polly after that, defending like a pack of wolves, but she still managed to grab the ball for herself and, with impressive lone runs, she scored twice more. Only Clara congratulated her, but Polly barely noticed. On her last shot, she pushed past Joyce so fast that her fellow striker fell to the ground.

'Sorry,' she mumbled. But at least it meant a hat-trick.

Joyce wouldn't last five minutes in a rough kick-about at Duke's, Polly thought as Tweedy blew the whistle for half-time.

'Hey, Nabb, you might try passing once in a while,' hollered Joyce as she picked herself up from the mud.

Polly pretended not to hear. If Joyce couldn't get a touch of the ball, that was her problem. Polly was scoring goals for the Red team and it was the final result that counted.

'Well done, Greens. Great play,' said Tweedy. Polly was incredulous. *Greens?* Had he got the teams muddled up? The Reds were winning four-one, and three of those goals were thanks to Polly. How could he compliment the Greens on a performance like that?

'Now!' he said, holding up his hand before the teams could divide and talk tactics. 'I am going to reduce the players from seven-a-side to six. Without discussing it, I want each of you to come up in turn, write a name on one of these slips of paper I have prepared and put it in my hat. The girl who receives the most nominations from her team will not play in the second half.'

A gasp went up from the squad.

'I can't do that,' cried Clara standing close to Polly. 'It seems so mean.'

Polly agreed. She wasn't worried for herself, of course – she had scored so many of the Red team's goals – but it did seem harsh to deny someone else the chance to practise playing for the rest of the match.

'No talking amongst yourselves,' reminded Tweedy. 'Just write down the name of the girl who you feel has not used this practice to develop a sense of sportsmanship amongst the squad.'

'Sports*woman*ship!' corrected Joyce and everyone gave a little cheer.

'Indeed.' Tweedy nodded seriously. 'Miss Shaw makes a good point. Folk are fond of telling you lasses how football is a man's game. How you have no business playing it. We're here to prove them wrong. That's why sportsma… sports*woman*ship,' he corrected himself, 'is so important.'

Polly listened. *But scoring goals is still what matters,* she thought.

Tweedy beckoned the Greens forward first. One by one, they each wrote down the name of the player they thought least deserved to stay on their side for the rest of practice.

Tweedy lifted the seven slips out of the hat and examined them.

'This is a close one,' he said. 'But, by a whisker, Phyllis Magnall will sit out the second half.'

311

'Fair enough. I wasn't at my best today.' A small, sandy-haired girl gave a deep sigh and walked over to the sidelines, limping a little.

'Probably wise to rest up with that knee injury still healing, Miss Magnall,' said Tweedy, and the Green team nodded vigorously. 'Now for the Reds . . .'

'This is horrible. I just want to get my vote over and done with,' cried Clara, springing to the front of the line. 'I don't want to pick anyone to sit out . . .'

'You do know you can't nominate yourself, don't you?' warned Tweedy with a gentle smile.

'How did you guess?' Clara crumpled.

'Call it manager's intuition,' said Tweedy with a chuckle.

'In that case, I need more time to decide.' Clara darted to the back of the queue.

That left Polly to go next. She had thought, with a brief unkind flash, of nominating Joyce. But she knew that wasn't fair. The captain was playing well and deserved the chance to carry on. Instead, Polly wrote down Dorothy Farnworth, the defender who had slipped up and given the Greens their only goal.

Then she stood back and waited, watching poor Clara wriggle with indecision.

'Right,' said Tweedy at last, sorting through the

seven slips in his hat. 'This one is much more decisive. Almost unanimously, the Red team have decided that the player who should sit out is Polly Nabb.'

For a moment, Polly thought she must have heard wrongly.

'Me?' she said. 'But I scored a hat-trick!' She scowled at her teammates. Most seemed unable to meet her gaze. Even Clara had her head bent and was intent on fiddling with a stray curl. Only Joyce glared right back at Polly, her eyes steely and unforgiving.

They're all jealous, thought Polly. *Every one of them. They've got rid of me because I'm the best player and they want to show off themselves.* She wished with a twist of fury that she had voted for Joyce after all.

'I'm not going to go,' she said, refusing to shift. 'I've got so much more I can show ...' She hadn't even had a chance at a header yet. Or scoring from a corner – that was one of her favourite tricks. 'I'm a good player. Really good ...' She looked imploringly at Tweedy. Surely he would see that her teammates' decision had been driven by spite. It was envy, pure and simple.

Tweedy cleared his throat. 'I'm sure you are a good player, Miss Nabb. You could possibly even be a great one,' he said. 'Nevertheless, we are here to build a whole team of great players, not just a single star.' He pointed to the sidelines where Phyllis Magnall was sitting on a bench with a rolled-up sweater under her swollen knee. 'I'm afraid your teammates have spoken …'

'Fine!' Polly stomped away across the pitch, flinging herself down on the bench.

At least Phyllis has the excuse of injury, she thought furiously as Clara sent a lovely cross to Joyce, setting her up for a perfect goal. Five minutes later, Mercy smashed in a header off a corner from Dorothy Farnworth, the player Polly voted to have sent off.

Polly sprang to her feet. She couldn't watch any more.

'Tell Tweedy I've gone for a run,' she barked at Phyllis. She didn't give a stuff if she got into trouble for leaving the training session. He was the one who'd said fitness was important and Polly was just wasting her time sitting around here. 'See you back at the factory!'

'But that's miles,' said Phyllis.

'I don't care!' Polly sprinted out of the ground and began to pound away along the hilly road back to town.

Behind her, she heard a cheer go up and Joyce's name being shouted. She must have scored again. Polly ran faster, her chest already thumping with pain – what sort of squad made a player like her sit on the bench? She'd scored more goals than anyone else.

She wished she had never come to Kerston and joined the stuck-up, know-it-all Sparks.

CHAPTER THIRTY-SEVEN

That night at tea, Polly was glad for Mr Venne droning on about tanks and guns; it meant she didn't have to talk to Clara about what had happened at practice. Tweedy said the vote against Polly was almost unanimous. Did that mean Clara had voted for her to be sent to the bench too, just like all the others in the team? Clara didn't seem to want to talk about it either and they had walked home from the factory in near silence, Clara scuffing her feet and not skipping for once.

'Aren't you hungry, pet?' asked Mrs Venne as Polly pushed the food around her plate. The beef dripping, with fluffy golden Yorkshire pudding, tasted like wet cotton in her mouth.

Polly shook her head. 'Not very.'

Her whole body ached from the long run, her feet

were covered in blisters and, although her tummy was empty, she felt sick.

'Well, there's a turn-up for the books,' said Mr Venne, slapping the table. 'The way you dug in this week, I was worried you were going to eat us out of house and home.' He roared with laughter at his own joke.

'Dad!' said Clara. 'That's not funny.'

'Leave the poor girl alone, dear,' warned Mrs Venne, shooting her husband an unusually stern look. 'Can't you see poor Polly's upset about something?'

Mrs Venne was right. Polly was upset. The fury she had felt running away from Steepside had unravelled inside her like a ball of string. Now it wasn't just anger she felt, it was something else too, all knotted up.

She had played well, but her team had thrown her out. Why? Had she done something wrong?

'Spit it out,' said Mr Venne. 'What's bothering you, lass?' He sat back in his chair, making a little steeple with his hands, as if he was sure to have the solution to whatever the problem might be.

'Just a bit of bother at practice,' said Polly. She was too tired and upset not to answer him truthfully. 'I didn't make the squad for the second half of the game.'

'There you are, then.' Mr Venne nodded, as if the answer was as plain as the nose on his face. 'You're obviously wasting your time with this silly football nonsense. You'd do well to let it drop and take up another hobby.'

'I—' Polly tried to interrupt, but Mr Venne went on.

'Encourage my Clara to quit along with you. Mrs Venne here enjoys knitting. The pair of you could help with that. Our lads at the Front can never have too many pairs of socks. Queen Mary herself is encouraging girls to knit. I believe you get a special badge if you work hard enough.'

'I don't think the queen would give me a badge,' said Polly in disbelief. 'And no solider would thank me for a pair of socks I'd knitted him either. There'd be so many holes the poor beggar's toes would drop off with frostbite.'

'Oh, Polly!' Clara snorted, smiling so widely the gap in her front teeth showed. It was the first time Polly had seen her smile all afternoon.

'Polly can't give up football, Dad,' she said in a serious voice. 'She's a wonderful player. Tweedy says she reminds him of young Ned Shorrock and she's going to be the golden light of our team.'

'That Tweedale wants his head seeing to,' snapped Mr Venne. 'No girl can play like Ned Shorrock. He's a legend, that boy.' Polly barely heard a word Mr Venne was saying even though he was close to shouting and thumping the table with his fist for emphasis. 'He had feet of fire, that lad.'

'Did Tweedy really say that about me?' she whispered.

Clara nodded.

'It's a disgrace to his memory!' thundered Mr Venne. 'Nearly all those boys he used to play with are lying dead in the fields of Flanders. Ned Shorrock amongst them.'

Polly winced. She hadn't known the legendary striker had been killed in the war. Joe would be sad to hear it too. She wondered, with a quick stab of pain, if her brother knew already, wherever he was – missing – out there on the battlefield himself.

'There! That shocked you, didn't it?' gloated Mr Venne. 'Well, young lady, perhaps you ought to think twice before you step into a dead man's boots.'

'I'm not stepping into anyone's boots. Dead or alive,' Polly snapped. Why did men always think women were trying to take the game away from them? Surely there was plenty of room for everyone to join in. 'I've got my own boots, Mr Venne,' she said as he glared at her down the table. 'I just want to play football in them.'

Mr Venne reeled as if she'd blown a big fat raspberry in his face. He clearly wasn't used to being answered back.

'I'm going to smoke my pipe,' he said, and stormed out of the room.

There was an awkward silence as the three women glanced at each other, then they washed and dried the dishes with barely a word.

'That Tweedale wants his head seeing to. Ned Shorrock compared to a lass!' they heard Mr Venne protesting to himself in the darkness.

'Oh dear. You've got him proper vexed,' whispered Mrs Venne. 'Best you two keep out the way.'

Mr Venne was still muttering in protest as Clara and Polly tiptoed up the stairs.

'Can I come in?' asked Clara as they reached the landing.

Polly shook her head. 'I'm dog-tired …' she said with a flash of guilt as she saw the hurt in Clara's eyes. 'Sorry about upsetting your dad.' She stepped into her bedroom and closed the door behind her. Polly couldn't face Clara's bright chatter tonight. She'd want to plait her hair or tickle her arm. Polly felt too hurt and betrayed for any of that. Everything was all mixed up.

Her team had banished her to the bench. Clara amongst them, probably.

But Polly had scored three goals.

It didn't make any sense.

Tweedy had compared her to a young Ned Shorrock. He'd called her a golden light of the team. Yet he hadn't complimented her on a single moment of play since she'd joined the Sparks. He'd barely said a word to her at all.

Polly fell on to her bed and kicked her feet against the mattress.

She wished Daph was here.

Daph understood things.

Daph would help untangle the knots.

But Polly was alone.

Chapter Thirty-Eight

On Saturday the charabanc took the team over the moors to a town called Oldport on the coast.

The Sparks were going to play against Oldport Rovers Munitionettes. The Rovers were pretty good they'd heard, winning four of the five matches they'd played since the team was set up.

This will be my chance to prove myself, thought Polly. There were only eleven of them on the bus. Phyllis Magnall still had trouble with her knee injury and had stayed home, while a couple of others had a spot of winter flu, so Polly knew she'd get a game.

She sat next to Clara at the back of the bus as usual, but things still seemed a little strained between them. As the charabanc rolled up and down the winding roads, Clara didn't chatter away like she normally did. Polly wanted to reach out and squeeze her hand but she didn't dare.

After a while Clara nodded off and her head rested on Polly's shoulder. Polly liked that. Even though Clara's hair tickled her nostrils, she didn't move a muscle. She sat still for miles, her tummy fizzing with nerves and excitement when she thought about playing her first proper game for the Sparks. As the bus came down from the top of the moors at last, Polly suddenly leaped to her feet and cried out in delight.

'Look!'

'What?' gasped Clara, eyes wide as she was jolted awake.

'The sea!' cried Polly. 'Look.'

A strip of silver-speckled water glistened between the hills.

'Oh!' Clara laughed. 'Is that all. I thought the bus had caught fire.'

'Have you never seen the sea before?' asked Mercy turning round in her seat.

'No.' Polly stood on tiptoe trying to get another glimpse of the sparkling water as the bus went down into a dip. 'Have you?'

'Of course.' Mercy laughed. 'I'm from the Caribbean. I spent every day of my life in the sea, until my dad came over here to fight in the British Army and I came with him.'

'Blimey!' said Polly. 'You must miss it.' She felt like she'd come a long way from Lowcross, but she remembered Miss Divilly pointing her cane at the pink-painted Caribbean islands on the school map. They were oceans away.

'I do miss it,' said Mercy, 'and if you're excited about that cold grey puddle' – she pointed to where the sea had come back into view beneath them – 'then you should see the water in the bay where I live. It's as blue as sapphires or ...' Mercy waved her hands in the air as if trying to think of something else bright blue, something they might actually have had a chance of seeing, as it was obvious none of them had ever caught so much as a glimpse of a sapphire.

'Clara's eyes?' said Polly, trying to be helpful, but she instantly felt like a fool. Girls weren't supposed to notice what colour each other's eyes were ... or certainly not compare them to jewels. Polly knew she wasn't meant to feel about Clara's beautiful eyes the way she did, that just looking in them made her happy.

Clara blushed like a tomato as Mercy leaned over and peered into her face.

'Yes, Polly!' she agreed excitedly. 'Clara's eyes are exactly the right colour: Caribbean seawater blue.'

'Don't be daft!' cried Clara, but she was grinning as Mercy turned round to face the front again.

'I like what you said about my eyes,' she whispered, squeezing Polly's arm. 'Fancy them being Caribbean seawater blue.'

'All right. No need to go on about it!' said Polly with a snort, but she smiled, feeling warm inside. They really were the most beautiful eyes she'd ever seen, and she was pleased she had made Clara so happy.

The ground where the Oldport Rovers played was high on the cliffs above the sea. Polly could smell the salt in the air as the charabanc juddered to a halt outside the white clapboard clubhouse.

'We're early,' said Tweedy, glancing around at the few spectators who were starting to arrive. 'That's good. Go and get yourselves changed and I'll see you out on the pitch.' He doffed his hat politely as usual and his grey hair was buffeted about by the sea breeze.

'I've got big plans for you today, Miss Nabb. The squad will be able to make grand use of your skills,' he said with a smile as Polly passed him.

'Thank you!' said Polly, excitement leaping in her chest. Clearly all that stuff about being a team player and sending her to the bench had been for training only. Tweedy had been impressed by her hat-trick after all. Now he was going to reward her.

In the changing room, Polly's shoulders were tight with nerves. It had not been easy joining the Sparks, things had not gone to plan that week, and she still felt like an outsider amongst the team. A tiny part of her still wished she'd stayed in Lowcross. The Ruffians might not be as ambitious as the Sparks, but they were her friends. The girls respected her. She was the one who got to make the decisions for the team. Here, she was like a marble rolling down a slide; she had no control over anything.

Yet, since that first moment Polly had seen the Sparks play on Christmas Day, she'd known they were something special. With this team she would get to play the very best games she could. Now, at last, Tweedy was going to make use of her skills.

As she pulled on the black-and-white jersey for the first time, Polly felt a shiver of excitement so strong it made her shudder.

'Exciting isn't it?' Clara winked. 'Don't worry, you'll be great out there, Polly.'

'Just don't be selfish. Pass the ball once in a while, Nabb. We're on the same team now, remember,' said Joyce, striding by.

'Yes, captain!' Polly seethed inside.

I'll show her, she thought. *We'll see who the team really respects when I put away double the number of goals Joyce ever could!*

She stamped her feet into the new boots she had been given the day before. They were the real thing – made by a company in Northampton – like the professionals wore! She clattered over the tiled floor towards the pitch and, in spite of feeling wound up by Joyce, Polly smiled. When no one was looking, she doubled back and circled the locker-room bench one more time just to hear the clack of studs on the floor.

Mr Venne had accused her of stepping into a dead man's boots. Well, she wasn't doing that now. These were her very own, brand-new boots – the first new shoes Polly had ever owned in her whole life. She ran out on to the grass feeling the studs sink softly into the turf.

'Blooming brilliant!' she grinned. There'd be no more slipping and sliding about or getting bogged down like she had in her old work boots.

She thundered across the pitch to where Tweedy had gathered the team around him.

'Listen up, please, ladies,' he said. 'I'm going to sort out who is playing where today. The team's changing a bit and growing, so don't be surprised if you find yourselves somewhere a little different from usual ... I'm just trying things out.'

Polly waited, her heart pounding in her chest.

Of course there were going to be changes, and to her advantage too. Surely that's what Tweedy had been hinting at when she got off the bus. Maybe she'd be centre forward, which was normally Joyce's role.

Polly was surprised then as the forward roles were all handed out: Joyce, with Clara on the left wing and Mercy on the right.

She wondered if Tweedy had forgotten all about her. How could that be possible ... he'd said he had 'big plans' for her only moments ago.

The pounding in Polly's heart shifted from excitement to worry. The midfield positions were given out too.

'What about me?' she cried.

Tweedy held up his hand. 'All in good time.'

'But—'

'Shh! Pipe down!' Joyce silenced her.

'Don't worry.' Clara smiled encouragingly.

Polly couldn't stand still. She began to pace up and down. There were only defence positions left, or goalie. Surely Tweedy wasn't going to put her in goal? Jessie

Jump – which really was her name, though the team just called her 'Jumper' for the way she leaped after the ball – still hadn't been picked and she was always the Sparks goalie.

Polly's palms were sweating. She respected people who could play in goal. She knew from Joe how tricky the position was. How crucial. But it wasn't for her. She needed to be out on the pitch scoring goals, not saving them. She was a proper butterfingers, as useless with her mitts as she was good with her feet.

Panic swirled inside her.

'Miss Jump, you'll be our usual safe pair of hands in goal,' said Tweedy.

Jumper beamed. 'Right you are, guv. For a minute there I thought you'd get me kicking something!' She pretended to faint with relief.

Polly couldn't laugh along with the others. She could barely even force a smile. She was desperately running through all the positions to see what had not yet been filled. Had she missed something? Left winger! Her heart leaped with hope … No. She remembered that was Clara.

She began to count heads again. Perhaps she'd been wrong, perhaps there had been more than eleven girls on the bus, after all. Was she just a reserve, here to sit and watch from the bench like she'd done in practice? Why wasn't Tweedy making use of her? Why had he told Polly he had big plans . . .?

'Miss Nabb,' he said, turning to her at last. 'Don't look so worried. I promised you your skills were going to be vital to us today. You'll be our left back.'

'Left back?' said Polly. 'But that's defence. What am I supposed to do there?'

'Defend,' said Tweedy calmly. 'The Rovers are a strong attacking team, by all accounts. Work with your fellow defenders and Miss Jump to protect our goal.'

'But that's the wrong end of the pitch for me!' Polly paced up and down with her hands on her head. Had Tweedy lost his mind? 'If the Rovers are an attacking team, then we need to match their score,' she cried. 'I need to be up at the other end, putting away goals. For us.'

'Perhaps another time,' said Tweedy. 'But today we are short on defenders, as Miss Magnall is still out with her knee.'

'That's madness!' Polly raged. Tweedy remained calm, even though, through the haze of her anger, Polly was aware she was shouting at him like little Bob or Tommy in a tantrum at home.

'For today, Miss Nabb,' he added, more firmly, 'I

don't want to see you anywhere near the Rovers' goal unless you're being pursued by a bloodthirsty lion.'

Some of the other girls laughed.

'Fine,' said Polly. 'I'll defend for you. I'll defend like I *am* the blinking lion.'

'I know you will, Miss Nabb,' said Tweedy, his kind eyes sparkling. 'I know.'

CHAPTER THIRTY-NINE

The match was tough and Polly did have to battle hard to defend against the Rovers. But as they pushed tirelessly forward, she pushed back harder, alongside the other defenders, to keep them at bay.

It looked as if it might all finish in a nil-nil draw. Then, minutes before the end, Joyce scored – a beautiful, sly little chip. Without thinking, Polly threw her arms in the air and cheered. Her heart soared. She realised, for the first time, she was thrilled to see a goal she hadn't scored herself. A moment later the final whistle blew.

'One-nil!' chanted the Sparks as Polly ran down the pitch to join the celebrations.

'Great shot, Joyce,' she called. She had to admit it had been a real beauty.

She was surprised though to see Joyce running towards her.

'Nabb! You were brilliant!' the captain cried, flinging her arm round Polly's shoulder. 'It could easily have been three-nil to the Rovers without your defending.'

'Thanks!' Polly flung her arm round Joyce's shoulder too as the pair of them strolled back up the pitch, discussing the details of the match.

'Shame that early cross from Mercy hit the bar . . .'

Polly felt warm inside, as if she'd eaten a bowl of hot, sweet porridge.

This is what it's all about, she thought as they reached the others and the Sparks flung their arms round each other whooping and jumping. There had only been one goal and it didn't matter who had scored it. They had won.

'Fish and chips for everyone!' announced Tweedy as they clambered back on to the bus. That caused a whole new round of cheering.

'Grand!' cried Polly, her appetite fully restored. 'I've never eaten fish and chips.'

'Never?' said Clara in amazement.

'I've had chips,' said Polly. 'And fish. Just not at the same time.'

'Never by the seaside either,' said Mercy. 'Just you wait. It's one of the things that makes this cold wet country worth the bother.'

'We'll need thirteen portions if you count me and the bus driver,' said Tweedy as the charabanc juddered to a halt by the pier. While the girls were all covered in mud, the dapper grey-haired gent still looked smart and crisp in his tweed jacket with spotless pocket handkerchief. 'Come along, Miss Nabb.' He beckoned to her. 'You've proved you're not afraid of a bit of hard work. You can help me carry.'

Polly followed Tweedy down the promenade. It was dark now and lights were twinkling on the water all along the beach.

While Tweedy went into the chip shop, she stood leaning on the rail outside, turning her face to the salty breeze blowing off the sea and listening to the waves rolling on to the shore.

'It's going to take them a while to fry that lot up,' said Tweedy, coming to stand beside her. 'You did well today, Miss Nabb.'

'Thanks,' she said, still feeling proud, but she knew she had to take her chance to speak to Tweedy. 'Thing is, I don't really want to—'

'Play in defence forever?' he said, finishing her sentence.

'Exactly!' Polly agreed.

'You think my brains have curdled, don't you?'

Tweedy lifted his hat a little as if to show her. 'Why would a manager invite a gifted striker to join his team and then stick the poor lass in defence? It doesn't make any sense, does it?'

'No,' said Polly, shaking her head.

'So do you think I'm mad?' Tweedy looked her straight in the eye.

'No,' said Polly truthfully.

'Well ...' Tweedy scratched his chin as if he was as confused as she was, 'if I'm not mad and you're a great striker, why did I put you in defence?' he asked.

'Was it because I didn't score the day the Ruffians played against the Sparks?' asked Polly. Was that where it had all gone wrong? Tweedy was yet to see her score a goal in any match.

'No.' Tweedy chuckled. 'I could see your potential, clear as I can see that seagull waiting for our chips.' He pointed to a fat grey bird perched on the rail a little way off.

'Then I don't understand,' said Polly.

Before Tweedy could answer her, the man from the chip shop came out, his arms laden with parcels of greasy newspaper.

'I've put salt and vinegar on all of them,' he said gruffly, and Polly's tummy rumbled at the hot, sharp smell.

Tweedy thanked the man, then gave Polly a few of the parcels to hold. 'That's a great help,' he said.

'You're welcome.' Polly sighed. That was it! The conversation with the manager was over and she was more confused than ever.

But Tweedy didn't walk back to the charabanc.

'Watch this!' he said, unwrapping one of the parcels and taking a chip. He tossed it in the air and the gull screeched and dived, catching the chip in its beak before it even hit the ground.

'She reminds me of you,' said Tweedy.

'Thanks a lot!' snorted Polly. First she was a blooming lion, now she was a seagull.

'She's hungry . . .' said Tweedy, and Polly's tummy rumbled as if to agree. 'And tough. She's a fighter, scrapping for what she can get.' He tossed another chip in the air and this time a whole flock of gulls appeared, screeching for the morsel of food. 'I am guessing that's what your football games have been like up until now?'

'Yes,' said Polly, beginning to see his point. Tweedy was right – she'd grown up fighting with the lads outside Duke's, desperate to get a shot at the ball, desperate to be allowed to join in at all.

'Well, you're part of a team now,' said Tweedy. 'A

great team, I hope. You're not just fighting for yourself any more. You proved that today.'

Polly nodded. 'I think I understand,' she said slowly. 'You're saying I can't just fly wildly after every goal ... I need to work with the other players. We're all on the same side now.'

The gulls were still screeching, tumbling over each other in a mess of feathers.

'Precisely!' Tweedy doffed his hat in delight, then strode off towards the charabanc. 'Come on,' he called over his shoulder. 'Let's feed those hungry pals of yours.'

Polly followed him back along the windy promenade, smiling to herself.

She was smiling even more by the time she'd gobbled up her newspaper parcel full of tangy salted chips and crispy battered fish.

'Delicious!' she declared, licking her fingers.

'Told you.' Mercy smiled.

'I saw you talking to Tweedy on the prom,' said Clara as the charabanc left the seaside town behind and began to climb the steep road back to the moors. 'What did he say?'

'He said I was like a greedy seagull,' said Polly. 'At least, I used to be, but I don't have to be any more.'

'A gull?' Clara looked horrified. 'What did he mean by that?'

'I think,' said Polly, crossing her fingers as she spoke, 'that if I stop being so much of a seagull, I might get to be a striker for the team.'

CHAPTER FORTY

Sure enough, at practice the following week, Tweedy confirmed a new line-up.

'Miss Magnall's knee has recovered so she can return to defence,' he said. Then he made the announcement Polly had been waiting for. 'After Miss Nabb's gallant team spirit and "sportswomanship" in our match against the Rovers, I'm placing her in an attacking position out on the left wing.'

Polly let out a whoop of joy. It wasn't centre forward as she had expected, but left wing might be just as good and the perfect position to score goals.

'As a fearless, left-footed player, it will suit you down to the ground,' Tweedy explained, smiling at her.

'Meanwhile,' he continued, 'I'll move Miss Venne to midfield where her quick speedy footwork will pay off.'

Clara looked pleased.

'That leaves you, me and Mercy, pushing hard at the

front together,' said Joyce, slapping Polly on the back. 'We'll be unstoppable!'

'You bet,' whispered Polly as Tweedy ran through the positions for the rest of the squad. Jumper was in goal, of course.

'This is the line-up I want to take forward from now on,' Tweedy explained. 'Learn to love playing together and to love the position you play.'

The more she thought about it, the more excited Polly was. Playing on the left wing really would suit her, making the most of her strong dribbling skills.

Tweedy held up his hand. 'One more announcement . . . We've got a big match coming up. I'm taking you London.'

Everybody cheered.

Polly gasped.

'London!' cried Clara. 'Can we go to the ballet?'

This set off a howl of giggles.

'No, we blooming can't!' For once even Tweedy's sense of composure slipped. 'But the FA are allowing us to play at Stamford Bridge, home of the famous Chelsea Football Club.'

'Who are we playing?' asked Joyce.

'I hope it's the Chelsea men's team,' said Polly, only half joking. At that moment she was so excited, she believed the Sparks could have beaten anyone.

'It's a group of women calling themselves the London Ladies,' said Tweedy. 'They've got fancy notepaper thick enough to eat your dinner off and their captain signed herself Dr Lavinia Dickson, so we best mind our Ps and Qs.'

'Just because they're posh doesn't mean they can play any better than us!' said Joyce firmly.

'Let's hope they trip over their big, fancy bloomers and fall flat on their faces,' snorted Polly.

That made everybody collapse in a fresh round of raucous laughter and Polly noticed Tweedy had gone a little pink around the ears. 'Rather than hoping the opposition trip over their underwear, we might do better to rely on training,' he said firmly.

Sure enough, the next few weeks were a blur of freezing-cold runs over the tops of the moors, javelin throwing and even gymnastics out on the field.

By the time spring began to appear, Polly could run laps of the pitch barely stopping to catch her breath and could throw the javelin almost fifty yards. She didn't even ache in the mornings when it was time to get up, either for training or the long boring days sorting nails and screws at the munitions factory.

'You've got proper colour in your cheeks,' remarked Mrs Venne.

'It's thanks to your cooking,' said Polly, and that was true too. For the first time in her life she was getting three proper meals a day. She had almost forgotten the dull ache of hunger that used to lie in her gut for weeks on end. The other ache, deep in her belly, had not gone though – the ache for Joe, the worry and the longing for him to come home safe and well.

She got in the habit of checking through the long, terrible lists of dead soldiers printed in Mr Venne's paper each evening.

As long as Joe's name wasn't there, she still stubbornly carried hope. Just as she had believed baby Queenie would grow strong and well, she believed in Joe too. As long as she never gave up hope, he would be found.

'You needn't bother scouring the paper,' said Mr Venne brutally when he caught Polly looking one night. 'That brother of yours won't turn up after all this time. Missing lads never do.'

Perhaps he thought he was being honest, or perhaps deliberately cruel. Polly didn't know and she didn't care. She walked away. She didn't need to listen to cold hard men like Mr Venne.

She froze on the stairs next morning, though, when she saw a letter in Mam's handwriting lying on the mat.

Was it news? Had they found Joe? She leaped into life and ripped the envelope open.

It was just a short note saying how useful the extra 'football' money from Polly was. The army had long ago stopped sending Joe's pay – just four weeks after he first went missing. It suited their purses to believe that he was dead and had no further need of cash.

What about his family? We've still got mouths to feed and no lad to bring home wages, raged Mam in her furious, thick handwriting.

Polly screwed up the note and threw it in the neat little wastepaper basket Mrs Venne kept in the hallway. She was pleased the extra money helped Mam, but she wasn't going to pay attention to what the army thought, any more than she'd listen to Mr Venne.

She had football to think about.

At last, on a sunny morning in late March, the Sparks climbed aboard the train for London.

As Polly leaned out of the window to watch the station disappear through the steam, her heart gave a tug of sadness as she remembered how she had seen Joe lean out of a window just like this. Remembering that day made her think of Daph too.

Polly missed her dreadfully. She'd made Clara roll

her eyes with the many, endless stories she'd told about her old friend and how she roared around the roads of Lowcross on the mighty Green Dragon. But Daph still hadn't visited Kerston. Polly began to wonder if there was a reason ...

Perhaps she's given up on Joe, she thought. *Perhaps she's stepping out with a different fellow and she doesn't want me to know.* It would break Polly's heart if that was true.

Before she could dwell on it, Clara grabbed her hand and pulled her into the carriage with the rest of the team.

The girls shouted over one another, discussing tactics for the game all the way to London. When the train finally arrived at the station, they had to make their way straight to the Stamford Bridge ground, passing lines of bloody, battered soldiers returning from the Front.

Outside on the street, other men, who'd returned much longer ago, were begging for pennies from passersby. One man, wheeling himself along on a homemade cart, grabbed at Polly's sleeve, but she had no money with her.

'I'm sorry,' she said as they fought their way on through the jostling crowds. At least they were playing for charity today as they always did. The takings from the match might help men like him – forgotten soldiers who badly needed medical care, which the army and government were no longer paying for. Like Joe, they had bravely done their bit but were now missing from the thoughts of those they had served. Polly looked over her shoulder and saw the man wheeling himself away through the crowds.

At last they found the right bus. Polly sat with her mouth open on the top deck, staring down on the hectic, jostling streets. She had never seen so many people, vehicles and buildings all crammed together. Kerston had seemed busy after Lowcross, but London was like a buzzing wasps' nest.

She thought she caught a glimpse of the Houses of Parliament, but there was no time for sightseeing. As soon as they arrived at the ground, they were bustled into the changing rooms and out on to the pitch just in time for the match to start.

Both teams lined up for the photographers as usual, along with Marie Lloyd – the famous music-hall star was going to have the first kick of the ball as a novelty for the crowd. She had signed the ball too and it was going to be auctioned for war charities after the game. Polly thought again of the solider on the cart and hoped all this would somehow help.

'I might bid for the ball myself if it goes for less than twenty pounds,' Polly overheard the captain of the London Ladies say. 'It would be a lovely memento of our day.'

'Twenty pounds!' Polly couldn't help blurting out. She had never dreamed someone might have that much money to spend on a football, even if it was for charity.

Dr Lavinia Dickson looked down the end of her nose at Polly and muttered something about 'factory girls'. None of the London women had East End accents like Daph – they all spoke more like Lady G.

Later, as the two teams were taking their places on the pitch, Polly heard another of the well-bred ladies telling her friend that these 'simple Lancashire lasses would be easy to beat!'

'We'll see about that!' said Polly; she felt as if there was fire in her feet, she was so desperate to get playing. She was in her new attacking position and the whole Sparks team was at the peak of fitness – even Phyllis's knee was holding up. If the London Ladies thought this was going to be a tea party, then they should think again.

As the whistle blew, Marie Lloyd, wearing a big, feathered hat, gingerly kicked the ball with her high-heeled shoe. The actress had barely teetered out of the way before Polly was picking up a pass from Joyce and kicking it on to Mercy, just as they had practised over and over again on their freezing morning sessions at Steepside.

Tweedy was right. Polly really did love playing on the left-hand side of the pitch. She felt more powerful on the field than ever. She loved being right amongst the action as a winger, shooting forward every time she saw an opportunity to score. The first chance came off a clumsy pass between Lavinia Dickson and another of her London Ladies.

Polly intercepted the ball and was away. She could have risked a run at goal but the path wasn't clear and she heard Joyce calling her name.

'Nabby, over here.'

Polly didn't think twice. She passed the ball to her captain, who was right on the edge of the box, and Joyce put away a lovely volley. One-nil to the Sparks! The girls threw their arms round each another, celebrating the goal that Joyce had scored and Polly had set up.

Polly's own chance came a few minutes later, getting her head on a perfect cross from Clara and sending it into the corner of the net.

The large London crowd seemed to warm quickly

to the Sparks despite them being from faraway 'Up North', and their cheers rang out from the stands.

Clara dominated the midfield, darting around the opposition like a twirling ballerina in studded boots.

The only player who seemed not to be having such a good match was Mercy. The London left back was sticking close to her and some of the crowd were shouting horrible, shocking things about the colour of her skin. Twice Polly saw the left back, who had long thin pigtails, deliberately kick Mercy's shins. The referee didn't seem to notice anything even though the crowd was bawling at him, and when they came into the dressing room for half-time, Mercy was hobbling.

She rolled down her socks and showed a ring of bruises all around her legs. 'They're fouling me again and again, and the ref is taking no notice!' She sighed. 'I heard two defenders telling each other they had to watch out for my "sort". I've got a pretty good idea what they meant by that.'

'You're a good player, that's what's bothering them!' said Joyce firmly. 'I never guessed a match against such fancy ladies would get so rough.'

'They're tiring fast,' said Polly. 'We'll run rings around them in the second half.'

'They're not going to like losing to a "bunch of factory girls",' warned Joyce. 'Someone's going to get injured if the ref doesn't sit up.'

'I expect they're used to bashing each other over the head with hockey sticks,' giggled Clara.

Tweedy had a word with the referee before the second half began and both the captains were called over for a pep talk, but the match still remained a sniping, scrappy one. One posh defender pinched Polly hard and another pulled her hair ... it was like being back outside Duke's with the Cogley clan.

She was right about the London Ladies getting tired though, and Mercy now escaped the left back easily to score a neat goal off a pass from Polly. Polly quickly followed this up with a volley of her own.

In the last ten minutes of the game, things got really nasty. Unable to keep up with Mercy, the left back began to hound Phyllis, who was slowing down a little with her bad knee. She slammed right into her with a filthy tackle and pushed her to the ground.

This time, the referee did see and blew his whistle, but not before the defender had kicked Phyllis while she was still lying down.

'You're a right cow, you are!' roared Polly as a free kick was awarded and the game played on.

Phyllis was clearly limping now and Polly saw the left back go in for another aggressive kick of her shins.

'Enough!' Polly charged down the pitch and, before the girl could attack Phyllis again, Polly yanked hard on her pigtail.

'Ouch!' The left back screamed like a banshee. She sank to her knees, clutching her head and wailing. 'Ouch! Ouch!'

For once, the referee was looking the right way and decided justice must be done.

Polly was sent off.

A roaring mix of boos and cheers rose up from the crowd as she stomped furiously across the pitch. As she passed Joyce, the captain patted Polly on the back.

'Don't worry! That girl had it coming,' Joyce said.

Polly agreed. They were winning four-nil anyway and there were only five minutes left of the game – what did it matter if she was sent off?

As she approached the bench, though, she saw Tweedy looking angrier than she had ever seen him. The crinkled smile lines around his eyes had shifted to a dark frown.

'That was not the way to deal with the situation,' Miss Nabb,' he said. 'You've let the team down.'

Polly bit her lip. That was easy for him to say, sitting on the sidelines watching.

Phyllis was limping badly as they made their way back to the station to catch the night train home.

'My poor knee. That brute has done for it,' she growled as they clambered into the carriage.

The exhausted girls huddled against one another, dozing off as the train rattled along the tracks.

Polly was the last to fall asleep. She stared out of the window, Clara snoring lightly on her shoulder, and watched the flickering lights of towns and villages flash by in the darkness.

Tweedy sat nearest the door with his hat pulled down over his face. Polly wasn't sure if he was sleeping but she was glad she didn't have to talk to him. A niggling sense of shame had crept under her skin. Tweedy was right. She was on the pitch to play football, not to scrap and fight.

When they arrived at Kerston station, the morning papers were just being put out.

'Come on, girls. Let's go and see,' cried Clara, grabbing Polly's hand. 'I bet there'll be a write-up on the match!'

'I saw Bill Allred from the *Kerston Star*,' said Joyce.

'He'll have wired something over right away. We beat those swanky London Ladies four-nil, remember. This place will be busting with home-town pride.'

The girls skidded to a halt beside a boy hawking papers from a cart.

'Sparks play soccer in London,' he bellowed.

Tweedy gave the lad some coins and unfurled the paper for them all to see.

There was a headline about the match, but it was not proclaiming a four-nil win as they had hoped.

'SHAME OF LANCASHIRE,' the front page read. 'Polly Nabb, first girl ever to be sent off in a ladies' football match.'

Polly felt her stomach fall away from her as she read the words. Her cheeks flamed and she glanced around, half expecting people in the station to stop and point her out.

'Oh, Polly!' cried Clara in horror.

The other girls looked shocked.

'I still think you did the right thing,' mumbled Phyllis. But she didn't sound very sure.

'Come on!' Tweedy tossed the paper into the bin. 'Folk will be eating their chips off those headlines by tomorrow. What's done is done.'

He smiled briefly at Polly, although she could still

see the disappointment in his face. 'Let's get you home,' he said gently.

Tweedy led the team out of the station. Polly came last of all as Clara linked arms with her.

'I wish he'd shouted at me,' Polly mumbled. That would somehow have been easier than Tweedy's kindness, knowing how much she had let him down.

CHAPTER FORTY-ONE

As spring edged towards summer, the warm bright mornings certainly made practising at Steepside less of a battle.

The Sparks continued to work hard though, and to win matches too. Polly always found herself on the scoresheet, and although she was pretending not to keep a tab, she couldn't help but carry a bubble of pride in her chest at the knowledge that she was the Sparks' highest scorer by far. Her total goals now outnumbered those of Joyce, Mercy and Clara combined. Determined not to bring shame to the Sparks' good name, she promised herself never to lose control and be sent off a football pitch again, no matter how furious she might feel inside.

Mr Venne, however, would not let the incident drop. He seemed to take every opportunity to bring the subject up and shake his head and tut, 'What a disgrace.' Polly had been in the paper many times since, but he never felt the need to mention those.

Unlike her husband, Mrs Venne kept a little scrapbook of everything the team did and there were endless photographs of Polly, covered in mud and smiling, as she held aloft a ball or trophy. 'PROUD OF OUR POL!' the *Kerston Star* had proclaimed just last week when she'd scored a final-minute decider in a tough three-two match against a team of munitionettes from Scotland.

Polly wondered if the *Lowcross Herald* had run a similar piece and if her family had seen it at home. Or maybe Lady G?

And Daph ... Her friend still hadn't come to visit. Polly missed her advice and support and their early morning kick-abouts. She also missed the chaos of Link Street in a funny sort of way. Frank Cogley too. She liked to think of them all reading about her in the paper. Especially Walter – it would get right up his nose!

It was impossible for anyone to ignore the Sparks' growing fame. They had become the highest-scoring and best-known women's football club in the country, just as Tweedy had set out to make them. One tobacco company was even making cigarette cards of the team so that people could collect the famous girl players – Polly hoped it was the brand that Don Sharples smoked.

Above the munitions factory there was a huge billboard which could be seen from just about anywhere in the town: HOME OF THE WORLD-FAMOUS KERSTON ELECTRIC SPARKS! Polly wondered if 'world-famous' was going a bit far, though there were rumours they'd been invited to play in France, and even America, as soon as the war was over.

Yet it wasn't all praise and glory. There were plenty of men like Mr Venne or Don who still thought girls had no business playing football. Groups of lads sometimes came to the matches simply to laugh or ogle or boo. Women showed their disapproval too, coming to the games to shake their heads and sneer, while others wrote letters to the paper saying things like, 'Do these girls have no shame, running around in little more than their knickers' or 'What unnatural lasses they all must be'. Mr Venne took special delight in reading one aloud which had been sent in by the wife of a local dentist, Mrs S. Mckenzie: 'I am aware two hundred pounds was raised for charity ... but fear girls like those playing on the pitch will end up spinsters – sad, unmarried and alone.'

'What a heap of nonsense!' cried Mrs Venne. 'Rip it into squares and we'll use it in the lavvy, dear. It's all that sort of spiteful blether is good for.'

Clara and Polly giggled, delighted at the thought of Mrs S. Mckenzie's letter disappearing down the lavatory bowl.

Mr Venne pushed back his chair furiously. 'I'm going to smoke my pipe,' he said, storming out as usual, the paper under his arm.

'It doesn't worry me. I don't ever want to get married anyway,' Clara whispered, leaning close to Polly's ear as Mr Venne slammed the door. 'But don't tell Dad that!'

Polly was amazed. She'd never met another girl who didn't want to get married. She thought Clara would be the sort to cut out pictures of brides from magazines and newspapers, sticking them in a secret book of plans for her own big day. Phyllis and Jumper had both shown Polly similar books, giggling as they asked her opinion on which veil Polly thought would suit them best or which frock or shoes. Polly had tried at first to say she didn't know – they all looked the same to her – but in the end, when the girls persisted, she picked out things at random to the delight of the would-be brides.

There were bigger protests for the Sparks to worry about than those from dentists' wives or Mr Venne,

357

though. The FA themselves had begun to ask questions about the women's game.

Tweedy received a report written on official FA headed paper. It turned out they had sent along a team of doctors and three officials from the leading men's football clubs to observe the game the previous Saturday. It had been a slow local match against Wardour Munitions, the team Polly had first seen the Sparks play all those months ago. It ended in an easy one-nil win for the Sparks, with Polly scoring from a corner, and no goals at all in the second half. The report painted a very different picture of a frenzied scramble with girls thundering around the pitch like horses and collapsing, near dead from exhaustion, at the end.

'I'm surprised you lot can even stand up this week,' said Tweedy, flicking through the opinions of the doctors and officials. 'Some surgeon fellow from Harley Street says he considers football, "a most unsuitable game for women … the kicking is too jerky a movement for their legs".'

'What do they expect us to do, if we don't kick,' cried Polly furiously. 'Blow kisses at the ball and hope it rolls along like that.'

As usual, she hadn't meant to be funny but the whole team collapsed in laughter. Even Tweedy chuckled.

'Hold on, you'll like this one,' he said. 'It's from Mr Turner, the secretary of Tottenham Hotspur: "Violent exercise such as football cannot be good for women".'

'Violent exercise? He should try doing a week's washing for a family like mine,' said Polly angrier than ever. 'A game of footie's nothing compared to that.'

'Or milking a herd of cows and getting the hay in,' said Jumper, who had grown up on a farm.

'Or building shells for the army,' said Joyce and Mercy at once.

Tweedy sighed. 'There's this from Mr Knighton, the manager at Arsenal, too: "The knocks and buffetings of the game mean that the girls' future duties as mothers could be seriously impaired".'

Joyce peered over Tweedy's shoulder. 'Is he saying playing football will mean we can't have babies?'

'I believe so,' said Tweedy, blushing slightly. 'It's all nonsense . . .'

'Of course it is,' said Jumper. 'I'm going to have seven babies. All girls. That'll show 'em!'

'And I'll have four daughters too,' said a midfielder called Alice. 'Two sets of twins. That way we can have a whole new girls' team of our own.'

Everyone laughed again, but Tweedy shook his head.

'I warn you, the FA are out to get you lasses,' he

said. 'This war has only got months left to run and they're starting to worry. What'll happen when the men come back? What about next season, or the one after that? Will crowds of people still come to watch you girls play?'

'Of course they will,' said Joyce.

Tweedy nodded. 'The FA thought women's football was just a novelty, but now they've seen you lasses can really play. They know the supporters love it too. They're worried you'll take their fans away. That's what this is all about. They're going to try to find a way to stop you girls, you mark my words.'

'They'll have to dig up all the pitches first!' said Joyce.

'I'll bring along a plough and make my own,' said Jumper.

There was a cheer of approval and a smatter of laughter, but Polly could tell the girls were uneasy. Tweedy too. He was humming under his breath and fiddling with his pocket handkerchief.

Trouble was coming and they all knew it.

CHAPTER FORTY-TWO

There was no official women's league as there had been for the men before the war, and no end-of-season cup, but the constant call to raise much-needed money for war charities meant that the Sparks played on through the summer.

Their main concern was with defence. Phyllis's knee was still giving her problems. It had continued to flare up ever since the London Ladies game and she was starting to miss more matches than she was fit to play. Her obvious substitute, a young woman named Kathleen, was expecting a baby – proof, if it was needed, that playing football did not stop women from starting families. As her bump began to grow, however, it was clear that it was time for her to take a break, until after the baby was born at least.

'There's no one as good as either Phyllis or Kathleen to take their place in the squad,' said Joyce glumly one morning as they lay on the heather, catching their breath on a run to the top of the moors.

'Daph!' said Polly suddenly.

'Daph who?' asked Jumper. 'Not old Daph from the canteen? She's about a hundred and two!'

'No!' said Polly, leaping to her feet. 'Daph Jenkins. She played with me in the Ruffians.'

'Short hair? Tiny? Kick like a mule?' asked Jumper. 'I remember her.'

'London lass? She was good,' agreed Joyce.

'Come on!' cried Polly, turning to sprint back down the hill. 'Let's tell Tweedy. He can telephone Lowcross and Daph could be here by tomorrow.' She was surprised she hadn't thought of it sooner. Daph could be playing with the Sparks in time for their match on Saturday.

Tweedy remembered Daph well and agreed to give her a trial immediately.

'She should be here by now,' said Polly, pacing up and down outside the gates of Kerston Electrics at lunch break the following day.

'I'm sure we'll hear her coming if she's riding that big motorbike you go on about all the time,' Clara sighed.

'The Green Dragon!' said Polly. 'You'll love it. Daph's so brave the way she rides.'

Clara rolled her eyes. 'Daph this, Daph that, Daph the other,' she snapped. 'Do you have to go on about how perfect she is *all* the time?'

Polly was surprised. She knew she did tell a lot of stories about Daph, but it wasn't like Clara to be so tetchy. The rest of the Sparks seemed excited to try out Polly's friend.

'There!' she cried, pricking up her ears. 'Can you hear it? Listen.'

The clattering sound of a distant engine grew louder.

But it wasn't Daph's motorbike that came rattling round the corner, just a delivery lorry bringing rolls of copper wire for the factory.

In the end, just as Polly and Clara were about to have to go back to work, another vehicle appeared. That wasn't the Green Dragon, either. It was Lady G's van. Daph was in the passenger seat.

'Pol.' Daph's voice sounded wheezy as she poked her head out of the window. Her face looked thin and her skin was far more waxy and yellow than Polly had remembered it.

Even so, Polly couldn't contain her excitement. 'Hello!' she cried, waving her arms in delight.

'Goof to seal you,' said Daph, strangely slurring her words.

As soon as Lady G had driven through the gates, Daph opened her door and half fell, half stumbled out of the van.

'Lady Gee grove me here,' she said, swaying from side to side.

'She's blotto!' cried Clara. 'Blind drunk!'

'No.' Polly shook her head. That couldn't be true. Daph never touched a drop. Not even a port and lemon at Duke's when boys offered to buy. 'Daph?' She stepped towards her friend.

Daph swayed and blinked.

'I've never seen anything like it,' said Lady G, coming round the back of the van. 'Daphne didn't feel very chipper this morning, so I offered to drive her over rather than let her ride that wretched bike . . .'

'Gween Dragon,' slurred Daph.

'No sooner were we on the road than she started to carry on like this.' Lady G sighed.

Daph steadied herself on the side of the van, trembling from head to toe.

'Hello!' a clamour of voices called from across the courtyard as Joyce and the rest of the team came hurrying out of the canteen to greet the new arrival. Their faces changed suddenly from welcome to shock as they saw the state Daph was in.

'Whatever's the matter with her?' asked Joyce.

'She's drunk,' said Clara.

'Completely sozzled!' agreed Lady G.

'But it's only just past noon.' Jumper giggled.

'You're wrong,' said Polly desperately as Tweedy appeared in the doorway too. 'Daph doesn't drink.'

Daph nodded as if trying to agree, then threw up all over the wheels of the van.

'Get her to the nurse,' said Tweedy gruffly as the bell rang for the end of lunch break. 'Polly, go with her. The rest of you, get back to work.'

Polly watched as her teammates walked away shaking their heads in disbelief.

'You're wrong!' she called after them. 'She isn't drunk!' Daph would never show her up like this, not when she was supposed to be trialling for the Sparks. There had to be some other explanation. Daph was her rock, the one person Polly could truly rely on ... Joe's sweetheart. She was fearless and rode a motorbike and took no nonsense from anyone. She wasn't careless, or silly ... or drunk.

'What a pickle,' said Lady G, putting an arm round Daph's shoulder and trying to steer her towards the hospital wing.

Daph sat down on the ground.

'I'm going to need your help, Polly,' said Lady G with a groan.

Daph collapsed and lay flat on her back.

'Come on!' said Polly trying to pull her up. 'The nurse will make you better!'

At last, with Lady G on one side and Polly on the other, they managed to bundle Daph across the courtyard.

Polly was amazed at how thin Daph had become. She had always been slight, but now she was skin and bone. As she put her hand firmly on Daph's back to guide her through the door of the hospital wing, she could feel the sharp outline of her spine.

'Hello?' called Lady G, as they entered a little white waiting room full of chairs.

'What have we here?' said a brisk Scottish nurse appearing from one of the sick rooms with a stethoscope round her neck.

'I'm afraid someone's been having a party all by themselves,' said Lady G as Daph staggered forwards, swayed, then sank to the floor in a heap. 'She's drunk!'

'I see!' The nurse was calm and efficient, seeming to scoop Daph's tiny frame up off the floor and into a nearby wheelchair in a single movement. 'She works with high explosives, that much is obvious from the colour of her skin,' she said. 'But I don't think this young lady has touched a drop.'

'I told you,' cried Polly.

'It's the effects of the TNT – the gunpowder – she works with,' the nurse explained. 'Chemicals have got into her bloodstream and affected her in just the same way that drinking a bottle of whisky would. I saw it once before when I was in a munitions factory near Carlisle. That poor girl was sacked before we even realised what was going on.'

'Oh, Daphne,' said Lady G. 'I should never have thought so badly of you.' She looked over at Polly and smiled apologetically. 'Trust you to stand firm, when others doubted.'

Polly smiled back. It wasn't Lady G's fault. Daph really had been reeling like a drunk – it was only because Polly knew her so well, that she hadn't believed it was true.

'This young woman is a hero for working with those chemicals, just the same as if she was fighting gas in the trenches,' said the nurse. 'They're poisoning her from the inside out.'

'Poisoning her?' Polly's brief sense of relief turned to panic. 'Does that mean Daph will be like this forever?'

'She won't always appear drunk,' said the nurse.

'That will probably wear off after a good sleep.' Daph was already lolling back with her eyes closed and her mouth open, breathing in loud, rattling breaths, which sounded like someone shaking a bunch of keys.

'So she'll get better?' asked Polly. 'Can she still try out for our football team?'

The nurse shook her head. 'I'm afraid your friend is very ill. Her lungs have been seriously damaged by the chemicals.'

Polly's skin turned cold.

'Daphne does have trouble breathing,' agreed Lady G. 'We always thought it was a spot of asthma but it's getting worse.'

'Will she die?' Polly blurted out.

She had to ask the question. But the nurse didn't seem to want to answer it. Not directly.

'She is extremely weak and she's going to need a lot of rest,' she said, wheeling the chair away. 'I'll see if I can find her a bed in a convalescent home. I suggest you stop worrying and get back to work ...'

'Chin up,' said Lady G, ushering Polly across the courtyard. 'Daphne's a fighter. She'll be haring round the roads again on that wretched motorbike in no time.'

*

'Has she sobered up yet?' asked Clara, as Polly walked numbly to her bench in the factory.

'I told you. Daph wasn't drunk,' Polly snapped.

'Will she be fit enough for the trial later?' asked Joyce.

Polly shook her head. 'She's been poisoned by chemicals in the explosives she makes. I don't think she'll ever play football again ...' The truth of it hit her as she spoke.

'Oh, that's awful.' Joyce looked surprised, then concerned. 'Who will we put in defence?'

'I don't know ...' Polly felt numb.

For once in her life, she really didn't care about the game. All she could think about was her friend.

What did it matter if the Sparks couldn't find the perfect player for their team? What did it matter if they never played another match? Nothing mattered ...

Just so long as Daph could get better.

CHAPTER FORTY-THREE

Polly went every evening to visit Daph at Broom Manor, the convalescent home where she was being taken care of.

It was a grand old house that had once belonged to some fancy family, up on the edge of the moors. Now instead of card tables and dancing, the rooms were filled with endless lines of hospital beds for wounded soldiers – officers on the sunnier south side of the building, lower ranks in the smaller, dark rooms at the back.

Daph was the only female patient in the whole place, other than a young nurse who had been wounded in an explosion at a field hospital in France. They each had a tiny servants' room up in the attics.

'Three flights of stairs. Perfect for someone who has to wheeze their lungs out to take a single step,'

Daph always joked – a good sign that she was growing stronger, Polly thought. But one evening, as they sat on a sunny bench in the garden, she seemed distracted and sad.

'I can't stay here any more, I've run out of money,' Daph blurted out at last, coughing so much that her shoulders shook. 'I no longer have a job at Lowcross and they won't take me on at Kerston Electrics if I'm not in the football team.' Munitionettes were being laid off everywhere now the war was nearly over. 'They don't need us any more, Pol,' Daph sighed.

'There must be something we can do,' said Polly, though she knew hospital care was expensive. Surely they wouldn't just turn Daph out on to the streets?

'I already sold the Green Dragon to pay for the last few weeks,' Daph wheezed. 'Jessie, back at the factory, arranged it all for me. You'll never guess who bought her.'

'No ...' Polly knew at once who it was going to be.

'Don Sharples.' Daph let out a long, rattling groan.

Polly growled. Trust him to be hanging around like a vulture.

'He never did go to the Front. Apparently he's left the factory now too,' said Daph. 'He's working for the FA. Having the Green Dragon means he can ride to matches all over the country.'

371

'We'll buy her back,' promised Polly, remembering how happy they'd been when they rode the bike over the moors on Christmas Day. 'Football sisters!' Daph had called them. That was before they knew Joe was missing ... Before Daph got seriously ill. 'We'll find a way.'

'It's more important to pay for my care,' said Daph. 'I'm not sure I'll ever be up to riding a motorbike again ...'

'Don't say that!' begged Polly, but she knew something had to be done about the hospital fees. 'You shouldn't have to pay anything,' she fumed. 'It's working for the war effort that made you ill.' She watched as a wounded solider hobbled by on a pair of crutches, his left leg lost from below the knee. Daph was just as much a victim of the war as that poor lad. At least he might be getting help from one of the charities ...

'Hold on!' Polly had a flash of inspiration. The Sparks were playing all these charity matches to help war victims. The girls in the team had raised hundreds of pounds – thousands even. Why shouldn't Daph get some of that money too?

'I'll write to Lady G,' she said excitedly. 'She's on endless committees and things. She'll know what to do.'

'Thank you.' Daph seemed calmer already. 'You know I did keep trying to come and visit when I was still at Lowcross,' she explained as they stared out over the garden. 'I just wasn't strong enough.'

'I see that now. But you'll come and see me play for the Sparks soon, won't you?' said Polly.

'Wouldn't miss it for the world,' Daph promised as the evening sun began to fade behind them. A few of the leaves were tinged with autumn gold and Polly wrapped a blanket around Daph's shoulders.

Across the lawn they could see Clara coming towards them with three steaming mugs of tea. After her initial sulky welcome, she had become good friends with Daph and often came to visit her with Polly.

'It's because I'm dying that she likes me now,' Daph laughed. 'She doesn't need to be jealous any more.'

'Leave it out!' Polly refused to even joke about Daph dying. Yet secretly she liked the idea that Clara might be just the tiniest bit jealous of their friendship … Could Daph be right? She watched Clara dancing towards them with a tray.

'If you two are talking about me, I hope it's all good things,' said Clara with a little pirouette as she offered them each a mug of tea.

'We're discussing football,' said Daph. 'I'm going to

try and see a game as soon as I'm strong enough. I want to check out this new defender you Sparks are all so excited about. I need to see if she's up to my job.'

A young Irish woman named Maeve had been playing in the spare defence role for over a month now. She was fast and strong and fearless – just what the team needed.

'You should come to the night match!' cried Clara, leaping up with excitement. 'It's going to be in the dark.'

'In the dark? I won't be able to see a thing,' Daph scoffed.

'No! That's the point. We're going to have electric lights at the game!' said Polly proudly. 'It's never been done before. Not even by the men. We'll be the first team ever to play a match with lights in the dark. It's not until November, though. So it gives you plenty of time to get strong.'

'I'll come!' promised Daph with a smile. 'Who knows, maybe this rotten war really will be over by then.'

Polly crossed her fingers and for a glorious moment she felt a tiny flickering leap of the hope that she still carried somewhere deep down inside her. The hope she refused to let go.

Perhaps Joe will be found when all this is over . . . and Daph will be well.

She imagined them sitting together in the darkness, holding hands, as they watched her play football on a floodlit pitch.

CHAPTER FORTY-FOUR

Once Polly had urged her on, Lady G worked miracles. It was agreed that the charities the women's football matches had raised money for would pay for Daph's care at Broom Manor for a month or two at least, even though she was not strictly a wounded soldier.

Daph got her wish about the war ending too.

The illuminated game took place on Saturday 16th November 1918, just five days after the armistice had been signed, and the Great War – the war that generals and politicians promised would end all wars – was over at last.

There was a carnival atmosphere, with laughter filling the air and people singing patriotic songs, as the team arrived at Steepside in their charabanc. Daph came with them so that she could get a ride to the pitch.

Crowds made their way up the hill in a torchlit

procession, led by not one, but three brass bands. Pathé News was there too, to film the whole thing.

Polly thought folk seemed freer and happier than they had been at celebrations in town a few days earlier, when peace finally came at the eleventh hour of the eleventh day of the eleventh month. Then, people had seemed sad as well as grateful that the madness was over and done with at last. There were too many losses for the town to feel truly happy – sons, brothers, husbands, loved ones who would never return.

Yet tonight, for the football game, there was a purpose to the jollity. Folk were going to see some fun.

'Lasses running around in the dark!' as one man loudly proclaimed

Polly of course couldn't help wishing Joe was there. There had still been no word of him. No magic letter the minute the armistice came, as she had so often hoped. No telegram saying: 'We've found him. He's here. He's alive.' No knock at the door. She was finding it harder and harder to believe. Yet, still she could not give up.

Daph was there, though. For tonight that would have to be enough. And Clara. Even Mr and Mrs Venne – though what Mr Venne was making of it all was anyone's guess. Polly didn't give a jot! She was proud to be there with her friends from the team. The Sparks were so famous now they were playing against 'The Rest of Lancashire', an opposition made up of the best remaining players from the whole county.

'Good luck!' said Daph, her voice sounding wheezier than ever in the cold air as she made her way to the stands, leaning on Tweedy's arm.

Polly, already in her kit, ran out on to the pitch with the rest of the team.

It was still dark as they came on to the grass, with only the light of the spectators' torches and a few flares by the turnstiles lighting the ground.

'Thank goodness we're dressed in black and white. Like a badger's face,' said Polly. 'I can see half the stripes, at least.'

The Rest of Lancashire had opted for a dark red kit to represent the Lancashire Rose. Unfortunately it meant they disappeared almost completely in the gloom.

'Will we even be able to see the ball?' asked Maeve, the new defender.

'Of course,' said Joyce confidently. 'They've whitewashed it for us.'

Like kicking the moon, thought Polly. Yet she felt anxious that the whole thing would be a joke. What if the lights weren't strong enough? What if they didn't work at all?

She needn't have worried. With a great drum roll from the band, two huge army searchlights sprang to life. The crowd gasped and cheered. There were forty carbide flares all along the sidelines as well. Polly shielded her eyes. Suddenly it was glaringly bright. Almost too bright.

'It's like being a dancer on a stage,' cried Clara as the whistle blew and the searchlights followed the players up and down the pitch.

A few minutes into the match, one of the searchlights failed.

'Air lock,' bellowed the operator as if that explained it, and the big light only flickered on and off for the rest of the game.

The remaining searchlight was so bright that every time Polly tried to make a run up the left-hand side of the pitch, she was blinded by the glare.

The crowd was raucous with high spirits.

'Off! Off! Off!' cheered a big group of women from the factory, pleading with the lighting operator to take their side when the Rest of Lancashire had a free kick.

The lass missed anyway. Polly smiled. She had never heard so many women's voices raised at a game before.

There must have been as many of them as there were men here tonight.

'Listen to the crowd!' said Joyce, echoing Polly's thoughts as she took the ball from her for a throw-in.

It wasn't the most serious or stylish match they had ever played, but it was fun. In the end the Sparks won and Polly scored a lovely header. It was nice to win, of course, it always was, but it seemed to be about something more as well. There was a sense of them all playing together just for the love of the game, both teams lit up like that – and the roar of the women in the crowd cheering them on. Polly wished her Queenie could have been there to see it too.

'We're making history,' said Mercy, as a cameraman from Pathé News ran on to the floodlit pitch to film their smiling faces.

Out of the corner of her eye, Polly saw a little girl – perhaps six or seven years old – run on to the pitch too and steal the white ball right out of the goalmouth where it had been forgotten.

'Hey!' cried the referee as the cheeky lass pelted past Polly. 'Grab that thief!'

Polly didn't move. Perhaps it was because she had just been thinking about Queenie, or perhaps because the little rascal reminded Polly of herself, but she wasn't going to be the one to stop a girl nabbing a free football.

'Run!' she cheered as the tiny figure bolted away pursued by a linesman. The last Polly saw, she had disappeared into the crowd still clutching the ball.

'You'll have to come and see the match on Christmas Day,' said Polly as Daph shuffled slowly back across the dark gardens of Broom Manor. Daph seemed especially slow and wheezy. The trip to Steepside had obviously taken its toll, but Polly was pleased her friend had come. Polly herself still felt light and giddy from the game and she couldn't help being excited.

'Tonight was fun but Christmas Day will be the real thing. It's the most important match of the year,' she explained. 'We'll be playing against the whole of the rest of England. Imagine that? Perhaps we'll have found Joe by then and he can . . .'

'Listen to me, Pol,' said Daph, stopping in the middle of the path. Her voice was quiet but firm. 'It's time to stop this now. Joe's gone. He's not coming back. You know that.'

'No!' Polly shook her head furiously. Why was Daph giving up on him now, of all times? The war was over. Joe would finally be safe. 'Perhaps he just ran away from the fighting and he's been hiding somewhere … in a barn or something,' she said, although she knew even as she was speaking, that wasn't true. Joe was a team player – he would never have run away while the lads around him were still fighting. In the moonlight, she caught a glimpse of the pain on Daph's face.

'It's time to begin to mourn him, Pol,' she said. 'Promise me you'll always remember him for who he really was. Talk about him. Celebrate his life: the brother you loved. The goalie. The daft lad I lost my heart to …'

'Stop it!' Polly turned her back – but, deep down, with a cold stone-heavy certainty, she knew that Daph was right. There was no hiding from it any more. None of the thousands of missing boys on the battlefield were ever found. They were lost forever and so was her Joe.

'He was a daft beggar, my big brother, that's for sure,' she said at last, and for the first time the tears began to flow. She hadn't cried when Joe had waved goodbye and walked out through the gate in the back yard. Nor when she had kicked that ball to him through the window of the train taking him away to fight. Not even when the dreadful letter had come on Christmas Day. 'Missing, presumed killed.' Now it was nearly Christmas again.

Stubbornly, for almost a whole year, when everyone

else had given up hope, Polly had insisted that the worst could not happen. She knew now that it had. Joe was dead. His breath, his stories, his love of football was long gone already. It was only his body that was lost, buried somewhere unknown out there in the mud and terror of that stupid, blasted, pointless war.

Daph squeezed Polly's arm. 'I'm so tired now,' she said faintly. 'I need to rest.'

'Of course.' Half dazed, Polly helped Daph to the bench where they'd had tea with Clara. 'Take a seat for a minute. I can wait,' she said, gulping back tears. 'Mrs Venne knows I'm going to be late home . . .' Tweedy had even given her money for a taxi, something Polly could barely believe.

'I mean a long rest,' said Daph, her voice so quiet that Polly had to lean towards her as she sank down on to the seat. 'It's time to face up to this too. I'm dying, Pol.'

'No!' Polly wished she could block up her ears. She couldn't take any more pain. Not tonight. But Daph held her hand and would not let go.

'Somewhere out there, beyond all this, I'll find Joe's spirit and we can be together again,' she said.

Polly felt how cold Daph's fingers were. 'You can get strong,' she pleaded. 'We'll raise more money. You can stay here at Broom Manor as long as you need to.'

'No. It's time, Pol,' said Daph. 'I've had enough. My chest aches. I can't breathe. I can barely walk ...'

'But ...' Polly tried desperately to interrupt. She wanted to stop the words coming out of Daph's mouth. She felt as if her chest had been ripped wide open. First Joe, killed by some unknown German bullet or shell. Now Daph was slipping away from her too, killed by the terrible weapons she'd been asked to make. Weapons that were meant to kill the enemy but had destroyed girls at home too.

'What will I do without you?' Polly sobbed, wiping snot and tears away with the back of her hand.

'You'll heal. In time,' said Daph, crying too. 'You're strong ... stronger than anyone I've ever met. Promise me you'll go on grabbing life with both hands ... or, knowing you, kicking it ... hard ... with your left foot.' They both laughed a little at that. 'Do it for me,' whispered Daph. 'For the girl I could have been.'

'I promise!' Polly breathed. 'I will.'

Daph smiled and rose shakily to her feet. 'Come on. Walk me up to the house now,' she said, taking Polly's arm, 'and tell me more about this game on Christmas Day.'

Slowly they made their way up the dark path together. The two friends laughed and chatted quietly about

Polly's hopes for the big Christmas match. As they walked, Daph grew very tired. Polly took her arm and helped her slowly up the long steep hill.

It was the last time Polly ever saw her friend.

That night, Daph died peacefully in her sleep.

CHAPTER FORTY-FIVE

On Christmas morning, Polly rose early and slipped out of the front door, leaving a note for Clara: 'Merry Christmas! See you later, at the ground.'

She didn't want to get in the way of the Vennes' family celebrations, but mostly she wanted to be alone before the big match.

She walked slowly up the hill to Steepside, remembering how fast and furiously Daph had driven as they roared up this very same road a year ago on the Green Dragon. How unstoppable Daph had seemed then ...

She thought too about Joe and how he had told her the story of the Christmas Day football match in the midst of war. How German soldiers and British boys had kicked a ball about together in no man's land.

She wondered what had happened to the battered,

precious football she had booted to Joe through that train window. She liked to imagine he'd had it with him on his final day. Perhaps he'd grabbed it in his arms – a perfect save – in the very last moments, just before he died.

She took a deep breath of cold morning air and remembered the promise she had made to Daph too. She was going to take hold of life and kick it, hard – joyfully – with her strong left foot. Today was the perfect chance to do that. It was Christmas and Polly wasn't going to allow herself to be sad. She was going to celebrate all those that she loved in the way she knew best. She was going to play a cracking game of football.

By the time she reached the turnstiles, the first of the crowds had already begun to arrive. She bought a hot meat pie and sat on a wall eating it.

The crowds around the gate grew thicker and thicker. Polly had never seen anything like it, not even at that first Christmas match, and there was still well over an hour until kick-off.

The turnstiles opened and people surged forward.

Polly jumped down off the wall. The charabanc would be here soon. There was a special players' entrance at the back. She'd go and wait for the team round there. Maybe the opposition had arrived already.

'The Best of England,' she muttered proudly. All the top girls from every squad had gathered a team together to try and defeat the unbeatable Sparks.

Good luck to them! thought Polly, but still she didn't leave.

She realised she was scanning the crowds of spectators, looking for someone.

'Hey, Pol!' Frank Cogley waved at her from the throng like a little jack-in-a-box, leaping up and down. He had his dad with him, home safe from the war, and a gaggle of the endless cousins too. 'Remember I taught you all you know!' he bellowed at the top of his lungs.

'Cheeky beggar!' Polly laughed as he disappeared through the turnstiles.

Still she stayed watching the crowds. She stood at a distance, her back pressed up against the low wall where she'd eaten her pie, watching and waiting.

Suddenly she saw Dad and Walter and the little boys.

'How do, our Pol,' they chorused. Even Dad looked bright-eyed and excited. Only Walter didn't join in shouting her name. He just stuck his nose so far in the air she could see right up his nostrils.

'Merry Christmas! I'll see you after the game,' she called. Then she turned to go. There was no point waiting any more ...

'Pol,' a voice bellowed at her and Polly spun round.

There she was – Mam – in her hideous best Sunday hat. She had come. She was clutching Queenie in her arms.

Polly couldn't believe how much her sister had grown. She wasn't a scrawny baby any more; she had rosy cheeks and a wild mop of thick black hair the same colour as Polly's – Joe's too, of course.

Polly ran towards them as Queenie squealed with excitement.

She recognises me! thought Polly in delight.

'I stopped to buy a meat pie,' boomed Mam. 'They're not half bad.'

Polly dodged through the crowd and flung her arms round Mam's huge waist, engulfing Queenie at the same time. 'It's so good to see you both.' She kissed Queenie's head. 'I missed you, Mam,' she said.

Polly expected Mam to push her away. To tell her not to be so soft. She didn't.

'I missed you too, Polly,' she said. 'I'm right proud of you, lass. Right proud.'

Polly held tight for a moment longer, just letting the feeling settle as the crowds thronged around her and she breathed in the familiar scents of home from Mam's clothes – coal dust, damp washing and pigs, of course.

Then at last she let go and kissed little Queenie on top of her head again.

'I'll score a goal for you today,' she promised. 'When you're big enough, I'll teach you how to play, then you can join a football team, if you want to.'

Queenie gurgled and clapped her hands.

'You know she'd smile at you like that if you sang "Ring-a-Rosie" too, don't you,' said Mam.

'Nonsense!' Polly shouted over her shoulder as she hurried away through the crowd. 'That lass is football-mad already ... and I've got a pair of boots just waiting for her to put on.'

As Polly rounded the corner to the players' entrance, she saw that the charabanc had arrived. The Sparks had already gone inside. All except Clara, who was standing at the back door of the changing rooms looking out.

'There you are. I've been waiting for you,' she cried.

Polly grinned and her tummy gave a leap, pleased that Clara had been keeping a special lookout for her.

'Have you heard? Tweedy says this is the biggest crowd there's ever been. The whole ground is sold out. Every ticket.'

'Bigger than the men's games, even.' Polly beamed. 'Merry Christmas, by the way.'

'Merry Christmas,' said Clara. 'I've got you a present.'

'Really?' Polly panicked. She hadn't got Clara anything. Not even an orange.

'You can have it now, if you want it,' said Clara.

'All right!' Polly grinned. She was never one to wait – although Clara didn't seem to be holding anything in her hand.

'I hope you like it.' Clara stepped forward and, taking Polly's face in her hands, planted a kiss on her lips. 'Merry Christmas, lovely Polly – that's for you from me,' she said. Then she skipped into the changing rooms and Polly stood alone for a moment, smiling.

Clara liked her . . . She had kissed her and called her 'lovely'. Her – Polly Nabb! Polly took a deep breath, then let it out again, very slowly.

She touched her finger to her lips and was still smiling as she kicked a stone across the ground. The pebble shot between two clumps of tufty grass as Polly heard a familiar sound. The spluttering roar of a motorbike.

'The Green Dragon!' Polly gasped.

Then Don Sharples sped round the corner and skidded to a halt.

Polly had almost forgotten the motorbike belonged to him – but the sound that had always promised such happiness now delivered her worst enemy to her.

Polly's heart sank.

'You're not the referee are you?' she asked, as he pushed up his goggles and grinned, his usual greedy, bully's smirk.

'No. The FA are training me up for the men's game. The real thing,' he said. 'It'll start again next season now the boys are back from war. Proper players. Then all this' – he pointed to the green pitch beyond the changing rooms and the stands packed with crowds – 'will be back where it belongs. With us. With men. We'll kick you girls out, you'll see.'

Polly sighed. The same old Don Sharples, always trying to take the ball away. Just like Mr Venne and Walter. Or Mr Graves, raging from his pulpit. Or the doctors who said women's legs weren't made the right way. And all the men at the FA, making and changing rules to suit themselves.

They're frightened of us! thought Polly, surprised she had never realised it before. *That's why they make such a fuss. They've seen that we're good – just as good as they are, and it scares them.*

She should have known it. That's why the boys outside Duke's would never let her join their games. It was the same thing for the Sparks, playing out here on the big, grand pitch with its clubhouse stuffed full of dusty trophies won by men.

Well, maybe it would be different from now on. Maybe girls like Polly and Mercy and Clara and Joyce, and those who had made sacrifices like Daph and the young bride Mary-Anne, and poor forgetful Olive – maybe they had all made a difference. Maybe, by the time her Queenie was ready to kick a ball, nobody would give a jot if she was a girl or a boy, just so long as she wanted to play.

Polly stared Don Sharples straight in the eye. 'You can do what you like,' she said, 'but football is ours now too. It belongs to us. Our beautiful game. You can never take it away.'

Without looking back, she turned and walked into the changing rooms where the team was waiting for her.

EPILOGUE

Don Sharples was right. Women's football was outlawed by the FA. Women were banned from playing on their pitches in 1921 and the exclusion was only finally lifted fifty years later, in 1971.

Yet Polly was right too. The legacy of those early women footballers has endured. Leading on from the example of players like Lily Parr, the passion for the women's game continues to grow, shown in the talent and commitment of teams like the Lionesses in England and thousands of others across the globe, ranging from national sides to local squads of women and girls playing with determination, skill and the sheer love of the 'beautiful' game.

The Sparks are closely based on the famous Dick, Kerr Ladies Football Club, a munitions team from Preston in Lancashire. For the purposes of my story,

I changed the dates a little but the Dick, Kerr team did launch themselves with a game on Christmas Day 1917 in front of a crowd of ten thousand people, which raised six hundred pounds for wounded soldiers.

They also played their most famous Christmas match on Boxing Day 1920 in front of a whopping fifty-three thousand spectators, with as many as fourteen thousand more locked outside because the stands were full. At the time, this was the second-biggest crowd ever recorded for any game. The match raised an unprecedented £3,115 for charity (which would be well over £145,000 in today's money).

Almost exactly a year later, in December 1921, the stifling FA ban was imposed amid growing arguments that football was unsuitable for women's bodies. This was clearly nonsense, not least because of the heavy war work munitionettes like Daph, Mary-Anne and Polly, had done in factories throughout the conflict. Many believe it was the growing popularity of the women's game and the sheer size of that 1920 Boxing Day crowd which led an unsettled FA, desperate to renew support for the men's leagues and worried that women's matches would draw away spectators, to ban their games. Perhaps it was that same fear – and prejudice about what women were capable of – which meant the ban stayed in place for fifty long, shocking years.

Although nothing can compare to the horror of fighting in the trenches, I was pleased in this story to be able to acknowledge the debt we owe to women working on the home front too. Many lost their lives or suffered life-changing injuries in explosions while working at munitions factories, and many, like Daph, died or had their health ruined by the chemicals and dangerous machinery they used. Despite guidance that only those over eighteen years of age should be allowed to work in the munitions factories, there is evidence that girls as young as eleven were frequently employed.

If you want to read more about the history of the Dick, Kerr team, including their role in making munitions, *The Dick, Kerr's Ladies: The Factory Girls Who Took On the World* by Barbara Jacobs brilliantly captures the atmosphere of the time. And *In a League of Their Own: The Dick, Kerr Ladies 1917–1965* by Gail Newsham is an absolutely invaluable source, as is the accompanying website: dickkerrladies.com, which is packed with information, and where you can see wonderful photographs of all the players of the past.

The FA ban did not stop the Dick, Kerr team – they might have been denied access to big grounds which could hold huge crowds but they continued to play whenever and wherever they could at home and abroad, including a tour of the USA where they played against men (and won a good smattering of the matches) when women's teams were not allowed to turn up.

They never gave up, but kicked hard and passed that treasured ball to all the women and girls who play today. In 2018, the Royal British Legion recognised the Dick, Kerr Ladies for their fundraising contribution during the First World War.

Acknowledgements

Writing a book, just like playing football, is a team game not a solo sport and I could never have written this story without the whole squad at Faber. Huge thanks to Alice Swan for sharing my excitement and commissioning the idea, Leah Thaxton and Natasha Brown for their endless support and Susila Baybars for her sharp-eyed edits. Thanks to Sarah Lough in marketing, Bethany Carter in publicity, Maurice Lyon for fantastic copyedits and Sarah Barlow for brilliant proofreading. Also to Claire Wilson – as ever – and Miriam Tobin and Safae El-Ouahabi at RCW. I am over the moon with Momoko Abe's lively cover design, which brilliantly captures the energy of the time. Sharing writing ideas with Sophie McKenzie always keeps me match fit – thank you for our invaluable early morning kick-abouts which have made such a big difference to this book!

I am enormously grateful to George Coombes for his patience and football knowledge both as a player and a fan. Thank you Robert Knox for digging into Lily Parr's genealogy and for bringing me a little closer to my own family history too . . . and, speaking of family, thanks to the team at home for putting up with me (and Polly!) while this book was being written.

It has been such a privilege for me to write a story based on all the brave, energetic, unstoppable women who worked so hard on the home front and played football in those world-changing years of the First War – thank you, above all, to them.